Sweet Scandal

SCARLETT SCOTT

Sweet Scandal
Heart's Temptation Book Four

For more information, contact author Scarlett Scott.
www.scarsco.com

ISBN-13: 978-1979465052

Dedication

This book is dedicated to the many NICU nurses who cared for our twins as if they were their own (especially Kelly, Kelsey, Fran, and Jade), who cried and laughed and cheered with us, who hugged us when we needed it most, and who were there for us and our precious girls when no one else was. Their kindness, compassion, and dedication to our children and countless others is utterly inspiring. To them and NICU nurses everywhere: thank you. Words can't describe what you do for the parents and tiny babies whose lives you change forever.

Contents

Part One

Chapter One

London, 1883

JUST AS SHE HAD DONE EACH MONTH she was in town for the last three years, Lady Helen Harrington stepped into the offices of the *London Beacon*. But on this day, something was frightfully out of the ordinary. She clutched her latest article to her silk pelisse as though it were a shield.

The *Beacon* had never been a bustling hub of activity. Indeed, as a journal concerned with egalitarian matters rather than societal gossip or daily news fodder, it had suffered from both lack of staff and funds. Often, the only soul in the office was the owner and editor, Mr. Bothwell.

And yet, somehow before her swarmed a veritable hive of activity. Men were everywhere. Wooden crates and plaster dust and papers littered the quarters. There was banging and clanging and shouting and, strangely, the entire building itself seemed to be buzzing.

No one appeared to notice her as she stood in the entryway, gawking at the commotion. A man bearing tools almost crashed into her in his eagerness to reach his destination. She sidestepped him and managed to run smack into a hard wall of chest instead.

Her papers and her reticule went flying and she nearly fell to the floor with the impact of the collision. Large hands caught her around the waist, pulling her far too close to an equally large, solidly muscled male form.

"Oh dear," she muttered, hastily stifling any quickening of her pulse that was inspired by the rather indelicate position.

"Steady," the man commanded in a distinctly American accent. One word and he'd given himself away.

She looked up into his impossibly blue gaze and her pulse exerted a will of its own, kicking back into a gallop. Good heavens, he was beautiful. There was no other way to describe him. His wavy, dark hair was swept back from his forehead, perhaps a bit too long for fashion, his lips molded with enough perfection that even she, dedicated spinster, was not unaffected. The finely trimmed beard covering his strong jaw made him appear intensely masculine in the very best way possible. If ever Helen had laid eyes upon a man who could shake her unwavering resolution to never again be wooed or misled by a man, surely it was he.

"I trust you aren't injured?" he asked, his words managing to pierce the London-like fog that had taken up residence in her brain. Oh yes indeed, very American, that accent. There were certainly enough of them traveling in her circles these days. But not this man. She would not have forgotten him.

"Madam?" he pressed when she failed to respond.

"No," she hurried to reply lest he realize the cause for her lack of alacrity. Goodness, she gawped at him as though she'd never before seen a handsome man. Or a man at all.

"Excellent." He released her and bent to retrieve her fallen papers and purse before handing them back to her. "Please see yourself out."

The tone of his voice was not one of concern but rather one of irritation. Had the man no manners? *He* was dismissing *her*, and with such insolence?

"Who are you, sir?" she demanded, unnerved by his rudeness and determined to get to the bottom of the tumult before her. "What is going on here?"

He raised an imperious brow at her. "May I ask who *you* are, madam?"

She blinked, finding his arrogance and audacity most vexing. "Who I am?"

"That is indeed the question I just posed." His expression remained an icy mask.

He wasn't about to budge. Very well. She too could be persistent. "Where is Mr. Bothwell?" she asked instead of answering him.

He waved a dismissive hand as though to suggest that Mr. Bothwell's mere mentioning was as bothersome to him as a fly. "Bothwell is gone. Off happily counting his pounds somewhere, I'd suspect." His gaze flicked over her person, boldly taking stock of her in a way that had her cheeks heating. "What business have you with him?"

"Business?" She frowned then.

Ladies of her station did not have business. No, indeed. The articles she wrote for the *Beacon* had initially earned her a bit of pin money, but as time had worn on and the *Beacon's* pockets were increasingly to let, she had merely volunteered her services instead. After all, it had been the platform she relished and not any meager funds once associated with it. The opportunity to give voice to the causes that were important to her was of the greatest significance. Through it, she and her fellow reformers had already done a great deal of good by raising funds and awareness both.

His sensual mouth compressed into a firm line. "Are you dimwitted, madam?"

The question took her aback. Of all the insolence she'd encountered in her life, the man before her surely took the proverbial cake. "How dare you?"

"Hang it, I haven't time to squabble with a woman who keeps repeating every word I say." He all but growled before hailing one of the men engaged in the industry of hauling away some battered old furniture. "You there, please see that this lovely, confused lady is taken to her personal conveyance at once."

And then without preamble, without even so much as another glance in her direction, he turned his back on her.

She had been dismissed.

Helen stared at his infuriating back, noting despite herself just how broad and well-muscled it appeared to be. Precisely who did he think he was? Did he not know she was a lady? That she was the daughter of an earl? That she ought to be at least treated with a modicum of respect if not gallantry?

Oh no he didn't.

She sidestepped the poor fellow assigned with the task of escorting her to her carriage and hurried after the source of her discourteous dismissal. "Sir, I must insist on an answer. What in heaven's name is going on here?"

He spun about on his heel, surprise evident in every line of his visage. Perhaps he had expected her to meekly do his bidding. If so, he was bound to be sorely disappointed. "Madam, kindly leave my building as you've been instructed. I have a great deal more important things to do than answer your hen-witted questions."

His building? His arrogance knew no bounds. And now he called her hen-witted? Surely the man must be daft. Either that or he was utterly mad, for there was no other explanation for such an appalling lack of couth. "This building belongs to the *London Beacon*," she pointed out. "I write a monthly column for the *Beacon*, and I won't be going anywhere until I can speak with Mr. Bothwell directly."

"Damn it all," he muttered, startling her by taking her elbow in a firm grasp and propelling her toward Mr. Bothwell's office. "Come with me."

He said the last as though he gave her an option. He hadn't. The man all but dragged her across the floor and into the room that had once housed Mr. Bothwell's sturdy old desk and a bookcase laden with fine literature. He slammed the door behind them, and she should have flinched or objected to the impropriety but she was too engaged in taking in her surroundings to notice.

Mr. Bothwell's office had changed. A brand new, fine mahogany desk with intricate carving and an inlaid mother of pearl monogram bearing an 'S' dominated the room. The carpet was lush beneath her feet and the gaslight had been replaced by gleaming electric globes. A fresh coat of paint had been applied, and it all looked very costly and very unlike any expense that could be afforded by the haphazard Mr. Bothwell.

Understanding dawned upon her at last. The forbidding man before her and his insufferable demeanor had so flummoxed her that she hadn't listened carefully enough to what he'd said. "Do you mean to say that Mr. Bothwell has sold the paper?"

The old rotter hadn't said a word to her when she'd last seen him. He had simply accepted her article and said he would see her in a month's time. Nothing had seemed out of the ordinary. Mr. Bothwell's fingertips had retained their typical ink stains, his thinning shock of white hair mussed as always. He hadn't suggested at all that anything was amiss.

"That is precisely what I mean to say." He towered over her, so near she could detect the faint, masculine scent of his soap. "I own this building and the *London Beacon* both. Mr. Bothwell won't be returning, and your services will no longer be required."

Dismay rattled through her. "But I have an understanding with Mr. Bothwell. I've been writing a monthly for three years now." The *Beacon* had been the only publication where she'd managed to publish her views. Bothwell espoused reform, and he'd been willing to give her free reign in venting her sometimes *de trop* and sometimes shocking notions. Indeed, the *Beacon* had always been a paragon of reform, at least until the interloper before her had greased the old man's palms. She very much feared she couldn't find another paper that would dare to publish her work, and she had yet so much to say and do. Why, she had only just begun.

He remained impervious to her pleas. "Whatever arrangement you had with the former editor and owner is no concern of mine."

Well. It would seem that he was equal parts good-looking and callous. He appeared quite inflexible. But she too was made of stern stuff. One had to be when one possessed three minx sisters and three wayward brothers. "You needn't be so dismissive, sir. I've put a great deal of research into this article, and it's about—"

"I don't care," he interrupted. "I don't care if it's about butterflies or your grandmother's shoes. It won't be published by my paper, and nor will anything else you write. As I said, your services will no longer be required."

The blighter. Butterflies and an old woman's shoes indeed. As though she would have nothing of greater import, no topic weightier than fripperies and nonsense to offer the reading public. Now her temper was rather beginning to get the best of her. "Sir, your manners are deplorable."

He flashed her a grin that wasn't polite or kind but somehow still had an effect on her. Dash it all, the man had dimples. Dimples, of all the preposterous things! As though he needed anything else to enhance his looks.

"Madam, if I had ever concerned myself with manners, I wouldn't have a cent to my name. As edifying as I find this discussion, I truly do have more significant matters requiring my attention. Would you care for me to have you escorted to the door or would you prefer to be thrown over my shoulder like a haversack and carted there?"

"Are you threatening my person, sir?" Surely he wouldn't dare.

He closed the distance between them, setting his hands upon her waist. Apparently he was and he would. "You have until the count of three, madam. One. Two."

She placed her hands over his, trying in vain to tug free of his grasp. It was a mistake. Even through her gloves, the contact felt somehow oddly, delightfully intimate. She gazed up into those ethereal blue eyes and realized he'd stopped counting. Her corset had grown unaccountably tight and an unsettling sensation had taken up residence deep within her. None of it made a whit of sense since each time the man opened his mouth the sentences he uttered were even more rude than the last. He was difficult. Arrogant. Irritating.

Handsome.

"Sir, you must release me at once," she forced herself to say in her haughtiest tone.

For a moment, he simply stared, their enmeshed gazes yielding a simmering tension that was as undeniable as it was unwanted. His grip on her waist tightened, almost becoming possessive. She found it hard to breathe. His head dipped to hers, his mouth alarmingly near. He was going to kiss her, she realized, and the prospect wasn't disquieting. Not in the least.

"Three," he said. "You had fair warning."

Abruptly he bent and did as he'd promised, scooping her over his shoulders, kilted skirts of her fashionable *polonaise* walking dress and all. She was treated to an upside-down view of his desk, shimmering in the other-worldly glow of the electric lights despite the gloominess of the outside day. She couldn't believe it. The man had actually thrown her, the daughter of the Earl of Northcote, over his shoulder. It was the outside of enough.

So she did what any lady in her incredible predicament would do when she'd finally caught her breath. She made a fist and pounded on his insufferable back.

Hang it, the woman was thumping on his back. She was a troublesome scrap of silk, this one. No doubt about it. She was as feisty as she was attractive, and saints be damned, he wasn't entirely immune to her more than ample charms. But that didn't mean Levi would allow her to meddle in his plans.

He hadn't traveled an ocean just to permit a blonde beauty with a sharp tongue to send his train rattling off the rails. North Atlantic Electric's success in dominating the market in England depended upon his maintaining a clear head. And by the time his work was done here, not only would all of London harness the power and function of electricity, but so would the entire country. From there, the rest of the civilized world.

What had begun in New York City as a business competing to create the most efficient light bulb would take over the entire globe. It all started right here in this newspaper office. He'd learned his lesson back in New York City. A man with a good mouthpiece could dominate anyone he wanted. And make no mistake, he wanted to win the race.

Never mind the minx draped over his shoulder and her ceaseless chattering about articles and old Mr. Bothwell. He wasn't a man easily deterred.

Neither, it seemed, was the lady in question. "Unhand me," she ordered as though she was in a position to do so.

But unfortunately for her, she was not in such a position. Rather, she was quite at his mercy. And at the moment, he was feeling considerably ill-tempered. His dynamo had nearly caught fire and a harpy had invaded his offices. It was not a good day on this side of the Atlantic.

"Silence," he ordered her when she refused to stop issuing commands against his back, adding a swat to her derriere to punctuate the order. This was not a request. He'd had enough of her disruption. It was time for her to be deposited on the street so he could proceed with lighting the world, lining his coffers, and growing his empire.

"I'll not be silenced, you brute!" Her voice was comically muffled. "Cease your manhandling of me at once."

Damn it all. He couldn't very well walk through his

newly acquired offices with a woman in high dudgeon tossed over his back. Could he? Levi briefly weighed the wisdom of doing so.

"I'll give you one final opportunity to conduct yourself with the comportment befitting a lady," he offered sternly, but only because he didn't wish to appear unhinged before his laborers and not because he sought to spare her feelings. She was the sort of irritation he didn't need. A burr under the horse's saddle, a bee abuzz about his head.

"Comportment," she cried, her voice strident despite being muffled in the fine fabric of his coat, "perhaps you ought to take your own advice, sir. You are certainly no gentleman."

Levi Storm hadn't built an empire on his reputation as a gentleman. Quite the opposite, as growing businesses and money both frequently called upon him to be merciless. Levi Storm's reputation in the business world was as well-known as *The Battle Hymn of the Republic*. He took what he wanted. Every damn time. He'd discovered over the years that if one had enough wealth, one could do nearly anything one wanted. And that included carrying a shrieking woman through the offices of the *London Beacon*.

"Very well. You had your chance, madam."

Without a moment of hesitation, he strode across his office and hauled open the door. As he crossed the threshold, he caught a few alarmed stares cast in his direction but he quelled each with an imperious arch of his brow. He didn't tolerate naysayers. Not even in matters as small as an English beauty with bats in her belfry.

She didn't stop caterwauling either, just kept on as though someone would rush to her rescue. No one dared and he carried on through the melee of workers and engineers. He deposited her with great care on her feet in the vestibule. She'd lost her hat, he realized, somewhere in the trek from his office to the entryway. A few tendrils of her golden hair had come free from her elaborately braided coiffure so that little curls framed her flushed face. She was even lovelier in her anger, her blue eyes flashing, her lush mouth pursed in disdain.

And then, as he stood there like a lad still in short pants, she walloped him with her reticule, landing a blow to his arm that actually rather stung. "You ought to be ashamed of yourself." He had no doubt her haughty tone could've matched the queen any day. "I've never been treated so poorly in my life."

To the devil. The brief moment of maudlin madness that had befallen him was thoroughly dashed. It was past time to see this bee on her way. "Apologies, madam." He held open the door for her since it seemed that all of his workmen were otherwise occupied. "But I do believe you were the one to have done me corporal injury with your reticule. I merely extracted you from a situation where you are no longer needed. By all means, have a lovely day."

There. That ought to do it. He waited for her to leave. She refused to move. The raucous din of the street filtered into the building around them as horses and conveyances rumbled by. Above it all, his dynamo could be heard running away, doing its work. It was a thoroughly satisfying sound. If he had his way, he'd have all of London ablaze with his electroliers in no time at all. The revolution had already begun.

"What is that noise?" she demanded to know, snapping the door closed and pacing a few steps away from him rather than leaving as he had so politely instructed her.

"It is the dynamo," he answered before his better judgment intervened. After all, he wanted her to go. Posthaste.

She blinked. "What is a dynamo?"

Of course she had more questions. Yes, the meddlesome woman likely had an endless supply of them. A legion, just waiting to barrage him with. "Listen here, madam, we aren't having afternoon tea. I'm running a business and I've had enough of your nattering."

He considered opening the door again and giving her a

gentle nudge over the threshold to be rid of her. There was a growing stack of correspondence on his desk, and he was waiting to hear from both New York City and Paris, and nothing so far had proceeded according to plan. His mood grew fouler by the second.

Her brows snapped together in a ferocious frown. It should have diminished the effect of her beauty but somehow it only served to enhance her definitively English looks. Her spine was stiffer than a ramrod. Her gown was very fine, he noticed for the first time. Everything about her said she was an aristocrat, including her shrewish nature.

"Where do you hail from, sir?" Her frosty question held untold implications.

The streets of New York City. The depths of hell. He could have told her any of those places and each would be equally true, but instead he put a hand firmly on her waist and steered her toward the door once more. "That is no concern of yours."

Touching her again had been a mistake. Her waist was small and well curved. For some irrational reason, he wondered what would happen if he slid his hand higher, all the way up her expensive silk to cup her breast. And then he cursed himself for a fool and dropped his hand away.

"I daresay you must be from some low part of the world to treat a lady with such an abominable amount of disrespect," she huffed.

"Very low," he agreed nicely and stepped closer, so close her skirts brushed his trousers. "If you'd like to find out just how low, I'll take you back into my office right now and show you."

Twin patches of color blossomed on her cheekbones. Her eyes widened. Good. He had shocked her. Frightened her, perhaps. He leaned down until their noses nearly touched. For the first time in their brief acquaintance, she remained gratifyingly silent.

"Do you want me to show you?" he pressed his advantage. Damn it, some insane part of him hoped she'd say yes.

He allowed his gaze to travel over the delicate planes of her face. Her skin was smooth and fair, the only hint of imperfection a pair of small lines at the corners of her wide, cornflower eyes. Someone had made this termagant smile, laugh even, enough times to leave a mark. It seemed impossible. He took in the lush fullness of her peony-pink mouth and longed to taste it with a hunger so fierce that it startled him.

Startled him, for not only was the reaction foreign in its intensity, but it was wholly unwanted and utterly impossible. The woman before him was taxing, but even if he'd been so inclined, he was not free to pursue her. He had somehow forgotten his obligations the moment her waist had curved against his palm.

It was precisely at that moment that the distinctive aroma of something burning reached his discerning nose. Damnation. What the hell had he been thinking, lusting after this woman so openly? And what the hell was on fire now? He straightened and stepped away from her as though she were the source of the flame.

"Sir."

He turned to find Edward Stillwell, his chief engineer and aide-de-camp, hurriedly approaching them. The expression on his face was not the sort to inspire confidence. "What is it, Eddy?"

"There's been an incident, I'm afraid." Eddy cast a meaningful glance toward the lovely interloper who had yet to leave. "Have you a moment in private?"

Ah, the perfect way to be rid of her at last. Levi glanced back at the woman who had managed to thoroughly upend his entire morning. She was a thorn in the side. He'd never see her again, and the thought gave him brief pause. A pity, that. But he had more important matters than a prettily nipped waist and a generous bosom and a mouth that begged to be kissed. He couldn't afford distraction. Didn't need it, in fact.

"Good day, madam," he said brusquely, for he didn't like the turn of his thoughts. Not one whit. He had obligations, hang it, and he had best remember them. "I've other matters to attend to." He opened the door to the bustle of the busy street again, guided her over the threshold, and closed the door at her back, sliding home the latch lest she decide she wasn't finished with her endless inquisition.

With the matter neatly settled, he turned on his heel to follow Eddy to the source of both his expression and the pungent scent tingeing the air. There was bound to be problems. With electricity, there seemed to be an equally endless ocean of possibilities and dilemmas. But Levi had great faith in Eddy's abilities. After all, he'd robbed him from Thomas Edison himself.

"What's caught fire now, Eddy?" he asked grimly as they passed back through the throng of men busied with the task of transforming the *Beacon* offices.

"Your desk, I'm afraid." Eddy winced. "One of the wires we concealed in the floor was faulty, and the deuced rug laid over it lit right up. We've doused the flames, but the room is rather ruined at present."

"Damn it, Eddy, I was just in my office and nothing seemed out of the ordinary." How long had he been distracted by his prickly siren? Too long came the obvious answer. Too damned long.

"It didn't take much time, I'm afraid," Eddy said. "Apparently, carpet is as good as a bundle of lucifers."

Levi was not pleased about this development, as much for the setback in his carefully constructed plans for North Atlantic Electric as for the fact that he'd once again be displaced. The Belgravia home he'd purchased was also in the midst of being wired for electricity, and the whole damn place was torn apart from bowels to rafters. He'd been relying upon the *Beacon* office as a quiet haven from which he could work—and more importantly—think. In peace.

He supposed he shouldn't be surprised. Nothing had gone right ever since his arrival in London. First, the work force of engineers and electricians charged with the task of outfitting the building for electricity had run across virtually every problem possible. All the while the rivals he faced, attempting to edge his company out of the race to light up England and the rest of the world, dogged him.

But if Levi had learned anything in his thirty-five years, it was that competition was the breeding grounds for brilliance. He had no doubt in his abilities or the abilities of the men he employed. There was a massive sum of money at stake in the conversion from gaslight to the infinitely better and odorless electric, and he meant to collect his fair share.

First, he needed to get his business matters in order.

"Let's assess the damage and get men working on repairing it," he told Eddy as they marched through the building to the office he'd just so recently exited and which had been so recently ruined. "We haven't time to waste on setbacks. Edison is making inroads here as well as in France and Germany, and his Pearl Street station has been running for months in New York City."

"Of course, sir. We'll have your office stripped and right as rain in no time," Eddy assured him. "We will show the others how it's done."

He crossed the threshold of his burned office. His desk was fit for the rubbish bin, the carpet badly singed and equally in need of being tossed. No, he acknowledged as he surveyed the charred remnants, nothing about this day had been to his liking. He had poured a great deal of his not-insubstantial funds into his England ventures, and he'd be damned if he didn't succeed.

He turned back to Eddy. "You're damn right we'll show the others how it's done. But hang it all, if we're going to best Edison, we need to stop catching things on fire."

Eddy winced. "Agreed, sir."

Levi sighed and consulted his pocket watch. He had very nearly lost track of the time with all the morning's distractions. An image of the loveliest of all those distractions rose unbidden in his mind and he tamped it down. "I've a meeting arranged with some engineers who just arrived in London from the Continent, and after that I've a dinner engagement with an old friend. I'll be back tomorrow morning, but if you need anything, you'll find me at my hotel."

It grieved him to stay at a hotel, regardless of how elegantly appointed it was, but his discomfort was a small price to pay for progress. He hadn't amassed businesses and a fortune by refusing to make personal sacrifices, that much was certain.

"Very good, sir. I expect to hear from Montgomery about the Paris station this afternoon. It should be fully operational and ready for testing by tomorrow. I'll send word to you as soon as I have any." Eddy was tall and dapper and his mind was as sharp as a rapier. He was more capable than anyone Levi knew, but electricity was a fickle mistress and sometimes bested even the most intelligent of men.

"Excellent." Levi would be mightily pleased when their latest station in Paris was live and generating electricity. Edison was a formidable foe, and he and his men were currently winning the race by more than a neck. "I'll leave everything in your capable hands, Eddy."

As he took his leave, Levi forced his mind to the next task at hand. North Atlantic Electric was by no means his only business, nor was it his first, but it was to be his greatest accomplishment. When he had been a small lad living on the streets of New York City, fighting for survival with the other pickpockets and waifs, he had dreamt of bettering himself. He'd built his fortune in real estate, but the wealth he'd amassed paled in comparison to the riches he could attain with electricity. Nothing would stand in his way now.

He was almost to the door, caught up in his thoughts, when he noticed something small and black, adorned by a jaunty feather and silk ribbon. So that was where the blasted woman's hat had gone. Levi glared at the offending frippery, for it reminded him of how breathtaking she had looked with blonde wisps framing her exquisite face. Fool that he was, he bent to retrieve it and discovered that it carried her scent, a delicate blend of rose and bergamot, unless he mistook his guess. Not the standard musk and ambergris so many women seemed to favor these days, but unique and somehow alluring, much like she was.

He ought to have a man return the hat to her, but he didn't know her name or direction. Very likely, he'd never see her again. It was for the best, but even so, a twinge of something like regret shot through him. The thought shouldn't give him pause at all, and that it did disturbed him. He didn't need vexing minxes to add to the many challenges facing him in London and abroad. He didn't need distraction. He needed focus, precision, boundless energy, and above all, success.

Perhaps the best thing to do would be to toss the hat away along with his burnt desk and carpet. He lowered it and continued walking lest one of his men catch sight of him standing about, mooning over a piece of headwear like a love-struck lad. It was utterly ridiculous to be so affected by a scrap of a woman he'd only met that morning. A woman who had disrupted and infiltrated his office so thoroughly he'd needed to throw her over his shoulder to remove her.

But damn it, part of him admired her pluck.

As he left the building, he carried the hat with him, his albatross. Perhaps he could discover who she was somehow, he reasoned, and return the damn thing. Yes, that was precisely what he would do. He would locate her, give her the hat, and forever remove it from his possession and her stunning face from his mind. All he needed to do was find her.

Chapter Two

"DEAREST HELEN, YOU LOOK QUITE OVERSET." A worried expression marred the otherwise serene beauty of Mrs. Jesse Whitney's countenance.

If Helen's extreme displeasure was that clear, there was good reason for it. He was a tall, decadently attractive American with the manners of a wild boar. *If you'd like to find out just how low, I'll take you back into my office right now and show you.* The sheer gall of the man. If only the reminder of those wicked words didn't now bring a sweet ache of something unfamiliar low in her belly. If only part of her hadn't been tempted for him to do exactly as he'd threatened. Dear heavens.

"I am overset, Bella," she confessed. "I've just had the most horrid experience with an appallingly rude man."

Bella had become a dear, if unexpected, friend to Helen as her sister Cleo had wed Bella's brother the Marquis of Thornton and their social circles had become hopelessly entangled. In the absence of her parents and siblings in town, Helen was enjoying the Whitneys' hospitality. It was

17

the devil of a thing to be a spinster sometimes, as she felt as though she were forever being foisted from one family member or friend's household to the next in the name of propriety. At thirty years of age, Helen was quite ready to be released from the silly snare of societal rules. After all, one couldn't ruin the already ruined. But she was the daughter of an earl and countess and her family was beloved to her and she dared not shame any of them.

So there she stood, in the entry hall of Bella's grand home, being relieved of her reticule and gloves. Her hat had gone she knew not where. In the rush of leaving the *Beacon* offices—nay, being lugged from the establishment over that scoundrel's shoulder—it had somehow fallen from her head and disappeared. She supposed she'd never get it back now.

"Oh dear." Bella eyed her gravely. She was a very striking woman, with black hair and bright-blue eyes complemented by her smart navy day gown. "I believe some tea and biscuits are in order. I've just put Virginia down for her nap and I'm in dire need of sustenance. You look as though you are as well."

Helen grimaced. "Perhaps something a bit stronger than tea would suffice," she grumbled. Something strong and mind-clearing. Something that would wipe from her brain all offending images of the dreadful man who had upended her day. It was truly unfair that he'd been so handsome. So tall. So potently masculine. Even now, her pulse still raced. She had been certain that he would kiss her, and she was ashamed to admit to herself that she had wanted him to.

But he had not. Instead, he had tossed her over his shoulder like the vagabond he undoubtedly was. No, she scolded herself, she must not think of him for another moment. She would strike him from her thoughts as surely as she would blot out an error in one of her articles.

Thinking of her article, forlorn and stuffed inside her reticule, brought a mantle of dejection settling over her as she sat down to tea with Bella in the otherwise cheery drawing room. When the servants had been dismissed, Bella was instantly ready for inquiry.

"Do tell me what has you at sixes and sevens." Bella took a delicate sip of her tea. "I've never seen you looking so distressed."

"Distressed does not begin to describe me at the moment." Helen sighed, wishing she had not allowed that dreadful man to shake her composure, that she had boxed his ears when he'd attempted to throw her over his wickedly broad shoulder. That she'd delivered a sound blow to his jaw when he'd proposed showing her how low he could be. The cur. "I stopped in at the *London Beacon* this morning to deliver my article to Mr. Bothwell as I've been doing for three years now, and he was gone. In his place was a horrid American." She paused, thinking better of her phrasing since Bella's husband Jesse hailed from the same land. "Oh, do forgive me, dear. I don't mean to insult Americans as a whole. Mr. Whitney is as fine a man as one could ever hope to find."

Bella smiled fondly at the mention of her beloved husband, and Helen knew a brief spear of envy at the sight. "Not to worry, dearest. You should hear the aspersions my mother casts upon Americans. They'd curl your hair."

The dowager Lady Thornton was well known for being a dragon and a curmudgeon both. Helen winced at the comparison. She hoped she wasn't yet so old and on the shelf or so ornery as Bella's formidable mother. "I didn't mean to suggest that all Americans are horrid, merely that the particular one I encountered was."

Bella raised an inky brow. "What in heaven's name happened? Shall I send Jesse round to give him a sound trouncing?"

Helen nearly spat the sip of tea she'd just taken all over her skirts. She swallowed hastily. "As satisfying as the prospect of that awful man being trounced is, I'm afraid fisticuffs is not the answer. Apparently, Mr. Bothwell sold the *London Beacon* and as the new owner informed me, my services are no longer needed. I'll be searching for a new home for my articles."

"Oh Helen." Her friend's pretty face was a portrait of compassion. "I know how much your reform work with the House of Rest means to you. Perhaps Jesse can help you to find another outlet for your articles. He counts a great deal of businessmen as friends and associates."

Jesse Whitney didn't merely dabble in trade; he owned quite a bit of real estate and businesses, both in New York City and London. Bella was unabashedly supportive of her husband's endeavors, despite what some old-fashioned members of their set thought.

"That would be very kind of him." Helping her fellow women in need had become one of Helen's greatest pleasures in life. She had long ago decided that she was not the sort of woman who was made for courting and marrying and producing the necessary heirs. One awful experience had shown her the path her life should take, and she had not looked back since.

"I take it that your upset has to do with more than merely losing a home for your articles, however?" Bella was perceptive. Too perceptive.

Helen wasn't certain she wanted to discuss the rest of what had occurred. She was still quite shaken by it. By him. But her friend's searching gaze was upon her, and her cheeks grew hot, giving her away. "The new owner of the *Beacon* was horribly rude, Bella. He was dismissive and arrogant, and when I would not do his bidding, he tossed me over his shoulder and carried me to the door."

Bella's eyes went wide. "He dared to throw you over his shoulder?"

"Yes." Over his broad, strong shoulder. And he had smelled wonderful. And his bottom had not been an unwelcome sight as she was carted away, nor had his hands been entirely unwanted upon her. *Oh dear.* Helen fanned herself, her discomfit even worse than ever. "Is it not exceedingly warm in here?"

This time, both of Bella's brows shot upward. "I don't

find it to be." A smile worked at the corners of her mouth. "Helen dearest, I wouldn't want to distress you by suggesting this, but perhaps—"

Helen feigned a large and unladylike sneeze to put a stop to Bella's dangerous words. Under no circumstances did she wish for her unfortunate and perplexing reaction to him to be examined. Besides, she certainly couldn't be attracted to a man who had shoved her onto the street and locked her out of the establishment as though she were a pickpocket come to thief his watch. She'd heard the latch slide home. No indeed, she had far too much sense for that. She wasn't a young girl who fawned over a fine-looking face or who was easily wooed by charming smiles and fast hands. Once, she had been. Never again.

"Oh dear, please do excuse me." Helen held a handkerchief to her nose, not feeling a jot of guilt for her subterfuge. She had been blessed with three sisters, after all, and she knew how to avoid an uncomfortable conversation when she wished.

Bella's expression said she was more than aware of Helen's ruse, but her manners kept her from pursuing the matter. "Bless you, my dear. I had word from Jesse this morning that we're to have a guest for dinner this evening. Another American, I'm afraid, but hopefully one that is more to your liking."

"Oh?" Helen was grateful indeed for the change of subject. If only her mind would depart from the topic as easily as her friend had. She could still see him glowering down at her.

Are you dimwitted, madam?

Such impudence. He had actually uttered those words to her. She should have walloped him with her reticule right then, in fact. But she had been too stunned by his masculine beauty. There was something indefinably magnetic about him, something that had called to her on a deep, primitive level that she dared not trust. She sipped her tea, hoping for distraction.

"Yes." Bella drew Helen's attention back to her. "Mr. Levi Storm is to be joining us. He should make for interesting company. Jesse says he is quite the talk of the town back in New York City. He's built up an impressive empire of businesses. Jesse has invested in one of his companies here in town. He's aiming to beat Edison at electrifying all of London. We're to have our entire house wired for electric lights. It's all quite exciting."

Electricity.

An American businessmen who was bringing electricity to London would be joining them for dinner. Helen allowed that news to settle into her mind as dread sank through her. It couldn't be. Could it?

"What is it, Helen? You look as if someone has cast up their accounts on your favorite dress."

Helen managed a tremulous smile. "Not as bad as all that, I hope. It's merely that I fear that your dinner guest and the boor from the *London Beacon* are one and the same."

Bella's expression clouded. "If that is the case, dinner tonight will be an interesting affair indeed."

"Indeed," she echoed weakly. Perhaps, she thought, she could cry off with the megrims. Anything would be better than seeing him again. *I'll take you back into my office right now and show you.* What would he have showed her? Good heavens, it was wicked for her to wonder.

More wicked still that part of her wanted to see him again more than anything.

Perhaps if she saw him once more, gave him the dressing down he deserved, she could forget all about him and his startling blue eyes and rakish good looks. Yes, that was what she needed. All she needed to do was make it through dinner, give him the earful she should have given him earlier, and forget all about him.

Hang it all, his vexing mystery woman was Jesse's guest.

What were the odds? Levi gambled, but only in business, so he was at a loss for calculating what he would have otherwise deemed the improbable chance that he would so quickly and easily find her again. Improbable no more, for there she sat across the table from him, her beauty unparalleled by Jesse's wife, exceptionally lovely in her own right though she was.

Her golden hair had been swept into woven coils with a waterfall of curls down the back. Diamonds twinkled from her throat. She wore a deep purple gown that set off her pale features and ample décolletage to advantage and highlighted her small waist. Damn it if she wasn't the most striking woman he'd ever seen.

At the moment, she appeared to be endeavoring to keep her gaze trained on their host and hostess, but her eyes had met his once and the effect had been startling, sending a physical jolt through him not unlike electricity.

No woman had ever affected him thus, and her effect upon him was quickly landing him in an even blacker humor than he'd already suffered after his day of burning offices and smoking dynamos. She was a noblewoman, which simultaneously relieved and disappointed him, for it meant that she was not the sort of woman with which one dallied, and he was a man who ought not to be thinking of dallying in the first place.

He was already engaged, after all, and he had carefully decided upon the match to further his business ventures and connections both. Constance VanHorn came from the most prominent and wealthy family in New York City. Her father owned half the city and beyond that, half the railroads in the entire country. Elias VanHorn had invested heavily in North Atlantic Electric. When he'd proposed the match between Levi and his eldest daughter, Levi had seen it for the rare opportunity it was and had agreed. He was willing to sacrifice his freedom for the greater good of his business, and VanHorn was willing to overlook Levi's dubious past to see his wayward daughter settled.

Levi had only met his bride-to-be on two occasions and that had suited him fine. He wasn't a man given to illusions of love, and he made no mistake that Miss VanHorn harbored any tender feelings toward him. Indeed, he scarcely recalled the stilted conversation they had exchanged and possessed only a vague impression of her appearance, which had been pleasant enough but rather unremarkable.

She was certainly not tall, blonde, and blindingly beautiful. He had never thrown her over his shoulder or yearned to carry her into the nearest empty chamber and kiss her delectable mouth. She had never irritated him or interrupted his day or spoken a tart word in his presence. She was a paragon, as uninspiring as an aspic, nicely formed but somehow unappealing just the same.

Miss VanHorn would complement his empire, enhance his holdings, and forge business relationships of the sort money couldn't buy. She was everything he had required in a wife, hailing from an old-money, blue-blood, New York City family he'd once looked upon with awe. He, Levi Storm, sometime orphan boy and ne'er do well, was marrying the daughter of the wealthiest man in America. It should have made him feel something more than ambivalence and a vague sense of disquiet. It should have pleased him and been enough to make him impervious to the charms of a maddening blonde with a penchant for penning drivel for a penniless London rag.

Somehow, it did not.

"I understand that you and Lady Helen are already acquainted, Mr. Storm," interjected Jesse's wife into Levi's thoughts, and unless he was mistaken, there was a sly undertone to her words. Her expression was bland and innocent enough, but he was not so easily fooled.

He cast a glance toward Lady Helen. Her name suited her, he thought, like Helen of Troy, an incomparable beauty. It was regal and lush, the same as she was. She looked at him at last, challenging him with her stare. He accepted her dare. "Lady Helen was kind enough to grace my offices with her presence this morning," he said, careful to keep his tone mild.

Lady Helen pursed her lips as though she'd taken a bite of something tart. "Indeed, but I'm afraid Mr. Storm was not altogether pleased by my unexpected arrival."

He couldn't stop staring at her. He wanted her, he realized then. He wanted her, and he could not have her. Or could he? The devil in him said maybe he could, that nothing in life was truly out of reach as long as one wasn't concerned with such things as honor and duty. "You have my sincere apologies if I caused you offense in any way, my lady."

"Your apologies are a bit tardy, sir." She was determined to rake him over the coals before the company, as politely as her manners would permit.

He had been rude to her, and he knew it as well as she. But niceties had never been his strong suit, and she had been equally tempting and irritating. He smiled. "Nevertheless, I am sorry for my cavalier treatment of you."

"Tossing a lady over one's shoulder is cavalier treatment?" She eyed him archly. "I confess, I hadn't realized your American customs were so decidedly different from ours."

If she was trying to embarrass him, she was failing miserably. He'd toss the bothersome woman over his shoulder again in an instant if necessary and relish every minute of it. His grin deepened. "Don't paint us all with the same jaded brush, my lady. Jesse here is as fine a gentleman as you'll ever find."

He and Jesse had been friends for some time. They both had earned their places in New York City real estate with nothing short of mettle and a fair dash of good fortune. They had kept in close contact over the years, and it had been Jesse who had prompted him to expand his business holdings to England, a land hungry for technology and change. The gateway to all of Europe.

His friend eyed him somewhat bemusedly. Damn it, Jesse ought to know he wasn't a dandy by now. He never had been and he never would be. He had fought his way up in life from lowly street urchin to respected businessman, but there were some roles he could simply never accept.

"Over your shoulder, Levi?" Jesse asked pointedly.

The woman was well-versed in the art of aggravation. Levi's foul humor returned. "I merely feared that Lady Helen would do herself injury," he improvised nicely. "My electricians were in the midst of a delicate operation. As it happened, she was removed from danger just in time."

"Danger?" Lady Bella echoed, her expression concerned. "Blessed angels' sakes, Helen, you made no mention of danger."

"Indeed." He met Lady Helen's narrowed glare across the table with a look of pure innocence. "There was a fire. The contents of my office were destroyed."

"Oh dear." Lady Bella pressed a hand to her heart, looking dismayed. "I hope your electric lights are safe, Mr. Storm."

"Perfectly," he answered easily. "Electricity is merely a feral beast that need be tamed, but I know of no better men to tame it than my own." He said the last with true confidence, for he was not lacking in conviction when it came to North Atlantic Electric and its men. Not for a moment. Electricity was the way of the future, whether the world was ready for it or no.

"Still," pressed Lady Bella, "fire is quite dangerous, Mr. Storm. Even you must admit that."

"It can be," he allowed, "but I think you'll find that, as with many things in life, the risk of electricity is infinitely smaller than the reward it brings." His gaze traveled to Lady Helen once more before he could think better of it.

The tension between them was nearly palpable. He yearned to have her alone, beyond the watching eyes of Jesse and his wife. To take her in his arms once more, but this time to do what he had so badly wanted to do that morning. Kiss her. Taste her. Strip her silk from her luscious curves and then sink his aching cock deep inside her.

Ah, he had gone far too long without a woman in his bed, and it was beginning to show.

"What are the rewards, Mr. Storm?" Lady Helen asked, even her voice a velvet seduction to his senses.

The look he cast her way was laden with meaning. "The rewards are many, my lady. Electricity is clean. It does not stink or smoke like gaslight. It's far brighter and more efficient. It is not what you are accustomed to, but once you have it, you'll never want to go back to the way you once lived."

He wasn't merely speaking of electricity and they both knew it. Very likely, Jesse and his wife knew it as well. He veered into dangerous territory. He was set to wed Miss VanHorn in a few months' time, and he had no business panting after a lady. Even if that lady was gorgeous and tempting and vexing and seated before him, nearly close enough to touch. But he wasn't sure if he cared at the moment. Hounds of hell. It wasn't like him to be so distracted by a woman.

Lady Helen gave him a small, nearly indiscernible smile. He longed to know what she was thinking, what mysteries hid behind her poised beauty. "I suppose we shall have to take you at your word, Mr. Storm."

"My word is my bond," he said without hesitation. It was the promise that had delivered him through endless business dealings. He had built his reputation upon it, along with the fact that he wasn't afraid to be ruthless when he needed to be.

"Is that why you bought the *London Beacon*?" she asked shrewdly.

She was a worthy opponent, this one. But he had never been fearful of an intelligent woman; rather, he preferred them to their insipid counterparts. "I purchased the *Beacon* for many reasons," he hedged with care.

"You didn't buy it so that you could propagate your own

interests?" Lady Helen's gaze was direct and unflinching. "It seems to me that when a man seeking to sell electricity to all the world buys a journal and turns out the paper's staff on their ears, he has only one thing in mind."

"And it seems to me that the *Beacon* and the way I choose to run it are not your concern, my dear lady." His tone was deliberately cool, all the better to discourage the current vein of conversation. She was right, damn her, but that didn't mean he would acknowledge it. He didn't like the swiftness with which she had seen through him, judged him, and he wasn't accustomed to anyone challenging him so directly. Not any longer, now that he was one of the wealthiest men in New York City.

"I'm sure neither are my concern, given that you've summarily dismissed me from my post." Her tone spoke of her pique.

He had not read any of the *Beacon* before purchasing it, had merely known that its flame was about to sputter out into darkness. Like the proverbial berry ripe for the plucking, it had been a promising lure. He'd required a press and its influence. One had been for sale, and for a very cheap price. He wondered now what she could have written that it meant such a great deal to her.

"Perhaps it's time that we took our leave of the gentlemen, Lady Helen," Jesse's wife suggested then, apparently seeking to avoid any further discord. He supposed it was the hostess's duty, quite customary and proper, but that didn't mean he appreciated the withdrawing.

Levi didn't miss the telling glance Jesse sent his wife's direction either. Their ease with each other and their quiet though obvious love was not lost on him. For the first time in as long as he could recall, he knew a prick of envy for the relationship between husband and wife.

He tamped the unwanted feeling firmly down.

He and Jesse stood in deference to the departure of the fairer sex from the dining room. To hell with society and its never-ending book of rules. He had just begun to enjoy himself. But as much as he didn't want to leave Lady Helen's presence, he also didn't wish to match wits with her in front of an audience. He wanted her alone, which he knew was an idea about as good as Pickett's Charge at the battle of Gettysburg. Which was to say not a good idea at all. Many a man never returned from that field.

"Ladies." He bowed to Lady Bella and Lady Helen, his gaze clashing with Lady Helen's once more as he did so.

"Mr. Storm," she acknowledged softly. Fire sparkled in her lively eyes. It was brilliant and bewitching. "Until we meet again, sir."

She was determined. He knew this would not be the last time they crossed paths or verbal swords. Desire stirred through him. There was that pluck of hers again. "Lady Helen, I shall look forward to it."

She turned and took her leave, and he couldn't help but admire the seductive nip of her waist and the beauty of the glow of the gaslight in her burnished curls. Lady Helen was a complication he didn't need. A siren calling him to the rocks. She was magnificent and brazen and opinionated and irritating. He had businesses to run both here and abroad. He had obligations from which he could not escape. He had engineers to worry about, competition and setbacks, malfunctioning stations and dynamos, and yet somehow, she made him want to forget about volts and amperes and ohms. She made him want to simply bask in her presence, ignore his cares and stresses, his duties and worries. She was altogether dangerous.

He decided in that precise moment that he was keeping the damn hat.

"I begin to think there is a great deal more to the story of you and Mr. Storm than you've revealed, Helen." Bella was being her usual direct self over tea in the drawing room.

Helen frowned. Her pulse was too fast for her liking, and no matter how she tried, she could not seem to purge Mr. Storm's handsome visage from her mind. Or the fact that even now, he was beneath the same roof as she, a mere room away. He took her breath and made her feel like a ninny. This would simply not do.

"There is no story of Mr. Storm and me," Helen assured her friend. "There is merely his appalling lack of manners and my reaction to it."

"I saw the way he looked at you at dinner." Bella's gaze was knowing.

As had Helen, and that was the precise, troubling reason her pulse was racing, she was sure of it. He had most certainly not looked upon her in such a bold fashion at the *Beacon* offices. "I don't know what you speak of, truly."

Bella grinned. "Nonsense. You know exactly what I speak of, which is exactly why your cheeks are going quite rosy."

Helen busied herself with taking a long sip of tea. Drat her observant friend. She was every bit as troublesome as Helen's own sisters. "I believe you've been spending far too much time with Cleo."

"I'll own your sister is prone to dramatics, but I'm not far off the mark and you and I both know it. You needn't worry on my account. I won't breathe a word of it to anyone, not even Jesse," Bella assured her. "Besides, no one knows better than I just how alluring an American man can be, much to my mother's dismay."

"You're right about one thing, Cleo is indeed prone to dramatics. I've never met another soul more adept at pleading the megrims at the slightest opportunity." She frowned then. "But I don't find Mr. Storm alluring. Not in the least. Not if he were the very last man in all of London. I'm a spinster firmly on the shelf, and I'm quite pleased with that fate."

Bella's expression still mirrored the proverbial cat who'd found her way into a saucer of Devonshire cream. "If you say so, my dear."

"I know that look, Levi." Jesse handed him a glass of amber-colored spirits he'd just poured from a crystal decanter. "American whiskey. I can't abide by port. You look as though you could use it."

"Hell yes." Levi accepted the offering and took a grateful sip. "What look are you referring to, by the way?"

Jesse sighed. "We're old friends, are we not?"

Hang it. Levi wasn't a fool, and he knew all too well where their conversation was headed. They had been business partners in New York City for a decade, had been friends before even then. He and Jesse had forged an unlikely friendship in the murky years following the war. Levi had enlisted in the Union army as a young lad. Jesse had fought for the rebels. There had been no enmity between them when they'd crossed paths one day in New York City, only the same fierce determination to make something of themselves from the ashes of who they'd once been.

"We're old friends," Levi acknowledged slowly, "but not so old I hope."

"I feel old some days." Jesse sighed, his expression pained. "Jesus, Levi, I hate to say this to you of all people, but I'm duty bound. Lady Helen is under my roof and under my protection."

Damn it to hell. He took another drink of whiskey, relishing its burn all the way to his gut. "I would not have tossed her over my shoulder had I realized she was a lady." Truth be told, he wasn't sure if that was an honest statement or not. She had vexed him mightily, and he had never been particularly polished or mild of manner.

"It's more than just that. Of course, you can't go tossing

31

gently bred ladies over your shoulder and carting them about, but you already know as much. I saw the manner in which you were looking at her over dinner. She's the daughter to an earl and the sister of my wife's sister-in-law." Jesse took a sip from his own whiskey. "I'm sorry, Levi, but I couldn't let it go unsaid."

The manner in which he'd been looking at her. Christ, the way Jesse said it made Levi sound as though he were a lion eying up a prized lamb. "What do you think I am, a monster? Hell, Jesse. I'm to be married." He thought again of Miss VanHorn and wished she inspired an eighth of the interest he felt for Lady Helen. Not even a stirring of his cock, damn it. "I have no interest in harming Lady Helen, of that much you can be certain."

Jesse sighed. "I fear I've turned into a snarling old papa bear now that I've two daughters in my charge. I've been having a hell of a time with Clara, but at least Virginia is yet a babe. I don't need to worry about men sniffing around her skirts for at least twenty years, I hope."

Levi couldn't fault Jesse for his sense of honor. Besides, his good friend wasn't wrong about his interest in Lady Helen. It was improper and altogether wrong and he had no business whatsoever panting after her like a lovesick swain. He knew all that just as well as he knew the inner workings of a dynamo. "There is no insult on my part, old friend. How goes it with your eldest daughter?"

Clara had not been present at dinner. She was the product of an ill-fated liaison in Jesse's youth, and Jesse had been candid in his correspondence about the difficulties he'd faced with her. Apparently, the girl was quite a handful.

His friend grimaced. "She's in finishing school, much to her dismay. We thought it best after she led her chaperone on a merry chase at a country house party some months back."

Levi was damn glad he had no children of his own over which to fret, at least not yet. The thought brought him back to Miss VanHorn and his impending nuptials. Eventually, he would have to return to New York City and take her as his bride. He drained the remnants of his whiskey. "And how is married life treating you, old man?"

Jesse grinned, exuding more satisfaction than a dog who'd just eaten a fine steak dinner. "All I can say is that I'm very happy. Happier than I ever thought or hoped to be."

"I'm glad for you." No one deserved contentment more than Jesse. He was a good man, a good friend, and he had suffered enough through the hells of war. "Mrs. Whitney is clearly too good for the likes of your sorry hide, but I'm glad for you nonetheless."

"I'll not argue with you on that score." He laughed. "Have some more whiskey, Levi. I've missed our banter. It's been far too long."

"It has indeed." He thought then of the work awaiting him at his hotel. Telegrams. The latest report from Eddy. Newspapers. Engineering journals. Headaches, the lot of them. "But I should get back to my hotel. I've a great deal of work to do tonight."

"To hell with work," Jesse dismissed in his easy drawl as he splashed a bit more whiskey into Levi's glass. "Work can damn well wait. In fact, my dear wife would have this sorry hide of mine tanned if I didn't offer you our hospitality. Stay the evening. Stay the week. You needn't be relegated to a hotel, you know. Don't argue, damn it. You're like family to me, Levi. I insist you stay. It'll be good for you and for business. We're hosting a ball in a few days' time, and it would be an excellent opportunity for you to meet some of the peerage. Think of all the houses you can light up."

The suggestion gave him pause. Ordinarily, he preferred to be alone, to throw himself into his work. He had precious little time or want for pleasure. Men didn't breed success by resting on their laurels. But there was a definite appeal to Jesse's words, and he was no fool. It had everything to do with one woman.

Lady Helen.

He should put down his glass, politely refuse Jesse's invitation, and return to the sanctity of his hotel, where there would be no lovely English spitfires to distract him.

He took another draw of whiskey. "Very well. I'd hate to be the one responsible for Mrs. Whitney doing you harm."

"Excellent." Jesse raised his glass in salute. "Now, tell me more about North Atlantic Electric and how your company is going to beat the tar out of Edison."

A welcome distraction. There was nothing in the world Levi loved more than business. "With pleasure."

Chapter Three

ELEN DIDN'T KNOW WHAT NONSENSICAL impetus had caused her to wander from her chamber in the middle of the night. But she had, and here she was, scouring the bookshelves in Bella and Jesse's library in search of something to read. Bella was infamous for being a voracious reader, and though the shelves didn't disappoint, Helen wasn't particular tonight. Anything to keep her restless mind off Mr. Storm.

She wished he had not been a guest at dinner.

In his dark, evening finery, he had been wickedly gorgeous. She'd never been so drawn to a man. Indeed, she had not been drawn to a man at all for many, many years. After what had happened that long-ago day, she'd been certain the part of herself that had once possessed romantic fancies had died. Her sisters Cleo, Tia, and Bo were great romantics, but she had remained impervious, a dedicated spinster with no wish to be at the mercy of a man ever again. She'd admired handsome men from a distance, flirted on the odd occasion, but beyond that, had remained happily a spinster.

Her reaction to Mr. Storm troubled her greatly. He didn't make her ill at ease. He didn't frighten her. Quite the opposite. He intrigued her. She supposed she shouldn't be surprised that he affected her. After all, he was beautiful in a way that no man ought to be. But she had thought herself made of sterner stuff, had thought she'd been hardened enough to know better.

She sighed, continuing her perusal of spines but not even really reading them. She was too flustered to read. Too flustered to sleep. Anthony Trollope. Charles Dickens. Fiction, poetry, Latin. Nothing suited her.

Bella's words returned to her. *I saw the way he looked at you at dinner.* Goodness yes, he had looked at her as though he wasn't certain if he wanted to toss her back over his shoulder or kiss her senseless. She knew she nettled him, and she had to admit she rather enjoyed that fact.

Thank heavens he was no longer beneath the same roof. He was off to whatever corner of London he belonged in, and she was where she belonged. Alone, with no one for company but an army of books she didn't care to read.

"What finds you in the library at this late hour, Lady Helen?"

The deep voice just over her shoulder gave her a start. Heart thumping, she spun about. There he stood as if she'd conjured him up, tall and lean, in only a waistcoat and shirtsleeves and perfectly fitted trousers, his jacket long gone. There was a dangerous air about him, even though his words were perfectly benign.

She pressed a hand over her heart, willing it to slow its pace. "Mr. Storm, whatever are you doing here?"

"The same as you, I suspect." That gaze of his scorched her with its intensity. "I couldn't sleep."

"Sleep?" Surely he was not staying beneath Jesse and Bella's roof.

"Ah, we've traveled full circle." He sauntered closer to her than necessary. "You're back to repeating me in question form. Is this an English custom to which I've yet to be introduced?"

She was not amused. Her cheeks went hot. "You are not being very kind."

"I'm not a particularly kind man." His countenance was solemn, indecipherable. She wished she knew what thoughts lurked behind those brilliant eyes. "Jesse has extended his hospitality and I've accepted. I've been hanging my hat at a hotel and I find I've grown weary of it."

Dear sweet heavens, he was staying here.

Beneath the same roof.

Of course that fact didn't affect her. Not in the least. She was unmoved. Let him stay where he would. She reminded herself that she was quite put out with him. "You are an old acquaintance of Mr. Whitney's?"

He nodded. "He's one of few men I count as true friends."

"Were you a soldier in the war as well then, Mr. Storm?" It was impolite of her to ask, but it was the witching time of night and she stood before him in a nightdress and dressing gown, and he looked as if he'd been tippling whiskey with their host. With his dark hair ruffled and his bearded jaw, he rather resembled a pirate in gentleman's clothes. She didn't truly think society rules applied to such a situation.

His jaw clenched, his gaze growing shuttered. "I was."

It explained rather a great deal about him, she thought. The disciplined air, the impassive expression, the complete disregard for societal niceties. She wondered then what must have happened to him during that infamous conflict, what he must have seen and endured to so harden him. Death, surely. Destruction too. Had he killed? Suffered a wound? She couldn't even begin to imagine the horrors he must have faced. It almost weakened her resolve to keep him at a distance and treat him like the adversary he surely was.

"I'm sorry," she said simply, seeing that the subject was one that weighed on him. "I shouldn't have pried."

"No." He flashed a brief, haunted smile. "You should

not have, but I've gathered you do quite a bit of things you shouldn't, my lady."

"Perhaps," she allowed grudgingly. "I've discovered that life is ever so much more interesting when one dabbles in what one ought not to do." Sometimes more rewarding, sometimes more painful. She had learned many lessons in her thirty years, and there were some she would've rather not learned at all.

She realized that her words implied more than she had intended when his gaze slipped to her mouth. An answering heat blossomed within her. Heavens, but her reaction to this man was most vexing. She turned her attention back to the shelves of tomes lining the wall. "However, that is neither here nor there, and I really ought to find a book and leave you to your evening."

"You ought to, yes." He touched her elbow, exerting just enough light pressure to turn her to face him once more, his touch a brand even through the fabric separating their skins. "Just as I ought not to be here."

She jerked her arm from his grasp. "And neither should you make so familiar with my person, sir."

"What happened to your enthusiasm for dabbling in what one ought not to do? I suppose it only extends to yourself and not others?"

Oh, he was troublesome indeed. "I expect I've misplaced it. Perhaps it lies with the manners you surely once possessed."

He flashed her a crooked grin that was oddly charming. "Forgive me, Lady Helen."

Helen's heart fluttered like the wings of a butterfly. If she had a sensible bone in her body, she'd flee from the library as though her virtue depended upon it. Of course, she'd never been particularly sensible, and her virtue was another dark matter all its own.

"I'm sure you aren't being sincere," she observed, something about him bringing out the boldness within her. "You don't seem to be one who offers apologies so easily."

"You're right." His voice was low and personal, decadent as honey. She noted how very large his hands were, and then she imagined them on her, how equally decadent that would feel. "On both counts. It seemed the thing one ought to say to a lady that one has flung over his shoulder."

She flushed, thinking again of how easily he had hauled her out of his office. He was quite strong and tall. She thought once more of how she'd been afforded an excellent glimpse of his backside during her trip to the door. It had met with her vigorous approval. "Do you make a habit of flinging ladies over your shoulder?"

"As it happens, I don't. You alone enjoy that rare distinction."

"Ah, then I shall cherish the honor." She smiled, rather relishing their banter despite herself. But there was still a question that had been plaguing her since their conversation at dinner. "What are your plans for the *Beacon*, Mr. Storm? You seemed very determined to stay your course earlier today."

He was silent for a moment, his gaze unwavering and intense upon her until she feared that he would once more dismiss her query. "The *Beacon* will be devoted solely to business moving forward, and its offices will be an exhibition of the capabilities of electricity."

Of course. She had not been wrong that he planned to further his business dealings by using the paper, but she hadn't realized it would extend to the building itself. She frowned. "It will be solely devoted to business?" She'd never heard of such a notion, and it certainly didn't bode well for the reformist circles who had faithfully subscribed to the *Beacon*. Or for herself.

"No more gossip columns or cartoons or fashion plates, I'm afraid."

His earlier words returned to her. *I don't care if it's about butterflies or your grandmother's shoes.* It occurred to her that he had never actually read a word of the newspaper he'd purchased. The *Beacon* was irrelevant to him in his pursuit of whatever it was he wanted—money, influence, power. He was a man determined to have his way in the world, and he wasn't about to let anyone or anything stop him, certainly not the plight of the horrifying lives of London's ladies of the night. He hadn't even bothered to see what it was he bought and dismantled, whose voices he silenced. Handsome he may be, but she very much doubted a warm heart beat beneath his broad chest.

Her blood went quite cold at the realization.

"You assume that because I'm a woman, my sole interests are needlepoint and drawing room whispers?" How condescending of him. She was tempted to deliver a sound blow to his arrogant head with one of the volumes on the shelves at her back.

He looked surprised. "Of course not. It is merely that most newspapers are filled with utter drivel rather than anything of import."

"It is apparent, Mr. Storm, that you never read a word of the *Beacon*. You found a small journal that was an easy prey with a greedy man willing to sell his soul and you pressed your advantage." She warmed to her task of serving him an ample slice of how-dare-you pie. Irritation felt far more reassuring to her than attraction. It was safer to detest him than to want him. "You are a heartless man."

His mouth tightened, but she couldn't discern whether it was from anger or irritation. "How easily you've judged me, my lady. Tell me, is it because I'm common?"

"Not in the least. It's because you couldn't be bothered to realize what you were destroying with your whims."

"I didn't destroy a damn thing." His tone went more frigid than Wenham Lake ice. "That paper had been run into the ground by Bothwell and was so far in debt it was never going to make its way out without my assistance. I don't operate on whims, my lady. I make my business decisions with the greatest of care. Hundreds of families put bread on their table through me, and I take that responsibility seriously."

His words gave her pause. Perhaps he wasn't entirely heartless after all. But there remained the fact that he had unceremoniously closed the doors on the *Beacon's* formidable legacy of reformism without even bothering to read a single article it had ever run. Not to mention his patriarchal assumption that as a woman, she would have no greater thoughts in her head than gossip and nonsense.

"The concern you place upon those in your employ is admirable, Mr. Storm," she allowed, "however, you're altogether missing the point of my argument."

"I reckon the point of your argument is that you enjoy arguing. You're the single most vexing creature I've ever met."

Truly. He thought *she* was vexing? She was of half a mind to box his ears. "I assure you that I don't find arguing with anyone even slightly pleasant, and arguing with you is fast proving a Sisyphean task."

"I might say the same, my lady."

They were at a stalemate. She'd never found another man so frustratingly stubborn. So arrogant. So altogether wonderful to look at.

Oh dear, now where had that last thought come from? It wouldn't do for her to notice how lean and decadent a figure he cut. Or for her to notice how sensual his mouth was, to wonder how it would feel if his lips trailed a path of fire upon her bare skin. No indeed, none of those things would do at all. They would only leave her mired in scandal and ruin, the likes of which she'd somehow managed to avoid for thirty years, against nearly impossible odds.

She sighed. Perhaps it was the lateness of the evening that rendered her maudlin, but she was fast losing her meager line of defenses, and he was her enemy at the gate. "I fear the evening has grown quite late, and I ought to retire. This conversation seems to be going nowhere at all."

When she would have turned and fled, he stopped her once more with a hand at her elbow. "Lady Helen."

"Sir?" Helen knew more than a thing or two about putting on airs. She gave him her sternest gaze to remind him that he encroached upon her territory. "It would seem we've once again traveled full circle. Here you are making far too free with my person."

His lips twitched, and she almost suspected it was with mirth. But his countenance remained serious. Almost grim. "I would apologize, but I do believe I've offered the maximum amount of apologies I'm willing to give anyone in the course of one day."

Helen almost laughed at his aggrieved proclamation. "You needn't apologize, Mr. Storm, merely unhand me, or I shall—"

"Or?" His tone went low and intimate once more. She had unwittingly presented him a challenge. "What will you do? Bring all the servants upon me? Crack me in the eye?"

"Both are tempting scenarios," she said tartly, but she was inwardly amused despite her best intentions. There was something indefinable about this man that simply got to her, cutting straight past all her barriers, common sense, and good Lord, even her intellect. Whatever it was proved more potent by the moment. She had to guard herself against him. Lowering her defenses just wouldn't do. She well knew where it had landed her in the past, and she didn't care for an encore. "However, I would prefer to keep my reputation and your eye both intact for the nonce."

He retained his grip on her elbow, but it wasn't forceful or painful. Rather, it was...compelling. "The first rule of business is that you should never make threats you aren't willing to carry out. Otherwise, you give the advantage to your opponent."

He had her there, the arrogant man. "I wasn't aware you were my opponent or that we were conducting business."

"That depends." His fingers traveled slowly down her arm to make a leisurely exploration of the bare skin at her wrist.

"Upon what?" Her voice was breathless, even to her

own ears. Traitorous body, responding to him thus. One would have supposed she would have a far stronger sense of self-preservation. All these years, she had held fast in her determination to keep every gentleman at bay.

But Mr. Storm was no gentleman, and he had told her so himself, had offered to show her. Perhaps that was part of his allure.

"Upon you, Lady Helen." He stepped closer, so near that she could smell his deliciously masculine scent once again. "Would you care to continue writing for the *Beacon?*"

She couldn't have been more stunned by his words if he had announced that he was the bastard son of Queen Victoria. "I thought my services were no longer required. Not even if my articles were about my grandmother's shoes."

Helen couldn't resist the urge to needle him, just a bit. He had been exceedingly rude, and thoroughly maddening. Both appeared to be character traits of his. She wasn't certain she trusted this sudden change of heart. After all, he was a businessman. There had to be some reason he'd want her to continue writing for the journal, and with the way he was looking at her now, she had a feeling she had an idea of what that reason was.

She swallowed.

Oh dear.

He smiled, and the effect was smoldering. His dimples carved matching grooves in his whiskers. How ridiculous, she thought, that a man of his beauty should also have a facial characteristic that only served to enhance and call attention to his looks. He waged a full war upon her senses, and it wasn't fair. "They aren't required. Merely requested."

No sense in beating around the proverbial bush. "Why?" she asked bluntly.

His thumb traced a circle over her wrist bone. "Perhaps you've worn me down, my lady. I've seen the error of my ways. I really ought to have read the journal before I purchased it. If your writing is of such great consequence to you, who am I to still your pen?"

Clever of him to phrase his reply in such a way, but Helen was no fool. Nor was she easily won. "Perhaps I have, or perhaps there are other motives for your sudden generosity of spirit."

"I reckon we'll just have to wait and see, Lady Helen." He took her hand then and raised it to his lips for a kiss that couldn't have been more polite if it had been done in view of a drawing room full of the highest sticklers in society. "What is your answer?"

She ought to tell him no. Of course, she should. Helen knew that. Continuing to write for the *Beacon* meant she would have to see him again. Seeing him again would likely hold a wealth of consequences. She was sure that he meant to seduce her. It was plain in his frank admiration of her, in the way he touched her. She was also sure that she may not be able to resist just such an effort. Worse, that she may not want to.

But her cause was also important to her. If she could continue to give a voice to those who had none, continue to try to drum up support in any way she could, then anything was worth the risk. There was so much more that needed to be said and done, so few people willing to stand up and act. Much of the world needed fixing, and Helen wanted to help mend it. Mending healed. It had healed her, once upon a time.

"Your answer, Lady Helen?"

She was about to capitulate, and they both knew it. Still, her conscience prodded her. "What do you want from me in return?"

"Not a thing you aren't willing to give," he said easily.

Double oh dear. "You'll print anything I write?" she pressed.

He released her hand, his expression as indecipherable as ever. "Within reason. I reserve the right to exert my editorial authority, but you are free to write whatever your heart desires."

"Very well, Mr. Storm." She took a deep breath, hoping she wasn't agreeing to her downfall. "I accept your offer."

Levi woke in a strange bed with the persistence of a whiskey headache thumping his skull. Murky memories of the evening before flitted through his brain. There had been dinner and the happy surprise that his unruly mystery woman also happened to be Jesse's houseguest. There had been tumblers of whiskey and camaraderie with his old friend.

And then there had been the run-in with a blonde beauty in the library. Damn it. What the hell had he been thinking, telling Lady Helen he'd print her articles? He'd already decided that he was taking the journal in a new direction, one dedicated to business and business alone, the first of its kind. He didn't even have an inkling of what sort of nonsense she might foist upon him for publication. For all he knew, she could very well write horrid poetry or insipid articles about the art of curling one's hair.

Yet he had invited her to continue writing for his paper. What worm had taken up residence in his addled mind? It was lust of course. Had to be. He wanted Lady Helen. Despite the reassurances he'd given Jesse, despite Miss VanHorn, despite the fact that the woman irritated him to no end, despite every law of reason in the land, he wanted Lady Helen. There had been a moment last evening where, in his whiskey-fogged mind, he had realized he could walk away and never see her again or he could somehow keep her presence in his life.

He had selfishly chosen the latter, and by the grim rays of the morning, he already knew it to be a mistake. Hang it, the light streaming in past the window dressings was decidedly bright. Too bright, which meant he'd slept far longer than was his custom.

Levi snatched up his pocket watch from the bedside

table and confirmed what he'd already feared. He was late. Levi Storm was many things, but late had never been one of them. He regarded punctuality as a virtue very near to godliness. Yet here he was, in bed with a throbbing head when he was an hour past the time he was to have met Eddy. Add to that his ill-advised bid to continue seeing Lady Helen, and well, the day was not precisely brimming in promise.

With a groan that was one part penitence, one part reluctance, he rose from the bed. He'd had a servant bring over some of his necessities from the hotel the previous night, but he had no man to dress him. He had never had a valet in his life and he didn't suppose he ever would. While he'd grown accustomed to a life laden with finer things, he could never bring himself to allow another to help him dress. It just wasn't in him. Now he almost regretted it as he performed his morning rituals and slowly turned himself back into a gentleman fit for society.

As he exited his chamber, he turned his mind forcefully toward the day's business matters that would require his attention. It felt reassuring to entrench himself in his work and cast all thoughts of Lady Helen from his mind.

And then just as quickly as he'd removed her from his thoughts, there she stood before him in the hallway, wearing a violet morning gown that accented her lush curves to perfection. Lust hit him with the force of a blow directly to his midsection.

Damn it all to hell.

She smiled when she saw him, warily, or so he thought. "Good morning, Mr. Storm."

"Good morning, my lady." It would seem he'd have to act the part of gentleman. He offered her his arm. "May I escort you to breakfast?"

She rested her hand in the crook of his arm and he wished he didn't like the way it felt but he did just the same. "That would be lovely, sir."

They were being very formal now, as if they had not met

in the early hours of the morning and clashed verbal swords. Perhaps it was for the best. For the scent of bergamot and rose taunted him.

"I trust you slept well?" he asked, careful to keep his tone cool and unaffected. Lovesick swain was not a role he cared to play.

"My sleep was utterly unperturbed," she said in dulcet tones, staring straight ahead.

He could not say the same, and he had to wonder whether she was being entirely truthful. He didn't think he mistook her reaction to him. Even now, she held herself stiffly, the perfect picture of elegance. Too perfect. "Excellent, my lady."

They reached the curved grand staircase and began their descent. "I'm very grateful to you for your change of heart, Mr. Storm."

Her soft concession startled him as much as it warmed him. It wouldn't do for her to think him weak, or worse, kind. "I wouldn't precisely deem it a change of heart, my lady."

She stopped right there on the step, forcing him to halt their progress as well, and turned to look at him again at last, her gaze searching his. "No? What would you call it then?"

Selfishness. Stupidity. His cock ruling his head.

But he wisely said none of the initial responses that came to mind. "I would call it good business."

Her hand tightened upon his arm. They were very close, and if he leaned down a scant few inches, he could take her lips and kiss her senseless right there on the stairs for all and sundry to see.

"You may refer to it as you like, but I remain grateful nonetheless. The *Beacon* is very important to me."

Damn it all, if there was ever an inconvenient time for his cock to go hard as a brick, surely it was now as he stood like a vassal in Lady Helen's gleaming presence, servants bustling below them, stopped on the fourth step down. He cleared his throat, ill at ease, and moved his gaze to the infinitely more innocuous pastoral painting hanging on the far wall. "Don't forget that I must approve your writing. I haven't given you *carte blanche*."

The instant he said the words, he regretted them. He stole another glance at her to see that she had flushed, her cheekbones taking on a brilliant pink tinge that did nothing to dampen the intensity of her beauty.

"I think perhaps we ought to go down to breakfast before we're missed," she said, deftly avoiding the implications of the phrase he'd unwittingly used.

Mistress.

Lady Helen in his bed.

To the devil. None of this was helping the inconvenient state of his trousers, which were suddenly too damned tight. "Yes we ought to," he agreed, his voice strained, even to his own ears.

What the hell was the matter with him? They descended the remainder of the stairs in silence, Levi thoroughly displeased with himself. He needed to get back to where he belonged. Fast.

He didn't care what convention or polite society required him to do. If he didn't leave immediately, he was going to do something inordinately more foolish than what he'd already done. So he stopped and bowed to Lady Helen, who appeared as perplexed as he felt by his actions.

"I regret that I must take my leave, Lady Helen. Please extend my felicitations to our hosts on my behalf. Good day."

He didn't wait for a response, merely turned on his heel and strode from Jesse's house as though Cerberus himself nipped at his heels. And perhaps in a sense, he did.

Chapter Four

ELEN WAS REASONABLY CERTAIN that accepting Mr. Storm's invitation to continue writing for the *Beacon* had been a grave mistake. For one thing, it would give her cause to be in his company. To seek him out. To be near to him, perhaps alone with him. For another thing, she didn't like him. He was arrogant, condescending, and utterly without manners.

And for yet another thing, it would require drastic measures on her part. She would have to do something sensational. Something foolish. Something downright dangerous.

Something she was currently in the process of doing.

The East End was not a place for a genteel lady who was the daughter of an earl.

But she wasn't there on her own.

There was precisely one person in the world she could entrust with aiding her in her cause, and that woman sat opposite her as their carriage halted on the street outside a rather notorious brothel. Mrs. Augusta Bennington was well known for her work with the Ladies' National Association for the Repeal of the Contagious Diseases Acts. The Contagious Diseases Acts had long been a contentious fight, for the legislation enabled the forced inspection of prostitutes for venereal disease and sanctioned their unwilling captivity in lock hospitals. Mere weeks ago, Gussie's struggles on that front had met with success, and she and Helen had been present in the Ladies' Gallery in the House of Commons for the motion that would surely herald the Acts' ultimate downfall.

Gussie was a voice for change and had fought on behalf of women for the last two decades. Though fine-boned and delicate of appearance, Gussie was a formidable woman. Helen had once seen her wallop a man over the head with her parasol for kicking a dog. The man had been duly chastised, and Gussie had simply scooped up the ill-used pup and taken him into her care. Helen could only aspire to such unfailing mettle.

"Are you prepared?" Gussie asked her.

"I'm not certain I'll ever be prepared." Helen paused. She had never witnessed the horrors of an East End house of ill fame firsthand, though she had heard ample stories from her fellow reformers. "But if I don't witness it with my own eyes, how can I write about it?"

"Do you truly think your Mr. Storm will publish anything about the hells we are about to witness?"

Her Mr. Storm. It was rather a needling phrase, and not in an altogether bad sense either. But he wasn't hers, and Helen knew that he never would be, no matter how the mere thought of him made some weak part of her stir with longing. Good heavens, she had known him for all of two days.

"No one has dared for fear of the obscenity laws, and I'm sure Mr. Storm will not be so inclined." Helen knew all too well society's penchant for turning their backs on scandal and vice. It was easier to look at a bandage than a bloody, gaping wound. Even so, she was hoping that Mr. Storm might be compelled to at least change his mind about the *Beacon*. Turning it into a business journal would deal a severe blow to their cause. "I cannot help but think that perhaps he will be willing to aid us in some way."

After all, he had never read a single word printed in the paper he'd bought. He still thought she penned odes to her grandmother's shoes. Surely any reasonable man, upon discovering the very important work of drawing public attention to the mistreatment of women and children, would do something to help. Oh, drat Mr. Bothwell for allowing his greed to get the best of him. They would never be in such desperate straits if he hadn't secretly sold the *Beacon*.

Nor, reminded a tiny, unwanted voice, would she have met Mr. Storm. Rational Helen knew that Mr. Storm was a man whose sole motivation was growing his businesses and coffers and that he was as likely to help her as he was to fall to the ground and kiss the hem of her skirts. But foolish Helen recalled just how impossibly attractive he was, just how tall and strong, just how desire snapped through her at the mere thought of his forbidding mouth on hers. He had not kissed her in the library two nights ago. And she had very much wanted him to.

Oh dear.

She couldn't afford to allow foolish Helen to make her decisions for her. She had not been foolish Helen in a very long time, and it wouldn't do for foolish Helen to make a return now.

"I pray that he will help us as you hope," Gussie said before flipping a veil down to conceal her face. "The fates of so many depend upon it."

The gravity of the situation fell upon her like the weight of a cartload of bricks. She settled her veil into place as well. "Even if Mr. Storm does not lend his hand to our cause, we will not be waving the flag of surrender. We'll find another way. Another newspaper if we must."

But even as she said the words, Helen knew that finding another paper would not be an easy feat. Newspapers tended to stay far, far away from stories about country girls tricked into prostitution and sent to the Continent against their wills. Or young girls groomed to be prostitutes from birth and mothers willing to sell their young daughters to strangers for ten pounds. And while their cause was not entirely without means, they certainly didn't have the funds to purchase a building and presses, or hire men capable of churning out papers on the scale the *Beacon* had, pockets to let though it had often been. Gussie's House of Rest for women liberated from brothels was already bursting at the seams. They needed more homes. More supporters. More money. More everything. They had come too far to stop now at this bump in the road.

Gussie nodded. "We will do whatever we must to ensure that something is done to help these poor women and girls. They have been ignored for far too long. Steel yourself, my dear. We won't be able to bring any of them back with us. It's too dangerous at the moment."

Helen and Gussie descended from their carriage into the teeming, noisy street. The brawniest footmen Helen could find flanked them, the better to ward off would-be pickpockets or worse. While she considered herself a true and dedicated reformer, she had never previously ventured through the East End. And she had to admit she hadn't quite been prepared for it.

A cacophony of sounds assaulted her, from drunken men bellowing, to others hawking their wares, to barking dogs and crying children. The faces and clothes in the sea of people thronging the streets were dirty with the exception of the well-dressed gentlemen arriving and disembarking from their carriages to enter the brothels lining this part of town. They posed a striking contrast compared to the unfortunates forced to earn their bread so ignominiously.

A drunken man stumbled into her suddenly and nearly set her on her rump. Only the staying presence of her footmen kept her from falling and being enveloped by the clamor. Thankfully, in another few steps, they entered a side door of the establishment where a young woman as pretty as she was scantily clad welcomed them with a signal not to speak.

"Come quickly," she whispered. "Madame Violette will return within the hour. Your servants must remain at the door. They would cause too much suspicion."

Madame Violette was the prioress of the establishment. Cruel and depraved, she ruled her house of ill fame like a petty empress. Gussie had recently taken one of Madame Violette's victims under her wing, and the poor girl had revealed an appalling tale of her mistreatment at the brothel and of how others she'd left behind dearly longed for escape as well. Many were being drugged with laudanum, held against their wills, some without food and water, in an effort to force them into the horrible task of satisfying the madam's wealthy gentlemen callers.

Helen and Gussie hastened to follow their guide, remaining utterly silent, through the dim back corridors of the establishment. It was imperative that their presence remain a secret. If they were to help anyone, Madame Violette could never discover that her business had been infiltrated by reformers seeking to aid the girls forced to work for her.

The woman stopped before a door and pulled a ring of keys from a pocket hidden in the pleating of her robe. "The girl within is new and she's unwell. She's been here less than a fortnight."

The door opened to reveal a small, windowless room with one lamp upon a table, a bed, and a chamber pot. A young girl of no more than fifteen lay huddled on the bed, her face tear-stained. Helen's heart wrenched inside her chest. She'd never seen another person look more helpless or alone.

"Go inside before someone sees you." The woman gestured for them to enter. Her face was impassive, as emotionless as a floorboard. Helen wondered what could have happened to her for her to be so unaffected by the scene before them. "I'll knock twice when the time has come for you to leave. If Madame returns earlier than expected, I'll knock thrice."

"Thank you," Helen managed past the emotions clogging her throat. She had not forgotten what it had felt like, knowing someone was stronger and larger and capable of forcing her to do something she didn't want.

She and Gussie entered the chamber, which was even smaller than Helen had originally supposed. There was scarcely enough room for the two of them to stand side by side.

"Who are you?" the girl asked, her accent revealing her as a country girl. It was common for country girls to be lured away to London with the promise of adventure or even marriage, only to be forced into working as prostitutes instead. With no funds and no hope of communicating to their families, the unfortunate girls had little choice but to obey the depraved whims of their captors. Society turned a blind eye to their plight.

Gussie sprang into action, flipping up her veil and going to the girl's side. She was no stranger to this. She'd rescued a number of girls from different brothels all over the East End. "I'm Gussie, and this is Helen. We've come to help you."

An awful, wracking cough shook the girl's body. In the dim light offered by the pitiful excuse for a lamp, Helen thought she looked flushed with fever. Poor, dear heart, suffering as she must be. Helen patted the girl's shoulder as gently as she would a babe. "Everything will be alright now. What is your name, child?"

"Maeve," she croaked. Another cough rent the air. "Please, I don't want to be here."

The girl was plainly very ill, in addition to being held against her will for nefarious purposes. And quite young. Helen looked to Gussie. "I don't care how dangerous it is. We can't leave her here like this."

"You know the rules." Gussie was firm. "We need time

54

to formulate a plan for extracting her without causing any harm to those who are helping us."

Helen knew there could often be a delicate balance between help and harm in their work. To a procuress, each girl was a valuable investment rather than a human being, capable of bringing her great returns. When a girl fled from her care, not only did she lose future monies the girl would bring but she also feared it would encourage others to leave as well, costing her even greater financial losses. If a procuress like Madame Violette discovered that any of her girls had assisted in another's escape, there would be reprisals. Girls had been beaten, starved, and worse.

But Maeve tugged at Helen's heartstrings in spite of what she knew, in spite of the potential dangers involved. She reminded Helen a great deal of her sweet, spitfire sister, Bo. If someone had done this to Bo, Helen would have battered down the door herself, armed with her father's hunting rifle and prepared to wage war.

"Please, ma'am." Maeve reached for her, her eyes pleading. "Take me from this place. He tricked me into coming here and sold me like a cow."

"Dear God." Helen took the girl's hand and held it reassuringly. Her mind was firm. "Gussie, we must do something."

The twin strain of worry and compassion marred Gussie's face. She nodded. "We'll act with haste. Don't worry, child. I'll send someone for you tonight. When he comes, you must go with him and be very quiet, do you understand? There are those here who are helping you at their peril and none must be the wiser for either your escape or their aid."

"I understand." Maeve squeezed Helen's hand. "I'll do whatever I must."

Three discreet knocks sounded at the door. Helen met Gussie's gaze. They needed to leave at once.

"I'm so sorry this has happened to you, my dear." Helen brushed a sweat-dampened lock of blonde hair from the girl's forehead. "Stay strong until I see you again."

As Helen and Gussie hurriedly traced the path of murky corridors back to the outside world, a new wave of determination hit Helen. She would write what she had seen, what others had reported, without care to the delicate sensibilities of society. She'd lay bare the ugliness of the underbelly of London, the way innocents were destroyed at the hands of the lecherous and the greedy.

And she'd convince Mr. Storm to give their cause a chance. She couldn't stand idly by knowing there were others like Maeve, betrayed by those they had trusted and left to suffer alone. She knew precisely what it had felt like to be helpless, and she'd do everything in her power to keep another girl from the same fate. She had some writing to do.

"I was beginning to think you a ghost, Levi," Jesse joked with good-natured ease as they took up residence in his study.

Levi had once again missed dinner, returning to find that the ladies had retired for the evening and only his good friend was afoot. His mind was certain that avoiding Lady Helen and his inconvenient state of perpetual arousal in her presence had been for the best. He had far too many headaches to deal with at the moment. But he couldn't deny the disappointment that had hit him when he'd realized he had missed seeing her for the second straight day.

"Business is a hell of a thing," he told his friend.

Jesse gave him a wry grin. "Everything worthwhile in this world of ours is, it seems." He took up a decanter. "Do I sense the need for a fortifying whiskey?"

"Hang it, you know I don't like to imbibe." But the thought of a nice, luxurious whiskey to balm his ragged mind was terribly appealing just the same. "The other night left me with the devil of a headache, and after the last few days, there's no sign of it stopping."

In business as in life, he'd learned long ago that everything seemed to happen all at once and when one least expected it. It was as if fortune's wheel spun with an innate sense of how to strike the most crippling blow.

"Do tell," Jesse drawled. Apparently, life in England hadn't taken the Southerner out of him one bit. He poured a whiskey for Levi and handed it to him.

Utter chaos had descended upon North Atlantic Electric. In addition to the fire and resulting damage in his personal office, his Belgravia home wasn't any closer to completion or any more immune to missteps and errors. And everything else, well, it had gone straight to hell just the same.

Levi took a sip of whiskey, enjoying the burn, then sighed. "Edison is suing us in America for patent infringement. I've just had it from my lawyers. I have no worries that our light bulb design infringes in any manner upon his, but this is meant to tie up much-needed resources and time, neither of which I can currently afford to lose."

"The devil." Jesse whistled. "It sounds to me like you've got his back up. It must mean he doesn't appreciate the competition."

Levi was more than aware that Edison sought to monopolize their fast-changing industry. At stake was not only his reputation but a vast amount of money. Like Levi and his investors, Edison was aware that electricity was not a fad but here to stay. Eventually, the entire world would need it, not just the wealthy and the factories and governments who were currently beginning the transition. The companies who could provide it would have the potential for immeasurable wealth.

"While part of me finds his concern gratifying, the other part of me, the part with the pockets to let, wholeheartedly does not." Levi took another swallow of spirits.

Jesse grinned at that. "I'd hardly consider you pockets to let."

That was the trouble. He wasn't, but he was.

"The lawsuit isn't the only wormy apple in the proverbial bushel." Jesse was not just his friend, but also one of a number of investors in North Atlantic Electric. He would not mislead his friend in the difficulties they now faced. "Materials are not being manufactured quickly or efficiently enough back in our New York City facilities for us to be as competitive as we need to be. I've put in some legwork here and abroad to develop manufacturing, but we're rather stymied by our cash flow at the moment, and that leaves us at a disadvantage."

Levi couldn't help but fear his company was being left behind like a passenger who'd arrived too late and stood, valise in hand, watching the train pull from the station. One thing was becoming steadily apparent. He had poured a great deal of his own capital into North Atlantic Electric's ventures both in the States and abroad. But it wasn't enough. To accomplish what truly needed to be done, he needed more funds, and more funds than he was currently able to provide solely from his own coffers. He preferred to invest his wealth in real estate and other businesses rather than watching it molder away in a bank vault, leaving him without the liquid assets for an instant influx of capital the size he now required.

It was going to come down to groveling for more from his investors.

Jesse's countenance turned serious. While theirs was an old camaraderie, neither was he a fool. "What do you propose?"

"More money," he said baldly. "And a lot of it. Electricity is an angry, demanding mistress. But without risk, there is no reward. Fortunately, I know where to find the capital I require. There's wealth, and then there's VanHorn wealth."

"I begin to understand." Jesse sipped his whiskey. "Do you think VanHorn will provide the funding you need?"

"I do, and no pun intended." He was practically selling himself to secure it anyway, what with his engagement to the man's daughter. "With our impending familial connections and the promise of a ripe turnaround on his investment, I believe he'll see the wisdom of such a move. We'll be a damn sight better off than we are now. Seeing this through to the end is going to require patience, vision, hard work, and money. But it'll be worth it."

Jesse raised his glass to him, shaking his head. "I must say, old friend, that no one else could do what you've done thus far. If there is anyone who can light up this dark world of ours, it's you."

Levi raised his glass right back. "Thank you for your friendship. It means a hell of a lot to me. As for the flattery—"

"There can be no flattery in truth," Jesse interrupted, his tone brooking no opposition. "I admire you, Levi. You've overcome a great deal to get to where you are."

He had, but he didn't like to speak or think of it. The past was something he didn't wish to dwell on. It was a closed door to him in every way that it could be. "We both have. War is hell on earth."

His friend met his gaze, his expression grave. "You know as well as I that I'm not merely talking about the war."

It was very late, after midnight, but Helen didn't give a fidget for that.

She hadn't seen Mr. Storm in two straight days. According to belowstairs gossip wrangled from her lady's maid, he had arrived very late, gone straight to his chamber, and emerged before dawn to return to his offices each day. It had occurred to her that he might have been intentionally avoiding her. Perhaps he'd thought better of his offer all while she'd been working hard to pen an article that would convince him of the importance of her cause.

And work hard on the article, she had. She'd spent all her waking hours crafting her notes into a coherent piece that represented the plight of the women and girls she'd met both at the brothel she'd visited and at the overcrowded House of Rest that Gussie had formed. Thankfully, word had arrived from Gussie that Maeve had been spirited from Madame Violette's house of ill fame as promised, giving Helen at least a small measure of relief to know the poor girl was safe at last.

But for every one girl like Maeve saved in London, there were at least one hundred more waiting for a rescue that would never come. With one last, deep breath to calm herself, Helen peeked out into the darkened hallway beyond her chamber door. She was about to do something quite scandalous. Something she knew she shouldn't do. Something very much like sneaking into a brothel in the East End.

This time, there would be no brawny footmen for protection and no calming presence of her friend to ease her worried mind that nothing could go wrong. It didn't matter. In for a penny, in for a pound. Clutching the draft of her article tightly in her ink-stained fingers, she slipped into the hall. The gaslights had gone down for the evening, enveloping the space in a murky stillness that would have been impossible to navigate without the presence of a window at the east end. There, a blessed amount of moonlight sifted into the corridor to produce enough light for her to find her way to the chamber she sought.

If she had been nervous closeted inside Mr. Storm's office, she didn't dare to imagine how it would feel to be inside his bedchamber. Alone. With no one in the world the wiser and no one but she and that arrogant, handsome man. If the thought produced a dizzying sense of warmth washing over her, she dismissed it as over-wrought nerves. Being alone with Mr. Storm wouldn't have any effect upon her. Her goal was merely an audience with him, a means of delivering her article.

Time was of the essence, after all.

She stopped before his door. A sliver of light glowed

beneath it, confirming his presence. Good. He was here, at last. Her heart beat much too fast. Without further thought or the opportunity for rational Helen to get the better of her, she knocked quickly and quietly upon the door.

It opened with almost alarming speed, as if he had either just entered or was himself about to leave. He loomed over her, an imposing presence. The light at his back rendered it difficult indeed to see his face. But she'd recognize his form anywhere. Forbidding, tall, and lean with a barely leashed strength.

He didn't say a word. If he was surprised by her presence at his bedchamber door in the midst of the night, completely alone, he didn't let on. He merely grabbed her elbow in that commanding way of his, and pulled her over the threshold. The door closed with a hushed snick at her back.

His gaze nearly took the breath from her lungs. It was direct and laden with something dangerously primal. He wore only shirtsleeves and trousers, and she had the impression that he had been in the midst of disrobing himself upon her knock. Had he no valet? She hadn't thought of the complication a servant might bring, but a thorough inspection of the chamber behind him now revealed no one.

Thank heavens.

"Lady Helen." His tone was almost harsh. He released her elbow and crossed his arms over his broad chest. "You look as grim as a temperance harpy attending the funeral of a drunkard."

His bald pronouncement nearly wrung a startled laugh from her. He was bold and improper and altogether rude. She had dressed with great care for this visit, wearing a simple, black gown buttoned to the neck. If she appeared mournful, it was only because she'd attempted to retain as much propriety as she possibly could while visiting his chamber at midnight.

"I object to your use of the term 'harpy,' Mr. Storm," she told him in the most august tone she could manage.

"Objection duly noted." He grinned, and the effect was devastating. His dimples were once more on full display. "Would you care to enlighten me as to why you're gracing my chamber wearing funeral weeds and ink stains?"

Drat him, that grin had her at sixes and sevens. Why did he have to be so fine-looking and so infuriating at the same time? "I'm not wearing funeral weeds, though I'll own the ink stains." She thrust her article toward him with a lack of grace she inwardly cursed. "I've finished my article, sir."

"Ah." He accepted the neatly penned sheets she proffered. "That was rather a quick turnabout, wasn't it? I reckon I should have known. You're as determined as a terrier when there's something you're after, aren't you?"

Helen frowned at him. "I'm not sure I care for your similes this evening, Mr. Storm."

His lips twitched in what she supposed might be suppressed mirth. "I'm sure you don't, Lady Helen." He glanced down at the article she'd given him, then back up at her, his gaze too perceptive for her liking. "Tell me, do you make a habit of invading the bedchambers of all Jesse's guests, or is the privilege mine alone?"

His words echoed her own when she had asked him about throwing ladies over his shoulder. Unless she was mistaken, he enjoyed this turning of the tables. Of course he felt the need to bring attention to the unseemliness of her presence here, in a space that was undeniably his. She didn't belong in his chamber and she knew it. But somehow, she couldn't force herself to beat the hasty path of retreat she'd warned herself she must.

She met his gaze boldly, never one to back down from a challenge, verbal or otherwise. "Can it be deemed an invasion when it was you who forced me inside?" Helen couldn't quite contain her pleased smile at her clever rout. After all, it was he who had hauled her into his chamber. She had very much intended to stay on the safe side of their societal line of demarcation. Truly, she had.

He let out a short bark of appreciative laughter. "Ever a

worthy opponent, Lady Helen. But I merely wished to protect your reputation by removing you from eye and earshot of our hosts and their servants. Besides, Jesse will flay my hide if he ever gets wind of the improper nature of this meeting."

"There is nothing whatsoever improper about this meeting," she objected. Was she not properly buttoned up, severely dressed, and standing a full two steps away from him?

Rational Helen reminded her that there was nothing more improper than being so near to a man who presented such a wrong-headed lure for her. After all, she had wanted him to kiss her in the library. She had spent time, much to her chagrin, imagining what that sinful mouth of his might do to her. But that had been foolish Helen, and there was far too much at stake to allow that Helen to take charge of her mind just now.

"My lady, surely you realize there is nothing proper about you in my chamber at this time of night." His tone was intimate and warm, sliding over her with the effect of a caress.

She swallowed. Oh dear. His bright-blue gaze traveled to her lips, then down to the line of buttons at her throat, then back to meet hers. There was no mistaking the frank perusal. He felt the sparks between them the same way she did, roaring to life like his electricity and every bit as capable of burning hot.

"Pray forgive me for importuning you, Mr. Storm," she said at last, forcing herself to be polite. Rational. Cool. To flee his chamber while a modicum of her good intentions remained intact. "I merely wished to deliver the article as expediently as possible, and since you've been absent from breakfast these last few days, I deemed this the best way. Good night, sir." She turned to leave.

"Wait."

He didn't touch her this time, but it didn't matter. She stopped, halfway to the safety waiting on the other side of his chamber door. It wasn't that she feared him or the situation. Rather, she feared herself. She feared that the convictions she'd lived with for most of her adult life were wrong and that perhaps she wasn't destined to be chaste forever. He was temptation indeed.

She spun back around, drinking in the sight of him as she had not allowed herself to do before. His white shirt was unbuttoned, revealing a tantalizing swath of his chest, and rolled up to his elbows. His feet were bare, his trousers hugging his long legs to perfection. He very much looked the part of the brash American businessman she'd come to know, the man who had thrown her over his shoulder rather than escort her from his building, who spoke bluntly and had a penchant for arrogance and who touched her with the familiarity of a lover without ever having kissed her.

But he also looked a bit wild, and it was that wildness that called to some primitive, wicked being within her. He was the only man who had ever tempted her to throw everything to the wind—her reputation, her resolution to never again allow a man to lead her astray. Yes, he was dangerous to her in every sense of the word. And it was a danger that made her pulse quicken and her body go hot.

The silence between them was charged with all that remained unspoken.

"Stay, Lady Helen," he said at last.

She stared, wondering if he was suggesting what she thought he was suggesting. Her wide eyes flew to the perfectly made bed at the far end of the room, then back to him again. Surely not. Surely he couldn't mean…

He flashed her a wry smile. "You've come this far. You may as well remain while I read your article." He paused. "If you choose, of course."

If she chose.

He had very carefully and cleverly made the decision hers. And he was right. She *had* come this far. She'd worked hard to write the words in his hands. She'd put everything at risk to visit a house of ill fame and then steal her way to his chamber after midnight. What could be the harm in lingering long enough to hear his decision?

"Very well," she decided before rational Helen could intervene. "I'm eager to hear what you think of it."

Of course, that wasn't the only reason for her to remain here where she'd already established she most certainly ought not to be, but she didn't dare dwell on that. Instead, she followed him deeper into the chamber to a small seating area arranged by the gaslights. Mr. Storm saw that she was seated before sinking into a chair at her side. His proximity to her was not lost upon her. His trousers brushed her black skirts.

"I'm afraid I haven't much to offer as a host, but there is a tray Mrs. Whitney had sent up for me if you're hungry. There's wine, hothouse fruits, and I believe some roasted chicken that's long grown cold." He gestured toward a low *Louis Quinze* table laden with not only the tray but also a neat stack of correspondence and an odd assortment of objects that appeared to be in various states of dissection. She recognized a dismantled pocket watch and mantle clock amidst various parts and pieces.

"Thank you, but no," she declined his offer, though the wine and fruits did hold some appeal. She couldn't shake the impression that indulging in anything, even something as innocent as a strawberry, would weaken her resolve to stay true to her purpose.

"Are you sure you wouldn't care for a glass of wine, my lady? You seem a bit on edge."

She looked back to him, startled. How was he so perceptive? "I'm perfectly fine," she lied. In truth, she questioned the wisdom of her actions. Instead of leaving without anything untoward having occurred, she had lingered, going deeper into the lion's den. Now, she sat at his side, so near to Mr. Storm that his delightfully masculine scent proved most distracting.

"As you wish." His tone made it clear he begged to differ, that he could read her as easily as the article he held in his hands. But he kept his silence and mercifully turned his attention to her words instead.

An indeterminate amount of time passed as she waited while he read. Not a hint of emotion showed on his countenance any time she stole a peek at him. She clasped her hands nervously in her lap and tried not to squirm too much. From time to time, she glanced at the items he had taken apart and wondered if he would be able to put them back together the way they had been. Something told her that he would. Those long fingers of his would be precise, agile as his mind.

Finally, just when she thought she could stand the suspense no longer, he broke the deafening silence.

"Lady Helen, you know very well that I cannot publish this."

Chapter Five

*T*HAT HADN'T BEEN PRECISELY what she wanted to hear.

Of course she knew he wouldn't publish the awful truths she'd exposed in the piece. Well, she supposed she *ought* to know that, but part of her had still hoped that he might surprise her and prove open-minded enough to print a subject that went far beyond the bounds of polite society.

She cared about the women she'd met. She cared about their plight, about the hopeless situations in which they'd found themselves ensnared. Who else could allow their voices to be heard? Mr. Storm possessed such power. He could print whatever he saw fit. He had untold wealth at his fingertips if Bella was to be believed, wealth not even she could imagine, having grown up in a well-heeled aristocratic family, the daughter of the Earl of Northcote.

"Have you nothing to say for yourself?" he demanded, quite as though he were a forbidding headmaster and she a recalcitrant pupil. The teasing, intimate demeanor of earlier was gone.

She met his stern gaze unflinchingly, even if she wished he weren't quite so magnificent and austere. "It is a story that needs telling, Mr. Storm."

He inclined his head. "Perhaps so, but the telling will have to be done by someone else at a journal other than mine. There are obscenity laws in this land of which you must surely be aware. I'm not certain if you're mad or if you've got the daring of a corps of soldiers facing a wall of enemy cannon."

Helen almost smiled at that. Almost. She wasn't mad nor was she particularly brave. She never had been. Tia was the brave sister, beautiful and bold. But Helen was determined to do something with her life beyond wearing out the soles of her shoes at society balls. "To be clear, sir, I was aware of the reception my piece would receive, and I am also acquainted with the Obscene Publications Act."

"And yet you wrote it anyway." His gaze was searching. "Good God, woman, I'm not sure which alarms me more, the thought that you endangered yourself by mingling in the unsavory neighborhoods haunted by these creatures or the thought that you enjoy goading me to this extent."

His blustering did indeed win a smile from her this time. Mayhap he did care for her, just a smidgeon. "Truly, Mr. Storm, your concern for my well-being is most appreciated. However, I assure you that I didn't pen this article with the sole intent of goading you, as you put it."

"Indeed?" He had risen from his chair and fairly towered over her before turning to pace the length of the chamber.

Helen stood too, just to keep them on even ground, trailing after him at a safe distance. "These creatures, as you call them, are women. They are flesh and blood just like you and me, though I wouldn't expect you to know anything about the sort of penury and danger they encounter every day. I suppose you never look down from your tower of wealth and privilege and remember the little creatures like Susanna and Maeve."

"Unlike you, I wasn't born to wealth and privilege, my

lady." He circled the room, stalking her like a caged tiger from a menagerie. "Everything I have was earned. By me. By my hard work. By my determination. I spent many a night on the street with nothing but a hungry belly and a head full of dreams."

She found that difficult indeed to believe. "Spare me your sermons, sir. What do you know of the kinds of women I'm trying to help?"

"My mother was a whore," he bit out, shocking her as much with the revelation as with the barely veiled anger in his voice.

Helen stared at him. Perhaps that was the source of the wildness she had sensed. He was every bit the elegant gentleman accustomed to his deep purses and the finer things. But he was more than that. Just beneath his perfect veneer was a history with all its thorns and scars, unknown by anyone who looked upon him.

Somehow, she thought she understood him, at least in a small sense, for the very first time. She laid a hand upon his bare forearm. "I'm sorry, Mr. Storm. I did not know."

"I don't require your pity, my lady." His tone, like his countenance, was grim. "I could buy and sell all the pity in the world and it wouldn't change a goddamn thing about who I am or where I've come from."

He was right. Pity didn't change anything. But it wasn't precisely pity she felt for him. Rather, it was something else, something indefinable and altogether dangerous to her determination to keep him at a distance. She didn't flinch away from him as he no doubt wanted. Instead, she stood her ground.

"You'll not be getting any pity from me. Merely compassion. There is a difference, you see, a vast one."

He startled her by grasping her waist and yanking her against him. It was the first time she'd come into such intense contact with him since the day he'd unceremoniously thrown her over his shoulder in his office. This time, her body responded in a decidedly different manner. Heat suffused her, from head to toe. Along with something else.

Longing.

There was no indignation now, no irritation or frustration. Not even a smidgeon of outrage. There was only want and need, a dizzying, all-consuming hunger. She wanted him to kiss her, she realized. Very much so.

"I don't need your compassion either. I've lived my entire life without compassion from a single soul, and I won't be begging for it now," he growled.

Helen did something exceedingly foolish then, but for the first time in as long as she could recall, she was allowing her heart to overrule her head. Foolish Helen had won. She settled her hands on Mr. Storm's broad shoulders. The warmth of him, coupled with the barely leashed strength of his muscled body, was a welcome sensation beneath her fingertips. "Perhaps it wouldn't do you harm to experience compassion. Perhaps it's just what you need."

"What I need is to kiss you, damn it."

The surly statement, so like him in its boldness and yet also so startling, shouldn't have affected her the way it did. Her stomach was filled with butterflies and her body was nearly weak from the headiness of his touch, his nearness, and his words.

"Then do it," she demanded, feeling intrepid.

A second invitation wasn't necessary.

His mouth was hot and insistent. He kissed her as though he was starving for her, his lips molding and coaxing, his tongue sweeping inside to tangle with hers. The scrape of his neatly trimmed beard upon her skin was a welcome abrasion. She wound her arms around his neck and rose on her tiptoes to be nearer to him, pressing her breasts against his broad chest. He groaned, deepening the kiss, his palms sliding from their possessive hold on her waist to caress the small of her back.

She had not been prepared for the way her body would respond to him, as though it had waited years for him to set her aflame. As though she was made for him, his touch, his mouth. He tasted of whiskey and sin, and she wanted more.

It didn't matter that he'd purchased the *Beacon* to transform it into a business journal. It didn't matter that he had just refused to publish her article. It didn't matter that he was forbidding and irritating and stubborn.

All that mattered in that brief, glorious moment was his kiss.

And then, it was over.

He muttered a vicious oath and set her away from him so suddenly that she nearly toppled to the floor. She stared at him, uncertain of what to expect. Her actions had been reckless and imprudent. It would seem she'd never learn when to force her heart to listen to her head. A few more kisses, and she would have been on her back on the bed. She would have allowed him to undress her, take her, do anything he'd wanted. Worse, she would have welcomed it.

"If you think you can persuade me to print this with your pretty mouth, you're wrong," he said coolly, making her feel even more the fool.

"I think no such thing," she denied, willing her heart to resume its normal pace. "It was you who wanted to kiss me."

He strode closer to her again, crowding her with his big body. "And you who invited me to."

She licked her suddenly dry lips, wishing very much that she didn't long for him to kiss her again. "It would seem we're both in err."

"Yes," he agreed, his gaze dipping back to her mouth. "We cannot engage in such nonsense again."

But he had caught her round the waist, drawing her against him, belying his words.

She was breathless. His lips were a scant few inches from hers once more. "It would be foolhardy indeed."

Mr. Storm bit out another curse. His palm traveled up her back, skimming past the laces of her corset, beyond her shoulders, to rest on the bare skin of her neck just above her collar. She leaned into his touch, looking up at him, her entire body aflame, wanton wickedness washing over her in lazy waves that threatened to overtake her.

He kissed her once more, this time lingeringly, nipping at the fullness of her lower lip. Her fingers sank into his hair. She kissed him back with a ferocity she hadn't realized was even within her. A sweet, languorous pleasure stole through her, and it made her ache. It made her weak.

Before she had even realized what he was about, he'd undone half the row of tiny buttons fastening the front of her dress. Cool air brushed her heated skin, and then his touch was there, a decadent brand, caressing the patch of bare skin at the hollow of her neck he'd revealed. His large hand slid to rest above her madly beating heart, beneath her chemise.

Dear sweet heavens. What was she doing? Surely there was nothing more ruinous than being alone with him in his chamber and allowing him to undo half her dress while kissing her senseless. She tore her mouth from his with great reluctance, her conscience and judgment uniting to remind her treacherous body that she was a lady and Mr. Storm was most assuredly not a gentleman.

"We cannot," she said, rather unconvincingly even to her own ears. Every part of her clamored for more. More of his kisses, more of his hands on her. More of everything.

"We can," he countered, his gaze penetrating and unreadable upon her. He had not removed his hand, and now his fingers slid beneath her corset to tantalize the top of her breast.

She gasped, but not because she was scandalized. Because she liked it. He found her nipple and the most exquisite sensation overcame her. Only a closed door and a dark hallway saved her reputation from utter devastation. Helen didn't care. If anything, it heightened the way he made her feel.

"We should not," she forced herself to protest even as she arched into his knowing touch. He rubbed her nipple idly, his gaze lowering back to her mouth.

"Cannots and should nots have never interested me, Lady Helen." His tone was low, almost hypnotic.

"I don't doubt that." In that moment she was heartily glad for it. She very much wanted him to continue the sinful magic he worked upon her. Her hands were still on his strong, broad shoulders.

"Stay with me tonight." His statement was abrupt, more directive than request. Not at all the soft cajoling one might expect from a lover. But then again, Mr. Storm was not a soft, cajoling sort of man. He was imposing, hard as granite, a puzzle she dearly longed to solve. "Come to bed with me. Let me pleasure you."

She felt suddenly dizzied. This was not an innocent invitation, but one laden with as much promise as sin. Staying with him, in his chamber, in his bed, should not have appealed to her as much as it did. In truth, she wanted nothing more than to remain with him, to know him as intimately as a woman could know a man. But just as badly as she yearned to say yes, a sinking knot of dread in her stomach told her she could not. Should not. Must not.

Would not.

"I cannot." She stared at him, memorizing the beauty of his face, for she was certain she would never again see him thus, vulnerable and stripped of his veneer. "I must return to my chamber before anyone is the wiser to my presence here. Thank you for reading my article. I hope that, if anything, it will give you pause, Mr. Storm."

His expression was inscrutable as ever. He gave her a mocking half bow. "I assure you that it has, Lady Helen. It most certainly has."

She didn't bother to wonder at the hidden meaning of his words as she fled back into the dark safety of the night.

Chapter Six

"THE CRIMSON SILK, DO YOU THINK?" Bella gestured to one of three ornate ball gowns on display in her dressing chamber.

The very latest from Worth, it was fashioned of a luscious, vivacious red fabric and trimmed with lace at the bodice and sleeves. It was a beautiful creation, truly, to behold, and on any other day, Helen would have loved nothing more than to drool over her friend's ridiculously lavish wardrobe. But today, her mind was rather burdened by far weightier matters.

Far more dangerous and wickedly handsome matters.

"I must say that I do so love the blue as well," Lady Bella went on, moving to the next dress and fingering its elaborately plaited tulle and satin skirts. "It is so very sumptuous and I want to make my mark on this ball. I want Jesse to like it, and he has always seemed partial to me in blue." She looked up at Helen and frowned. "You haven't heard a blessed word I've said, have you, dear? My heavens, I'm beginning to sound like one of those empty-headed ladies who corners you in a ball to natter on about herself, aren't I?"

"Of course not," Helen rushed to answer. "You mustn't think anything of the sort. I fear that my mind was wandering a bit and it is I who has become empty-headed. Pray forgive me, Bella."

"Fiddle." Bella waved a hand as if to dismiss Helen's protest. "I know when I'm being a bore. I daresay this isn't like me at all. Ordinarily, I'm quite content to keep my nose buried in my books, but tonight is very important to Jesse and I want to look my best for him."

Helen envied the passionate marriage Bella shared with Jesse. How could she not? One couldn't help but to notice their private glances, their subtle touches. Jesse treated Bella with a reverence that was as touching as it was blatant. And even Helen, firmly on the shelf, self-declared spinster that she was, could see their love and wish she too had experienced something like it, even if just for a fleeting moment.

"Don't be a ninny. You could dress in rags and still please your husband, and well you know it." She paused, considering the third dress Bella had instructed her lady's maid to set aside for their inspection. It was a deep, riveting shade of emerald and its *tablier* of satin fairly shimmered by the light of day. "But I do understand your apprehension. Tonight's ball has been the talk of the town. The green, I think. It's quite unique and you'll be utterly magnificent in it."

"Is our little ball the talk?" Bella gave an excited clap. "I hope it will go smoothly. One never knows with this sort of thing. Throwing a ball, I've discovered, is a bit like having a child. You think you know what to expect, but you're entirely wrong, and at the end of it all you've experienced something miraculous and wonderful but you're tired and every bone in your body aches."

Helen laughed. "From what my sister tells me, you aren't alone in that sentiment on either account." Cleo had a son and was expecting her second babe. Helen adored her nephew. She loved his chubby face and tiny toes and sweet giggles. Sometimes, she still felt a wrench in her heart to know she'd never look upon the face of her own child. But the feeling inevitably passed, and she was above all else a woman who knew what she was meant to do with her life. She didn't require a husband or a child to find fulfillment.

Bella laughed. "Well I suppose it is good to know one is not alone, is it not?" She gave Helen a quick hug before pulling away to search her gaze. "I'm so happy you're here with us, Helen. Your company has been very good for me. Thornton is a wonderful bear of a brother, but I've begun to realize I was desperately in need of sisters all this time."

She smiled, touched by her friend's words. Having grown up with her gaggle of sisters, Helen had never paused to wonder what it might be like without them. Horrid, certainly. "You are an honorary Harrington girl. We've brought you into our flock, and we absolutely refuse to let you out of it."

"I am glad." Bella tilted her head in that way she had, her dark curls like a halo on her head, considering Helen too closely for her liking. "Tell me, Helen, what is on your thoughts this morning? You are not your usual self, and I fear something is amiss."

Oh dear. There it was. Apparently, she was as transparent as a window pane. And she'd thought she'd been hiding it so well. She bit her lip, wondering how much, if anything, to reveal to her hostess. For while Bella was her friend and very much like a sister to her, she was aware that her actions could nevertheless meet with censure. Shock. Perhaps she'd even be turned out. It was what a proper lady certainly ought to do. Genteel ladies didn't go about visiting a gentleman's chamber after midnight, no matter how noble the cause.

She chose her words with care. "There is something. I must apologize. I should have told you before now."

"You have a *tendre* for Mr. Storm."

Helen stared, aghast, and instantly thought better of her

confession after all. "No. Of course I have nothing of the sort."

Bella gave her a knowing look. "You needn't worry. I shan't tell a soul."

"I most certainly do not have a *tendre* for Mr. Storm," Helen protested, perhaps, as Shakespeare was wont to point out, too much. "Indeed, I daresay I don't even like him."

"Oh?" Bella plainly did not believe her, and her arch expression said as much.

"Bella." Helen fixed her most ferocious frown upon her face, the one she thought her best impression of her miserable old governess, Miss Hullyhew. "Mr. Storm is the most arrogant, infuriating, wrong-headed, stubborn, supercilious man I know. I most certainly do not feel anything for him."

"You did both say arrogant and supercilious," Bella pointed out in a conciliatory tone.

Helen heaved a sigh. "I'm aware they have essentially the same definition. Mr. Storm is merely so arrogant that I needed to say it twice."

"If you insist." Bella shrugged.

"What does that mean?" Helen demanded.

"It means that you needn't be so defensive." Her friend gave her an almost pitying look. "I've been in your slippers, my dear. I've also seen the way Mr. Storm looks at you. Your feelings aren't precisely unrequited."

She was flummoxed. Utterly flummoxed. Yes, of course she enjoyed the man's touch and his kiss. Being alone with him in his chamber had been equal parts temptation, frustration, and bliss. Yes, the plain truth of it was that he was vexing. He was infuriating, and wrong-headed, and every other thing she'd thought to call him. But there was something about him that spoke to her, to the deepest, darkest parts of her that she hadn't even known existed. Something indefinable and wonderful and frightening all at the same time. It wasn't just that he was handsome, though he was, and devastatingly so. It wasn't that he was intelligent or clever or that he'd built something astonishing for a man who had been the son of a prostitute.

It was more. It was simply *him*.

Her stomach felt as though it fell straight to the carpet at her feet.

"You look as if you've seen the ghost of your great-grandmother," Bella said with a grin, helpful soul that she was.

Helen would swear her friend was enjoying this, watching her fidget about in uncertainty. "I don't believe in ghosts." And she didn't. Not now that she was a woman grown. Helen was far too no-nonsense for spirits and sprites and superstition. She believed in reason, in certainties. She believed in love, but only for others. She had a higher calling. A purpose. She simply had to excise Mr. Storm from her mind and continue on with her purpose true and strong.

"It was a figure of speech, dearest Helen. You mustn't be silly." Bella winked, lightening the mood. "There will be plenty of time to see what happens tonight at the ball. Have you already decided upon your dress, or are you fickle as I am?"

"I've decided," Helen said, and in that moment, she had. It was a daring dress, the kind she'd commissioned, packed, carried about, and then never had the gumption to wear. But perhaps tonight would be just the night for it. "What do you mean, see what happens?"

"A great deal can happen at a ball," Bella said archly. "Trust me on this, if nothing else. A ball is a place of true possibility."

Helen stared at the gowns, wondering precisely what her friend meant, too afraid to ask. She didn't dare think of what sort of mayhem she could get herself into in a darkened alcove with a man like Mr. Storm. No, she didn't dare at all.

Damn it all to hell, he'd forgotten about the ball.

The crush of carriages and glittering lords and ladies swarming about Jesse's house that evening as he approached instantly reminded Levi that his host and hostess had invited him to the extravagant affair. He had walked the distance from his offices as he often did wherever he was in the world, finding the solitude and rhythmic motion an excellent boon for his harried mind.

But as he came upon the throng of revelers, he wished he had not walked tonight after all. In his rumpled work clothes, he hadn't a doubt that he was conspicuous as a regimental deserter walking through Mayfair. Perhaps it wasn't too late to sneak inside through the servants' entrance and straighten himself into some semblance of proper gentility.

He swept past a woman alighting from her carriage with diamonds winking from her throat and hastily descended to the tucked-away portal reserved for the echelon of society to which he truly belonged: commoner. He was proud of that, actually. He'd never understand the European penchant for aristocratic family trees. In his book, the beauty of life was that a man could be born anywhere, to anyone, and become whatever and whomever he chose to be.

If the servants bustling about belowstairs found it odd to have an interloper amongst them, they didn't show it. The underbelly of the house was a hive of activity as the ball got underway, the servants so busy that they hardly even spared him a glance. Maids in black dresses, white aprons, and white caps and footmen in formal dress went about their duties. He didn't envy them their endless tasks.

At least his day, apart from playing the part of gentleman, was largely done. He had telegraphed VanHorn and his other investors back in New York City, explaining the urgent need for a greater investment than the amount he'd initially requested. Of course, he didn't expect wrangling more money from the wily bastards to be an easy feat, but he had no fear that he could persuade them the risk was far worth the ultimate reward. And it would be. Yes, his affairs were finally getting back to their proper order. His house was nearing completion at last and his office would soon be habitable once more.

If only he could steer his thoughts away from the one person who threatened to undo all the order he'd sternly created.

Lady Helen.

No matter how hard he focused on his work, she was there, fluttering at the edges of his every thought like a shadow he couldn't shake. He had underestimated her, and the fact unsettled him as much as how sorely she tempted him did. She was no spoiled aristocrat as he'd wanted to believe. She was a spitfire with a cause, and she didn't write gossip or fashion drivel. No indeed, she wrote about the plight of women born without the protection her wealth and privilege afforded her. Something inside him, some icy part he'd kept long buried and frozen, thawed a bit as he thought of her. The feeling jolted him so much he nearly collided with a harried footman.

Damn it, he had to collect his wits. Forget about the way she had looked in his chamber, beautiful despite her prim black dress. Forget about how she'd responded in his arms. Forget the fact that she had put herself at grave risk to infiltrate a house of ill repute just to write an article he had summarily refused to print.

Ah, her article. It was profane. Shocking. There was no way he could print it even if he'd wanted to, for the damage it would do her. She could be jailed, earl's daughter or no. He could be jailed. Neither of them could afford the risk, and she had known that but she had cared enough to do it anyway.

At first, he'd been somewhat surprised to discover that the cause she so ardently supported was not only a worthy one but the very sort of cause that most women of her station would have ignored. But the more he read, the more he realized it was precisely what he would have expected of the bold, lovely woman he'd only begun to come to know.

Of course, when he'd read that she herself had entered such a den of vice, he'd wanted to shake her. Levi had been in brothels. He'd grown up flitting in and out of them, for God's sake, hiding in back rooms while his mother earned their rent. He knew what happened within those walls. What could have happened to Helen, had she not been so lucky. Jesus, but the thought of anything happening to her—some swine assaulting her, or far worse—was still enough to make his fists ball with impotent rage even now.

It wasn't lost on him either that his reaction rendered him the worst sort of hypocrite. He was ready to wage war on her behalf against some unseen assailant, and yet he had taken advantage of her last evening himself. She had come to him with a noble purpose. He'd known that having her in his chamber, such a decadent temptation within reach, was a mistake. Yet, he'd allowed it. And he'd allowed his emotions, made raw by reading her article and the ugly memories it visited upon him, to get the better of him. Hang it, he never should have kissed her.

He would see her tonight, surely, though he would do his utmost to keep his distance. Levi climbed the servants' stair and slipped into the upstairs hall, where his determination was instantly put to the test by the sight of none other than Lady Helen gliding down the hall like a princess come to walk amongst the lesser beings in her castle. She wore an ice-blue dress with a cluster of damask roses on the bodice and a full, draped skirt of tulle over silk that showed off her figure to perfection. Her low décolletage revealed a swath of creamy skin, her breasts full and lusciously displayed. Golden curls were artfully arranged at her crown, diamonds winking from her combs and her throat.

The full impact of her beauty hit him in the chest like a physical blow as he met her gaze. "My lady," he said formally, stiffly, even to his own ears. He had held her in his arms last night, and now she stood before him as a cruel reminder that the heady wickedness of the evening could not be repeated. Dared not be repeated.

"Mr. Storm." A telling flush splashed across her cheeks.

She had to be thinking, as he was—as it seemed he could not stop—of their last meeting. The conscience that had been aggravating him all day returned.

"I must apologize for my actions," he forced himself to say. "I am very sorry for the insult I paid you. It was unconscionable."

Her eyes widened. Perhaps she had not expected him to speak of their midnight meeting. He knew well it was not done, that he should not mention it by the light of day. But he had never cared for rules, and it grieved him to think of how callous he had been. She was too good to be propositioned as if she were no better than a dockside doxy.

"Pray do not worry yourself over it, Mr. Storm. We both erred. It shan't happen again." Although her tone was calm, her fingers betrayed her inner agitation, picking at the delicately draped paniers of her skirts.

He nodded. "Of course. Thank you for your understanding, my lady." Damn it all, he hated being so polite, so cold.

What he really wanted was to throw her over his shoulder as he'd done the first day he'd met her, carry her off to his chamber, and finish what they'd only just begun the night before. As gorgeous as she was in that dress, he couldn't help but long to strip it off her and throw it in a heap to the floor.

Hang it, he needed to get ahold of himself or he'd be on his knees before her soon, begging to kiss her ribbon-trimmed hem. Since when had he become this weak-willed? This affected by beauty, a lush form, a woman, any woman? He had no right, he reminded himself harshly, no right at all.

"Will you be attending the ball tonight?" she asked lowly.

"Yes." He didn't dance at society functions, but the

thought of holding her soft body to his was enough to make him wonder if he should. "Save a dance for me?" The words had escaped him before he could think better of them. He needed, just once more, to hold her in his arms.

She gave him a stunning, if wistful, smile. "Of course, Mr. Storm. Until then."

Without further words, Lady Helen spun on her heel and swept away just as smoothly as she had arrived. It was best. Had she lingered any longer, he very much feared his limited ability to restrain himself and remain cool and unaffected would have diminished entirely. He stood there in the hall, watching her go, wondering just what the hell it was about her that drew him in a way no other woman before her had. If he had a modicum of common sense left in him, he'd retreat back to his offices and forget all about her soft skin and tempting curves and the overwhelming need to have her in his bed.

But obviously, he didn't possess a shred of common sense any longer, for he beat a hasty path to his chamber so that he could change into his gentleman's clothes and attend a damn ball and hold Lady Helen in his arms again. He was a lunatic. An idiot. A fool.

Just one dance, he promised himself. One dance and then he would say his goodbyes this night. By morning, he would return his life to its peaceful routine of work, sleep, work again. If his house wasn't habitable, he'd go back to a hotel. Any hotel would do. Anywhere he didn't share a roof with a gorgeous golden-haired siren. Of one thing, he was deadly certain. He couldn't remain. She was too much a temptation, and he was too close to achieving what he'd always wanted. He had never been one to allow his prick to rule his brain, and he surely wouldn't begin now. There was too much at stake. He had come too far to sacrifice everything he'd built.

As the ball wore on, Helen wondered if perhaps Mr. Storm had thought better of his request to spare him a dance. She had never overly thrilled to the notion of a ball. There was something about all the dressing and preparing, the prancing about in tight heels for hours, and the general tedium of it that quite wore her out. But this ball in particular meant a great deal to Bella, and Bella in turn meant a great deal to Helen, so she pasted a smile on her lips and kept a glass of champagne close at hand.

Her friend was doing an admirable job as hostess, and if the crush of glittering lords and ladies was any indication, the ball would be deemed a first-rate success by society. Helen fanned herself as she sipped her champagne from her station on the outskirts of the revelries. She had danced with a handful of lords, one of whom had been an old suitor of her sister Tia's. The Earl of Denbigh was a widower now and had recently begun his return to society. He had broken poor Tia's heart once, but in the end it had all worked out, for Tia had found a love that was truly meant to be with her husband Devonshire. Denbigh had been kind, charming, and witty as ever. But it had all been rather lost on Helen, who had spent each of her dances scanning the crowd for a sight of Mr. Storm, only to be disappointed every time.

She sighed, wishing she wasn't such a ninny. Heaven knew there were matters of far greater import in the world than whether or not she danced the quadrille with Mr. Storm. Perhaps she should simply slip away from the festivities and go to bed. After all, she was tired from the late nights and early days she'd been keeping of late.

Helen turned, thinking to do just that, and there he was. Mr. Storm.

She stopped, her gaze clashing with his, the same, familiar heat sliding through her veins at the mere sight of him. He was so striking in his evening finery that it quite took her breath. "Mr. Storm."

He bowed with a cagey elegance that was patently his. "My lady."

84

Mayhap she would stay at the ball after all.

"I scarcely recognize you, sir," she teased him, unable to resist. When she had come upon him earlier, he had been dressed in his work attire, looking rough and uncivilized with a hint of sin. Now he was as polished and refined as any duke in the ballroom. She wasn't sure which she preferred, the rough and wild or the gentleman in him. Certainly, both made her yearn for something she had no right to want.

He took her hand and raised it to his lips for a kiss that was almost reverent. A new awareness settled over her, mingling with desire. In that moment, she caught a glimpse of the same in his startlingly blue eyes. All that had transpired between them the night before hung in the air between them, sparking like a live electric wire.

"Even a stray dog can clean up well with water and soap," he said with that wry grin of his.

"I'd hardly characterize you as a stray dog," she said softly. No indeed. Not a single soul looking upon Mr. Storm in the ballroom would consider him anything less than the picture of masculine beauty. He made her ache. "More like a wolf."

He laughed. "I suppose I'm deserving of that barb."

She hadn't been referring to what had happened last night in his chamber. Rather, she'd been thinking of how she saw him, fierce and dangerous, powerful and yet best kept at a distance. But now she couldn't help but think of his kisses, his caress on her breast. Her madly thudding heart reminded her that it hadn't been long since his palm had pressed there, intimate and warm.

"It wasn't a barb." She realized belatedly that he still held her hand and extricated it lest any of their fellow revelers happen to take notice. "It was a compliment." Helen paused then, wondering how much she should say, if anything, before plodding on. "And you needn't have apologized earlier. I wasn't insulted by you yesterday."

His expression became unreadable. "You should have

been, Lady Helen."

"I wasn't." She didn't know why it was important for him to know, but somehow it was. Her reason for fleeing him, she realized now, had been self-preservation and nothing else. She hadn't been shocked. She hadn't been outraged. She had been tempted then, just as she was tempted now, to cast aside the rigid rules of society and dare to experience passion just once in her life. Just once, and then she could go back to being proper Lady Helen, maiden aunt, spinster sister, dear friend, respectable reformer.

What was the harm, some forbidden force within her wondered, in allowing foolish Helen to experience one giddy night of pure, unadulterated hedonism in the arms of the man before her? Her breath caught at the notion, so wicked and yet so very wonderful all at once. The champagne must have bollixed her brain.

He looked at her as though he wanted to devour her. "It was exceedingly unwise of you to make that confession to me."

She raised a brow, feeling wicked. "Oh?"

"It means you have forfeited your advantage. In life, as in business, you should never reveal too much too soon, or your opponent will seize upon your weakness."

Was it always about business with him? This was not the first time he had spouted a maxim to her. But the very thought of him seizing upon her weakness, as he so politely phrased it, was enough to send a sharp tug of yearning though her. Oh yes, something strange had come over her. She thought then of Bella's earlier words. *A great deal can happen at a ball.* Perhaps the time to see about that had come. "I'm sure I never had an advantage over you to begin with, Mr. Storm. Now, have you come to dance with me, or have you come to stand in the corner arguing with me all evening long?"

It was his turn to raise a brow. "Duly reprimanded, my lady. There's nothing I detest more than the quadrille, but hang it, I'll not have it be said that I stood in the corner arguing with the most beautiful woman in attendance all night long."

The most beautiful woman in attendance.

Surely he didn't think so. And of course, she wasn't. There was a whole host of lovely ladies gathered tonight, Lady Bella with her raven hair and creamy complexion among the loveliest of all. Helen couldn't hold even a candle to them. But the way he looked at her, the way he touched her, the way he had held her yesterday and kissed her with such fierce hunger…it made her believe.

He led her to the dance floor and they took up their positions as the familiar tune began to play. Although they were surrounded by others, they could have been the only couple in the room, so thoroughly were they aware of each other. Their eyes locked as they traveled through the steps, side by side, opposite, twirling together as if one. His hand on the small of her back was like a brand through the layers of silk and boning she wore. Mr. Storm stood apart from all the other men at the assemblage with his height, dark hair, and commanding presence. This night, she had eyes only for him. She was dizzied. The dance seemed to be too short and never-ending all at once.

Helen didn't know if it was the dance or the champagne or the heat in the ballroom generated by the crush of guests, but as Mr. Storm led her from the floor at the quadrille's completion, steeped in formal politeness, she felt suddenly faint and unsteady. He noticed instantly, for she felt a staying hand on her waist. Her vision blurred around the edges like a watercolor painting.

"Oh dear," she said. "I fear I may swoon."

It wasn't like her. She was made of much sterner stuff, but she didn't wish to embarrass herself. She needed some air. Her corset seemed too tight. Her entire body was flushed and heated. If she didn't get away from this clamor at once, she didn't know what would happen. It would have been the perfect moment for one of her sisters to accompany her to the retiring room where she could regain her composure as they gossiped about all the lords and ladies in attendance. But her sisters weren't here, and she was alone with Mr. Storm in a sea of people.

How she missed Cleo, Tia, and Bo in that moment.

Everything sounded as if it were very far away, carried to her on a lush summer breeze. Maybe she should not have consumed quite so much champagne. She'd lost count of how many flutes she'd drained over the course of the ball. Good heavens, had it been more than five? A fresh wave of dizziness assailed her and she stumbled against his powerful, lean frame. He smelled divine, she thought fuzzily.

"Come," he ordered, ushering her hastily away.

She collected her thoughts enough to protest. "Where are you taking me?"

He couldn't simply escort her out of the ballroom and into a private room. Propriety certainly didn't allow such a thing. *She* ought not to allow such a thing. Would not if it weren't for the spinning of her head. As it stood, she was ineffectual as a fly at the moment.

"Hush." He steered her around a tittering countess and a footman bearing a tray of champagne flutes.

"But—"

"My lady, hush."

"Someone will see."

"No one will notice. Everyone here is either far too inebriated or preoccupied."

Casting a quick look about, he led her from the ballroom, down the hall, and into another chamber. As the door closed at their backs, stifling the cacophony of sound from the ballroom beyond, Helen realized they were in Jesse's study. Alone. Still dizzied, she clutched Mr. Storm's arm. "We are in our host's private study. We cannot be here together."

"Jesse won't mind," he assured her, guiding her to an overstuffed chair and easing her into it. He sank to his knees before her, his expression for once unguarded. "Are you unwell, my lady?"

He was concerned. A strange, new warmth stole over her. The world came back into crisp focus but her heart hammered furiously against her breast. She still felt off-kilter, almost as though she were out of her own skin, almost as if she were giddy.

Oh dear. He was before her like a knight of old, so striking and elegant, so unlike the arrogant stranger who had unceremoniously removed her from his offices the day they'd met. This Mr. Storm was different. Or maybe she was different. Or the night was different. Or she was hopelessly, thoroughly in her cups. She didn't know which.

"I am fine," she forced herself to say. "I daresay I sampled too much of the champagne this evening and that is all."

"You don't seem fine, my lady." He frowned. His hands bracketed her skirts, near enough to her that he almost touched her, and the thought of those big hands of his on her made her quite weak. "Can I fetch you something? Some water, perhaps? Some ice?"

She licked lips that had suddenly gone dry. "There is nothing I need other than for you to return me to the ball. This is quite scandalous, sir. If someone should come upon us, it would cause us no end of trouble."

"No one will come upon us. I've locked the door."

His casual pronouncement did wicked things to her body that she was sure had everything to do with the blasted champagne. The door was locked. No one could disturb them or happen upon them. They were free to do what they chose.

Yes, she was in her cups alright, she had to be. There was no other reason for her to lean forward, set her palms upon Mr. Storm's shoulders, and press her mouth to his. No other reason save for the fact that she had been thinking about him all day, about how he had touched and kissed her, how he had made her feel, how he had wanted her in his bed. She kissed him just for the feeling of his mouth upon hers once more, because she couldn't help herself, because she couldn't *not*.

And he kissed her back. Kissed her back with a ferocity that belied his every proper, polite conversation with her that evening. Kissed her back as though he hungered for her. He caught her waist and slid her closer to the edge of the chair, angling his lips over hers with just enough pressure to make her long for more. If she'd thought she was near to swooning before, she had been dead wrong. His tongue swept inside her mouth, claiming and seductive all at once.

He dragged his mouth down her throat, kissing and nipping and tasting. He caught her earlobe with his teeth and tugged, sending a white-hot spiral of desire straight to her core. She slid the rest of the way from the chair until she too was on her knees on the soft, rich carpet, skirts pooled around her. Her position was made somewhat awkward by her corset and the heap of her elaborate dress. She didn't care in that moment if it was irreversibly crushed or if she'd have to find the nearest servants' stair and run to her chamber in shame after Mr. Storm was done having his way with her. All that mattered was his hands and his mouth upon her, making her want him so much that she ached with it.

He pressed an open-mouthed kiss to her neck again and then traced a path of fire straight to her décolletage. With one swift tug, he pulled down her bodice, revealing her corset cover. She hadn't bothered with a chemise because of the cut of her sleeves, and she was glad for it now. One less layer between them.

He lowered her corset cover and unfastened the first two closures on her corset. The breath left her lungs as the reality of the situation pierced the fog of lust and spirits that had cloaked her sense of reason. She was on the floor of Mr. Whitney's study with Mr. Storm in the midst of a ball with hundreds of people beneath the same roof, allowing him to undress her. It was sheer, sanity-defying foolishness.

Before she could think further, he lowered her corset to

expose her breasts completely. The tight fabric of her bodice and corset made them jut upward like an offering. Cool air hit her flushed skin just an instant before he lowered his head and took her nipple in his mouth. She hadn't been prepared for *that*. Good heavens. He sucked the hardened bud, then caught it lightly between his teeth, and tugged. She arched into him, moaning.

"Mr. Storm." She meant to say his name in protestation. The last shred of her common sense told her that she could not writhe about half-naked on the floor with a man without it leading down a dangerous and irrevocable path. But the moment his name left her lips, it resembled more moan than dissent.

He tongued her nipple and then looked up at her, the picture of wicked masculinity. Their gazes clashed. In that instant, everything changed. "Levi," he said.

"Levi," she repeated, liking the sound of his name, the feel of it on her lips. "Levi, this is madness."

"Utterly," he agreed politely. "And yet I find myself not giving a damn." He pressed a kiss to the curve of her breast and cupped the other tenderly in his hand. "Tell me to stop, Helen." But he belied his words by continuing to rain hot, decadent little kisses all over her bare flesh.

That was the trouble. She didn't want him to stop. And whether she was buoyed by the champagne or the sensual power he wielded over her, she couldn't say the words. Foolish Helen was firmly in control now, her virtue galloping away into the horizon like a driverless carriage. She didn't give a fidget. Not one. What had she been saving herself for? When had she ever felt anything so all-consuming, so desperately exquisite?

"I can't tell you that." Her fingers sank into his silky dark hair.

Her confession wrung a curse from him, and she knew that he was as torn as she, torn between desperately wanting more and knowing they should cease their lovemaking immediately before they went even further than they already had. He sucked her nipple again before kissing the hollow of her throat, his tongue lapping against her skin. And then he claimed her mouth once more in a plundering series of kisses.

He tore his mouth from hers, framing her face in his hands. "My God, sweetheart." His eyes burned into hers. "If I kiss you one more time, I'm going to take you right here on the floor of Jesse's study."

His confession, raw and oh-so-wicked, produced a fresh onslaught of molten desire coursing through her. There was a throbbing between her thighs, steady and insistent, an answer to what he'd just said. No one had ever made her feel this way before, as though she had to have him, all of him, now. As though she'd perish if she couldn't satisfy this sinful hunger he'd brought to life within her. She should have been shocked. She should not have longed for him to lift her skirts and do precisely what he'd warned her he'd do. Take her.

Too much champagne indeed.

She responded by kissing him again. This time was different, tinged with an underlying understanding that there would be more, far more, to come. Acceptance. Invitation. He groaned into her mouth and caught her to him, their tongues tangling, bodies frantically straining to be closer. To be one.

His hand slid beneath her voluminous skirts and petticoat, finding the slit of her drawers. His fingers skimmed over her hot, sensitive flesh once, twice. He found the aching nub at her core and teased with just the right combination of pressure and rhythm. Her hips jerked forward and she cried out at the unexpected sensation. A feminine moan of satisfaction hummed from her. The things he was doing to her…good heavens. It felt wonderful. Heavenly. But still, it wasn't enough. She wanted more.

He caught her lower lip between his teeth and tugged before tearing his lips from hers. Rocking back, he stared down at her, his breathing as ragged as hers, his expression unguarded and laden with sensual promise. "Goddamn it," he swore, removing his hand from beneath her skirt. "We cannot do this here."

She felt suddenly bereft. Her mind spun as reality returned to her. She was on her knees in Jesse's study, half dressed, and Mr. Storm had just kissed her senseless while he had a hand up her skirt. There was a ballroom overflowing with about two hundred of London's finest lords and ladies mere yards away. The faint strains of the orchestra and the rumble of conversation and laughter filled the air. She was certain that she should be scandalized by what she had done, what she'd allowed him to do to her. Yes, propriety told her she ought to be horrified. Ashamed.

But she felt none of those things as she met his gaze unflinchingly. If this was scandal, it was one sweet scandal indeed, and she didn't regret casting herself directly into its flame. Let it burn.

"Where shall we go?" she asked him, as if she hadn't a care in the world, as if they discussed nothing of greater import than the color of her dress.

"We aren't going anywhere together. You should go somewhere alone. Somewhere very far out of my reach. On the opposite side of a locked door rather than the same." His gaze lowered to her bare breasts, then traveled to her mouth, then back to her eyes. "Hell. What have I done?"

In that moment, she was rather more concerned with what he hadn't done than what he had. Indeed, she ached with the unfulfilled need he'd sparked to life. "I don't want to be out of your reach," she said softly.

"You don't know what you're saying."

"I do." She had never been more serious or more certain. Perhaps the headiness of all the champagne she'd drunk was still wreaking its havoc upon her, but she knew her mind well enough to understand that it wouldn't change by morning. It wouldn't change at all. She'd given up trying to figure out what it was about him that affected her so.

Nothing mattered other than the way he made her feel, as though she were truly experiencing life as it was meant to be for the very first time.

He crushed her to him again, framing her face in his hands. "Damn you. You're playing with fire." He lowered his mouth to hers for another possessive kiss. "Helen, sweet Helen. I'm not the man for you. I have obligations back in New York City that I cannot escape no matter how much I want you. I never should have been so reckless with you, and for that I am damned sorry."

Helen wrapped her arms around his neck. "I don't care about any of that. I've lived a proper life and obeyed all the rules for thirty years. For once in my life, I want to do something because it feels good, without a care for the consequences."

"Everything has a consequence, my lady." His eyes blazed. "Perhaps you've lived too sheltered a life to realize that."

"Oh, I'm aware of consequences." She didn't flinch. "More than you can possibly know."

He caught a tendril of her hair that had come loose from her coiffure and swept it gently aside, his fingers grazing her cheek. "You're the daughter of an earl, and I'm the son of a whore. You're as regal as any duchess. I'm a street urchin and common thief."

She kissed his fingertips. He couldn't help the circumstance of his birth any more than she could hers. If anything, the way he had made himself into the man he was only heightened her feelings for him. She would not be dissuaded by whatever attack of conscience that had suddenly come over him. "I don't give a fig about any of that."

"But you ought to. Damn you, woman, I'm doing my utmost to be honorable." His expression was grim. "It's taking every last bit of restraint I have not to toss up your skirts and finish what we started. But I won't. We need to get you out of here before I do any more damage."

As he spoke, he went to work hastily repairing her undergarments and dress to their proper order. He was actually quite proficient with her many layers, which told her that he was certainly no stranger to helping a woman dress. Or undress. Helen didn't like the thought of him visiting the same sensual torture upon other women, either before or after her. A stab of jealousy shot through her.

"I daresay you know your way about a corset," she observed tartly. She didn't want him to be honorable, not now. She wanted him to be daring, to take her, as he'd threatened, right there on the floor with a ballroom full of people making merry just on the other side of the hall.

He sent her a wry grin. "Sweetheart, if I didn't know my way about a corset, you wouldn't want me so much."

Her eyes narrowed. Perhaps he was right about that, but she most certainly wasn't about to admit it aloud. In no time, she was refastened and laced, her bodice back in place. He took her hands and pulled her to her feet. While she was no longer indecent, a quick review of her skirts revealed that they had been hopelessly wrinkled, the damask rose trim crushed. One look at her gown, and it would be plain as day to anyone what she'd been doing locked inside Mr. Whitney's study with Levi Storm.

"We'll leave separately," he ordered, no nonsense now, as if the passionate lover of mere moments ago had vanished. She thought, not for the first time, that his surname was a fitting one. He was very much like a storm, this man, passionate as a summer thunderstorm one minute and then cool as a chill winter wind the next. "You shall go first. Your dress is ruined, I'm afraid. Go to the nearest servants' hall and find your way to your chamber. If you act normally, no one will notice. People are trained to only see what they think they see. No one will be the wiser."

No one except for her and Levi, and Helen wouldn't ever be able to forget what had transpired between the two of them. Not his kisses. Not his touch. Not a single, blessed second. How could she return to polite conversation with him when she saw him next after he had kissed her the way he had, after he'd touched her in places no other man ever had? After he had changed everything for her?

Perhaps she should be grateful that he was being the gentleman at last and refusing to take what she had so plainly offered. But all she felt as she followed him to the door of the study was a searing sense of disappointment.

He stopped and took her hands in his, raising them to his lips. "My lady. I am, as ever, your servant."

A bitter irony permeated his words. She searched his face and wished she could read him well. But he remained very much a mystery to her, a man who was at turns cold and arrogant, but one who also became a sweetly passionate lover when he wished. There was a hard shell about him, one she dearly longed to crack. She wondered if she could. If anyone could.

"No more 'my lady,' if you please. It must only be Helen now," she told him softly, unable to keep herself from reaching out to tenderly trace his stubborn jawline one more time.

"Helen," he agreed, his countenance as severe as it had ever been and every bit as starkly beautiful. "This is goodbye, sweetheart. I'm leaving in the morning."

He was leaving? And yet he called her sweetheart, and had just held her in his arms? Dread assailed her, odd for she had known him for only a short length of time. But he had made such a great impression upon her, as strong as a brand. She hadn't expected this, neither her reaction to him nor his impending departure from her life.

With reluctance, she pulled away from him, eying him warily. What had been his intent? To woo her and then disappear? Had he meant to lure her into the study to make love to her before he left? A confusing torrent of questions washed over her. "Are you returning to New York City, then?"

"Eventually that time will come, but for now, no." He ran a hand through his dark hair. "I will be in London, but

I think it best that we no longer see each other."

The urge to lash out at him was strong. How dare he? How dare he touch her the way he had, kiss her as he had, peel her out of her gown, only to button her back up and tell her he'd never see her again? But Helen had always prided herself on her strength. She had met with a great deal of heartache and pain in her life, betrayal too, and she had never faltered. She had simply bore it all with dignity and grace.

As she would now. She inclined her head. "As you wish. I've thought you a great many things since I first met you, Levi, but until today, coward wasn't one of them. Goodbye."

With that, she unlocked the study door and sailed out into the hall, not bothering to look back. She maintained her calm to the nearest servants' stair, not even running across a single soul. Somehow, she managed to make it all the way to her chamber in her ruined gown before she broke into tears.

Chapter Seven

*L*EVI HESITATED IN THE DARKNESS OF THE
HALLWAY. He had waited until the ball's end. He'd
drunk a glass of champagne and chatted with people
he didn't give a damn about. He'd met more lords than he
could name on two hands. He'd bowed to his hostess, the
incomparable and kind Mrs. Whitney. He'd gone to his
chamber and paced. He'd reassembled a pocket watch that
he'd taken apart the day he'd arrived at Jesse's house. He'd
drafted a list of all the reasons why he should stay the hell
away from Lady Helen. He'd burned it in the goddamn fire.

And now, despite all of his good intentions, despite the
incredible restraint he'd shown earlier in the study, despite
all reason and the fact that he had managed to somehow not
sink himself into Helen's delectable and willing body, he
stood outside her chamber door. The last place he should
be. The last place he meant to be. A sliver of light shone
beneath it, taunting him. When he'd first set out from his
chamber, he had initially promised himself he would take a
walk to reaffirm the wisdom of his decision, to remind
himself that though he'd been born to the gutter, he still had

his honor.

But his walk had inevitably taken him here, to the one place he knew he had no right to be but to the only place he wanted to be. Just a piece of wood and the thin remnants of his decency kept them apart. His decency was waning, and the wood was a small matter indeed.

He wasn't going to knock. By God, he wasn't. But something kept him rooted to where he was, unable to leave. Was it her unrivaled beauty? The unadulterated passion she had shown him? The way she had tasted, the way she had responded to him, the way she had been so wet for him? When he had touched her there, in the sweet spot hidden beneath the slit of her drawers, he had nearly lost his ability to stop. But his responsibilities had come crashing down upon him. He couldn't offer her anything. He was duty-bound to wed Miss VanHorn in the space of just a few months.

Helen was a lady, his conscience reminded him. She was more than a beauty. She was kind and compassionate, caring, and fierce, and everything he admired in a woman. She was everything he didn't deserve, everything he couldn't have. He might be betrothed to the daughter of the wealthiest man in all of America, but for him there was Lady Helen and then there was everyone else. And no one else would ever, could ever, compare.

It scared the hell out of him. *She* scared the hell out of him. Yes, she'd been right to call him a coward. He was all that and worse. A bastard. A selfish, weak-willed man.

Still, try as he might, he couldn't seem to shake her. Couldn't seem to stay away from her. As he stood in the hall like a thief about to make away with the household silver, he knew that he couldn't go back to his chamber. Not without seeing her first. There had been hurt in her eyes. He hated to know he'd been the cause of it.

Then he had told himself, as his feet had carried him to her chamber, that mayhap he ought to seek her out, if only to explain himself. It had been a lie. He couldn't simply seek her out. There was only one thing that would come of his visiting her chamber, and he couldn't deny it any longer. He wanted her. Wanted her more than he wanted the breath in his very lungs.

He shouldn't, of course. He had no right. He was promised to marry another, albeit in a cold-blooded union he had very much begun to dread. But still, he couldn't ignore the feeling that if he didn't go to her tonight, he would regret it for the rest of his life.

He knocked on the door. Lightly. It was very late, and not even the servants were about, no doubt having been completely worn out by the evening's festivities and all that entailed. If he had a shred of sense, he'd leave now. Leave her to her peace and beat a hasty retreat before he did something incredibly foolish.

Her door opened a crack. He caught a glimpse of her lovely face. Her long hair trailed unbound around her shoulders. "Levi?"

She was so goddamn beautiful it hurt just to look at her. What the hell was he doing here? She was too good for him. Far too good for him. And yet, he couldn't bear the thought of her belonging to anyone else. He had watched her dance at the ball in the arms of half a dozen other men. It had thoroughly rankled him. No sane, breathing man could look upon her and not want her. Seeing the others trail after her, touching her, twirling her about, had brought out a primitive instinct. One he hadn't known he'd possessed. Maybe that was why he'd reacted as he had in the study, why he was at her chamber, why he was riding hell for leather in the exact opposite of the direction he should be headed.

She held the door open for him, her eyes wide. She wore a dressing gown tied loosely at the waist and some sort of lace confection beneath. His cock went instantly rigid at the sight.

He stepped over the threshold, into her territory.

"What in heaven's name are you doing?" she demanded, half whisper, when he was inside her chamber and the door closed at his back.

Her expression was wary. She didn't trust him. He didn't blame her one whit. He didn't trust himself any longer.

"I don't know," he answered honestly. "I tried to keep to my own chamber and heed my inner sense of logic and reason. Believe me, I did."

Helen crossed her arms over her waist in a defensive gesture that only served to emphasize her tiny waist and generous bosom. He wondered if her lace nightgown was as transparent as it appeared. "But you are here now."

"Yes."

She stared him down, every inch the ice queen. "Did you expect me to launch myself into your arms just as foolishly as I did earlier and thank you for changing your mind?"

She wasn't going to take it easy on him. But then, she never had. She was the wiliest opponent he'd faced since the rebs back during the war. Strong and proud to the last. "I didn't expect anything," he answered honestly. "Were I you, I'd show me to the door and bar it and never look back."

Helen gave him a small smile then. "I ought to. Tell me, Levi, is this still goodbye?"

Hang it, he had sworn it would be. But he didn't fool himself any longer. He stepped nearer to her, closing the distance between them. Bergamot and rose teased his senses. Her hair was incredibly long, with a slight curl. It looked soft as goose down. He caught her waist and dragged her against him rather than answering her, relishing the chance to hold her without the interference of corset boning and petticoats. His fingers found the cord holding her dressing gown in place and he wasted no time in undoing it.

The lace was transparent. Jesus, he could see her nipples quite plainly through it. He eased her dressing gown from her shoulders until she stood before him clad in only the nightdress. For a moment, he could merely stare at her, mesmerized by her lush form and haunting loveliness. Nothing mattered with her standing before him, nearly nude, his for the taking. His, if for tonight alone.

"To hell with goodbye," he all but growled. And to hell with obligation. To hell with everything but Helen and her sweetly willing body. He pressed his palm to the lace above her left breast, absorbing the rapid beats of her heart. Just another scant inch and her breast would be in his hand. "Do you know what I think, sweetheart?"

She stared, looking a bit like a doe startled in the wilderness by the sudden presence of man. "What do you think?"

"I think," he began, sliding a slow caress down until the soft curve of her breast scorched him through the lace separating them. He heard her swift inhalation of breath, felt the hardened peak of her nipple, and knew an answering surge of arousal. "I think that you want me very badly."

"And I think you must also want me very badly, else you wouldn't be here." She caught her lip in her teeth and he almost groaned aloud at the fresh arrow of heat the sight sent straight to his cock. "Why *did* you come here tonight, after all that happened earlier?"

"I couldn't stay away," he said, the admission torn from him. It was the bitter, absolute truth. She had undone him. In the span of a week, she'd wreaked havoc upon all the plans he had so carefully laid, like Grant had taken Richmond. "If you have even a shred of reason, my lady, you'll tell me to go now. My intentions are anything but honorable. This is my very last attempt at being a gentleman."

"I don't want you to be a gentleman, Levi."

It was all he needed to hear. In the next instant, his mouth was on hers.

Helen clung to Levi and kissed him back with all the pent-up passion that had been building since she'd met him. She'd thought he was lost to her forever, that she'd never cross paths with him again. But now he was here, and she was in his arms, and for the moment, she couldn't shake the feeling that all was at last right in the world. Let tomorrow bring with it what consequences it would. Tonight, foolish Helen firmly held the reins, and she relished every second of her power.

Perhaps she had been too easy on him. Very likely she should have shown him the door as he'd said, and never looked back. But it wasn't that simple. Nothing between them was, despite their differences and difficulties.

He dragged his mouth down her throat, nipping and licking a path of fire as he went. His thumb toyed with her nipple, and his other hand cupped her bottom, angling her body against his so that she could feel every part of him thanks to the thin lace of her nightdress. He was heat and muscle and grace, and he was very, very hard. Everywhere.

Dear heavens. She was not entirely ignorant of the mechanics of a man and a woman making love, and she knew precisely what the rigid length jutting against her belly meant. An answering bolt of pure, molten want shot straight to her core.

He kissed her again, his fingers going to the line of pearl buttons keeping her nightgown in place. "Last chance," he muttered against her mouth. "Tell me to go to the devil."

She framed his face in her hands, kissing him once more before meeting his gaze. "I'm yours, Levi."

Their mouths met in a hungry, possessive kiss before he broke away again. "I want to go slow, but I'm not sure if I can. Darling, have you ever…" He allowed the soft question to hover, half unspoken, between them.

Helen hesitated, thinking of a long-ago, awful day. A day she had done her very best to forget each day since. It was as if a bucket of ice water had been thrown upon her. Time did not entirely dull the pain, and to have the ugliness return to her abruptly in the midst of a moment of such beauty reminded her of that.

"Forgive me," he hastened to say, pressing another kiss to her lips. "It doesn't matter. I only wanted to know how

103

slowly and gently to proceed. I don't want to hurt you."

He had obviously misread her silence. Old shame crept over her. She'd done her best to suppress it over the years. In her mind, she knew she hadn't done anything wrong, anything deserving of embarrassment in the slightest. But reliving what had happened inevitably brought with it a resurgence of painful emotions. After all, theirs was a society in which men scarcely suffered blame.

"I haven't," she blurted, not knowing what else to say. Truly, she wished she hadn't carried this burden. "That is to say, there was an incident. No one knows of it, not really."

He stiffened, searching her gaze, too perceptive and clever for her liking. "Don't tell me some bastard mistreated you."

She swallowed, wishing she hadn't chosen this moment to reveal to him what she had not divulged to anyone in all the time since. Not even her sisters, who were her dearest and best friends. "Please, think nothing of it. It happened a long time ago."

"What happened?" He caressed her cheek, the gentleness he exuded making her heart ache. "You can tell me, sweetheart."

"My parents were hosting a country house party," she began. Her vision blurred with tears despite her best efforts to keep them at bay. "I was young and quite naïve, and when my brother's friend happened across my path while I was out riding, I thought it a coincidence." She knew now looking back upon the entire scenario that he must have intentionally followed her with the sole goal of leading her somewhere no one would ever hear. She had been lucky indeed that her brother had accidentally stumbled upon them.

"Did he hurt you?" Levi's tone was lethal.

"Not as badly as he could have." An image of the Earl of Wainross crept into her mind. He had been dapper, friendly. She had seen him many times as he was a good friend of her brother's. She had trusted him when he had encouraged her to ride into the woods with him, had been charmed all too easily. But what had begun as a lark quickly devolved into a situation she hadn't been equipped to handle. He'd grabbed her in his arms, not listening when she told him to stop, tearing at her dress, pinning her to the ground. "My brother stopped him before he could do worse."

"I'll imagine your brother tore the son of a bitch limb from limb." There was a fierceness in Levi's expression she'd never seen before, a barely leashed violence. She realized he very much wanted to do harm to Wainross himself.

"Actually, quite the opposite," Helen said, unable to keep a trace of bitterness from her voice as she recalled. "My brother defended his friend."

He went still. "Your brother came upon you being attacked by his friend and instead of delivering a slow and merciless death to him, he blamed you for what had occurred?"

"Yes." She had not understood Bingley's actions that day. Indeed, she had come to realize that she likely never would. He had been beloved to her out of her three brothers, and she'd been shocked and wounded when he had gazed down at her with contempt and blamed her for luring Wainross into the forests at Harrington House. "Perhaps I was to blame in part," she acknowledged. "I was too foolish and trusting. I should never have gone into the woods alone with anyone."

"The fault is not yours but the monster who led you into the woods with the sole intention of misusing you. My God, Helen. Who is he?"

She shook her head. "It doesn't matter."

"It matters to me, damn it."

Helen was taken aback by the vehemence in his tone. Would he think her damaged now? Would he no longer be attracted to her because of what she'd revealed to him? Perhaps she should not have been so honest. Heaven knew she had never been so before. In all these years, no one other than Wainross, Bingley, and Helen knew what had happened in the woods at Harrington House. Bingley had helped her to get back to her chamber without detection. Wainross had been relieved not to be held accountable for his actions. Helen had simply done her best to work through the shame, had kept her secret, and had devoted herself to a life of helping women less fortunate than she had been.

It took all the strength she had to meet his gaze. "If my shame repulses you, I understand. If you don't want me—"

"Of course I want you," Levi interrupted. "How could you doubt it? The man's name only matters to me because I want to make him pay for what he did to you."

She wondered for a brief, silly second if Levi would beat Wainross to a bloody pulp. He was strong and broad and untamable enough to do just that. But while seeing the earl get his comeuppance would be incredibly satisfying on some primitive level, Helen knew it wouldn't solve any problems. It certainly wouldn't erase the wrongs that had already been done. It would only reopen wounds she had tried with all her might to heal.

"It was many, many years ago, Levi. I've had time to move past what happened."

He framed her face in his hands, staring hard into her eyes. "You damn well shouldn't have had to go through that, sweetheart. I'm so very sorry." He kissed her softly, almost chastely, then.

"You may kiss me harder," she told him with a smile. "I won't break. What happened that day made me stronger."

"You are strong," he agreed, kissing her more lingeringly this time. "And kind, and good, and so damn beautiful. Far too good for the likes of me." He gripped her waist and held her away from him. "I don't deserve what you're offering me. I don't deserve you, my lady."

"You needn't deserve anything." She caressed his whisker-stubbled jaw, loving the freedom to touch him as she pleased. "What I have I give to you freely. If you still desire me, that is."

"Stop saying that." He reeled her back in, her body pressing against his hard muscles from top to bottom. "Stop thinking that. I desire you more than I desire breath in my lungs."

"Then why do you hesitate?" Her gaze slipped to his mouth, so often stern and forbidding, set in hard lines. Now it was soft. She knew how it felt against hers. Possessive and altogether wonderful. She grew bold and ran her thumb lightly over the seam of his lips.

"I can't offer you marriage, and you deserve nothing less."

"It isn't marriage that I want." She understood that he had his business and his life in American to return to, that everything they shared was fleeting. But she didn't care. She had long ago accepted the fact that she would never wed, never bear children. She'd made peace with it. Now, it seemed that there was a fleeting opportunity for her to at least taste passion. If only for a night. "All that I want is you, Levi."

Before he could exercise any more gentlemanly inclinations, she undid the remaining buttons on her nightdress and shrugged out of it. The lace fell to her feet with a whisper of sound. She stood nude before him, and it was apparently enough for him to overcome any niggling sense of honor restraining him. Tonight, she regained the power that had been taken from her all those years ago. She would no longer allow the past to haunt or curse her or make her fear. Tonight, she was Helen and he was Levi, and she wanted him atop her, inside her, touching her, kissing her, taking her. Everything. She wanted everything.

"My God, Helen." He picked her up in his arms as though she weighed no more than air and carried her to her bed, laying her gently upon it. He joined her in an instant, his big body against hers, his hands on her, tracing her curves. "We will go very slowly, my darling. As slowly as you need. Tonight, I'm yours to rule. We won't do a thing you don't want, do you understand?"

His tenderness tugged at her heart. He had no way of knowing that there had never been another man since that awful day, that she had never wanted anyone until he had appeared in the offices of the *London Beacon*, hell bent on throwing her out on her ear. But as always, he was incredibly observant. He could be painfully kind when he chose to, and she was grateful for this side of him now. Somehow, he was precisely what she needed.

He caressed her waist, the soft roundness of her hip. "You are so very exquisite. I'm sorry that I was rough with you earlier. If I had known, I would've damn well controlled myself."

"Hush." She pressed a finger to his lips. "You were never rough. You couldn't be. And I've already told you that I'll not break. Make love to me, Levi."

He kissed her deeply, passionately. Together, they tore off his shirt so that his bare chest was at last revealed. It was a thing of beauty, sculpted and hard, stippled with just the right amount of masculine dark hair. His arms were muscled in a way a gentleman's were not, and a long, jagged scar marred the otherwise perfect flesh of his left arm.

She touched him there. "What happened?"

"A minié ball during the war. I'm damn lucky it grazed me or I'd have lost my arm."

Dear God. Helen tentatively traced indented, smooth skin. "It would seem we're both revealing our scars tonight."

"Does it offend you?" he asked, a note of hesitation in his voice that told her it had offended someone else before her.

She kissed the imperfect flash, thankful he hadn't suffered worse. "It's a sign of bravery. How could it be anything but beautiful?"

She raked her fingers up past the scar, across his broad shoulder, tracing the line of his clavicle and then down over his taut belly to his trousers. She wanted them off as well, until there was nothing between them. No more barriers.

Levi caught her fingers before they could investigate the length of him, the very part of him she was so curious to see and touch. "Slowly, sweetheart. Slowly."

His mouth was on hers. He kissed his way down her throat to her breasts as she settled for resting her hands on his shoulders instead. His skin was sleek and smooth and hot. He sucked her nipple into his mouth, teased it with his tongue and teeth. She rocked into him. The hand on her hip dipped between her thighs, touching her as he had before with the perfect balance of pressure and skill. Pure pleasure shot through her, beginning in the center of her body and radiating outward like a shining sun, every bit as white hot. As he moved to her other breast, nipping and sucking, his fingers slid over her slick folds and then a lone finger dipped inside her ever so slightly. She bucked against him, wanting more.

"Slowly," he reminded her, kissing the valley between her breasts and then down her belly. "Tell me what you need, sweetheart." He kissed her hip bone and glanced up at her, so sinfully good-looking the sight of him made her weak.

"I don't know," she confessed, breathless. "You."

He gave her a wicked smile before lowering his head and kissing her *there*, where she wanted him most. Shock warred with need within her. Dear sweet heavens. Breath hissed from her lungs and she arched into him. Surely what he was doing to her was incredibly indecent, and yet she had never experienced anything so wildly wonderful in her life. He sucked the sensitive nub hidden in her folds into his mouth, worked it lightly with his teeth. Then his tongue slid straight across her aching seam.

She cried out, unable to stop herself despite the danger of being heard. He continued doling out his torturous pleasure, not once stopping. The rational part of her reminded her that she ought to protest, that surely it was wanton and depraved of him to do such things to her.

"You shouldn't," she tried to protest. He worked her nub again, playing his tongue over it. A quiver went through her. She felt as if her entire body were a spring, coiling ever more tightly. Something would break. She would break. The pleasure was mind-numbing. "Really, Levi. You ought not…"

But his fingers had now joined his tongue, and she was robbed of speech entirely. Her hands sank into his thick, dark hair and her hips pumped into him. She had never felt more thoroughly, wonderfully alive. And then it came, swift and sudden upon her, a release so forceful that she swore she'd broken into a hundred pieces. She arched into him as his mouth absorbed the ripples of her pleasure. Another cry escaped her as aftershocks rocked her body. Nothing could have prepared her for this. For him.

Slowly, he had said. Perhaps he intended to kill her with pleasure.

He made a deep, low sound of appreciation in his throat and kissed her one last time before dragging his wet mouth back over her skin, across her belly, back to her breasts. He sucked first one nipple, then the other. His fingers were between her legs again, working the hungry, slick flesh that had so recently capitulated.

"I'm going to kiss every inch of you," he murmured against her skin, and then he proceeded to do as he'd promised. Random, decadent kisses rained across her naked skin. Her breast, her stomach, her elbow, the curve of her knee, her inner thigh. Until she was nearly out of her mind with wanting him, more of him.

All of him.

When she swore she couldn't stand another moment more, he kissed a path from her throat to her ear. His breath was hot upon her as he kissed her earlobe first and then the shell above it. His touch dipped back between her thighs, a slow and steady caress.

"Are you absolutely certain, darling?" he asked, still leaving her in control of everything that happened between them.

It was precisely what she needed, and it stirred her even as she knew she must guard herself against falling for this man. He was not of her world, nor would he remain a part of it. He was a temporary distraction with unknown obligations half a world away. Falling for him would simply not do.

"I'm certain," she managed to say past a swelling tide of need.

He left for a moment to shuck his trousers and drawers before returning and pressing his heated, solid body to hers. He cupped Helen's face, his eyes as intense and piercing as she had ever seen them. They seemed to cut straight to her heart.

"You are very sure?" he queried again, almost as if he needed to reassure himself as much as he wanted to reassure her.

She had seen him, every bit of him, as he had joined her on the bed. He was almost unbearably beautiful to behold. She knew a brief, passing flurry of nerves before dashing them away. He jutted against her belly, hot and hard. She was as ready as she would ever be to know him in every way she could.

Helen framed his face, his beard a delicious prickle against her palms. It seemed impossible to believe that this man, strong and handsome and so much an enigma to her, was hers to touch. "I am sure."

He kissed her then, long and deep and tenderly. And at last, he rolled them as one so that she was beneath him, her legs falling apart with his gentle guidance. He teased her with his fingers before finally the rigid length of him met her precisely where she longed for him to be.

"This will hurt a bit at first, sweetheart. I'm sorry for that," he whispered.

With one slow, swift thrust, he entered her. She knew a sharp twinge of pain as her body accepted him completely, dragging him deep within her. He stilled, his breathing ragged. She knew he would stop if she asked it of him. But she didn't want him to stop. She moved against him, urging him to continue. She wanted all of him. Wanted everything. With a muttered curse, he withdrew almost completely and then slid home inside her once more. Gradually, the discomfort subsided as her body grew accustomed to this new, delicious invasion.

As he moved within her, he kissed her, his tongue tangling with hers, claiming her with his mouth as surely as he claimed her body with his. His fingers slipped between them to tease her as he had before. The ache building between her thighs grew, and this time it was even more insistent. She felt as if she soared higher and higher, as though at any moment her body would come apart in shuddering surrender again. Levi knew just how far to go, how slow and then how fast, how sweetly and how passionately she needed him to take her. It was as if he knew her better than she knew herself.

Her entire body had come to life, and she was hyperaware of every sensation, from his fingers stroking her to the gentle abrasion of his stubble upon her cheek. She arched into him, preserving as much of this moment in her memory as she could. Surely nothing would ever compare.

Spasms shook her as she once more reached her peak. She cried out, her breathing ragged, holding him to her, kissing him everywhere she could. His ear. His chin. His strong jaw. And then he too was coming undone, going faster, sliding inside her until his entire body stiffened and she felt the hot spurt of his seed within her.

She cried out again as a series of small aftershocks shook her, but the hazy fog of pleasure surrounding her was dashed when he abruptly withdrew from her, rolling onto his side and jamming his hand through his hair.

"Damn it," he swore, his breathing as affected as hers.

Helen stared at the length of her body, flushed with passion and his kisses and touch, and then to him, so large and distinctly male. Even his feet were perfect, as finely shaped as the rest of him. Her modesty returned to her as she realized who they were, what they had done. She lay nude next to a man who had just taken her maidenhead with incredible, wicked skill only to curse and withdraw from her as if she'd burned him. She clutched at the bedclothes, drawing them over her. Perhaps he regretted what he'd done. Lord knew she should, but her throbbing body knew not an ounce of repentance.

"I'm sorry, Helen," he said into the silence that had fallen between them. "I didn't hurt you too badly, did I?"

She shook her head solemnly and met his gaze. "No. What's wrong, Levi?"

"Nothing." He took her back in his arms, pulling the bedclothes over them both and tucking her into the comforting, solid warmth of him. "Not a thing." He pressed a kiss to the top of her head. "You should rest."

She wanted to protest, but there was something about lying in his protective embrace, the steady thud of his heart beating beneath her ear, that lulled her into the most sound and dreamless sleep she'd had in a long time. But just before she succumbed to slumber, she thought again of the way he had withdrawn from her, and she was sure that he had lied to her when he had said there was nothing wrong. Something had troubled him. She would have to do her best to learn precisely what it was.

Chapter Eight

*L*EVI WOKE TO THE EARLY STRAINS OF DAWN casting its bright light through a small gap in the window dressing. For a moment, he was disoriented. This was not his chamber. A soft, plump breast swelled beneath his hand and the tempting curve of a derriere nestled against his already hard cock. The bed smelled of bergamot and rose, and lustrous curls fanned on the pillow before him. Lady Helen lay in his arms, her steady, even breathing telling him she was still asleep.

Holy hell, what had he done?

He had taken her. Had kissed and loved and tasted every gorgeous inch of her body. Hang it, he'd fallen asleep in her chamber as though he belonged there, sleeping all night with her in his arms as he'd never done with another woman before her. Worst of all, he had lost control and spent himself inside her.

He hadn't meant to do any of those things. From the time he'd been a lad who ran off to join the war and make something of himself to the day he'd met her, his entire life had been rooted in reason, order, duty, function, and routine. He had never, not once, allowed his baser instincts to rule his better judgment. He was cautious. Careful. Precise. He didn't engage in affairs with innocent ladies. He didn't cast his plans all to hell because a beautiful woman kissed him in a locked study. He didn't forget what it meant to be a man of honor simply because the most maddening woman he'd ever met had offered herself to him.

But he had committed all those sins. Every last, damn one of them. By God, he had taken the innocence of a noblewoman beneath his own friend's roof. A woman who was outspoken and ferocious, sweet and lovely, kind and good, and his better in every sense of the word. He ought to be drawn and quartered. What had he done to deserve her, the precious gift of her passion and her body that she'd so freely given? And he had taken, Lord had he taken. Like the thief he'd once been as a boy, he'd taken what didn't belong to him not only because he needed it but because he could.

She'd been a virgin, her only experience prior to him a violent farce forced upon her by some faceless bastard Levi still longed to beat to within an inch of life. He understood her now, not only in an elemental way but beyond that. Her devotion to her cause made bitter sense. She was driven to help other women escape a world that rendered them powerless. Because she knew how it had felt. She too had been defenseless once, and it would seem she'd been trying to atone for that by making certain she was never powerless again, by making certain that others were never powerless either.

Helen stirred then, burrowing closer. A bolt of pure lust drove straight through him. He wanted her again, and with a fierce need that shook him. Levi damn well knew better, but he couldn't resist parting the silken cloud of her hair to drop a kiss on her throat. The thought of leaving her, of never touching her again, left him stricken.

If he possessed a shred of conscience, he would get out of her bed and out of her life forever. He kissed her ear, inhaling deeply of the scent that was innately hers. Somehow, this feisty aristocrat had laid her claim upon him. No, not even a shred of conscience at the moment. Nothing had ever been so wrong or felt more right.

Just once more.

He reckoned there was about an hour until the servants were afoot and even longer before the rest of the household was, having been kept up half the night with festivities. No one would be the wiser. He caught her nipple between his thumb and finger and tugged.

She exhaled on a throaty moan and arched into him. All he needed to do was roll her onto her back, take her mouth, and slide sweetly home inside her. He ached to do precisely that. But he had no right. He'd already made enough transgressions in the span of one day to last him the rest of his life. Responsibility came crashing back down on him. He couldn't afford to linger, invite more ruin for either of them. No, he would slip from the bed and be gone before she rose. A shred of conscience after all.

"Levi?"

Damn it, she was awake. She turned in his arms so that she faced him, the bounty of her breasts against his chest. His rigid cock nestled between her thighs now. He couldn't shake the feeling that he was exactly where he belonged.

She blinked sleepily, and she'd never been more gorgeous to him than she was in that instant, unguarded and naked in his arms, her hair a riotous halo about her pretty face. He kissed her because he couldn't resist.

"Morning." He pressed another kiss to the corner of her mouth, drinking in the sight of her.

"Good morning." She flushed beneath his stare, no doubt feeling shy after the intimacies they had shared. "Is it wise for you to be here?"

"No." But he didn't move just the same. He liked the way she felt, her soft skin teasing his, her warmth a seductive invitation against his rigid arousal.

"Levi." She cast a glance about the chamber. "Good

heavens, you can't remain here. The servants will surely be about any minute."

Odd that she was the one so concerned with propriety. Of course, it should have been him. He should've been strong enough to let her go, but somehow he couldn't. "It's too early for the servants." His right hand went to her waist, anchoring her to him, his left into the sweet-smelling skeins of her hair.

Her eyes went wide then, bluer than a country summer's sky. "Levi, you must go. We cannot."

Hell. Maybe she regretted what had happened between them. He hoped to God she didn't, but he couldn't read her. The morning light had dashed the magical spell of the night, and with each increment the sun rose in the sky, they traveled further and further from where they'd been. It was as if she was slipping away from him, and he didn't like the feeling. Not one damn bit.

But he wasn't a fool. He hadn't dug himself out of the dirt, survived the hells of war, and gone on to build a successful business empire by allowing his prick to rule his brain. Far better that they should return to their separate lives and never again repeat this folly. Far better, far wiser, and necessary. He was pledged to another, damn it. Guilt skewered him. He should have told her everything. Should have given her the chance to truly turn him away. But he'd been selfish, greedy. He'd taken what he wanted, and now he still wanted more.

"Oh dear," she said, interrupting his thoughts as she pushed away from him and rolled out of the bed. She took the counterpane with her, dragging it around her with as much august dignity as a queen donning full court dress. Perhaps she had forgotten just how thoroughly he'd loved, kissed, and tasted every part of her luscious body. "I almost didn't recall that I promised to meet Gussie this morning."

He rose from the bed, not bothering to hide his nudity for the sake of her modesty. Her gaze traveled his body, dipping to his cock before she flushed an even brighter shade of scarlet and turned away.

"Who the hell is Gussie?" he growled in irritation. Wasn't he the one who was supposed to have the willpower to leave her behind? Instead, he had been lingering in the bed like a lovesick swain while she couldn't wait to put distance between them.

"Gussie is my dear friend." Helen presented him with her back as she shimmied into a shift beneath her mantle of bedclothes. "She runs a House of Rest for the ladies we've managed to save from brothels and for others who have escaped on their own."

Levi was sure the woman must be an agitator. He knew the sort. He made a noncommittal sound as he took up his discarded drawers and stuffed a leg inside. "Tell me this isn't the biddy who took you to that den of vice you wrote about."

Her shift firmly in place, Helen dropped her counterpane and turned to face him. Although her lithe form was covered by fabric, it did little to hide her. Indeed, he swore it was thin enough that he could see the peony pink of her nipples straight through it. Damn but it was difficult for a man to put on his drawers when he was stiffer than a ramrod. She quickly averted her gaze when she realized he was not yet decent.

"Yes, it is, and do keep your voice down." Her tone was prim, as though she hadn't turned into a wilding in his arms mere hours before. "I'll thank you not to refer to her as a biddy. Gussie is a wonderful woman, and I admire her greatly. She's devoted her life to helping those women and girls."

Perhaps the woman was a saint, but she was also the cause for Helen putting herself in grave danger, and he was determined not to like her. "Why are you meeting her?"

"The home that she runs is quite out of lodging space, and we are taking in more girls all the time. She found a building that she thinks we may be able to afford in the East End." Helen busied herself by stepping into her underclothes and buttoning and fastening herself back into her elaborate fashion for the day. "It isn't in the best neighborhood, but our funds are short. In the end, any roof will do, as long as it's a safe and dry place."

He strode across the room and caught her arm before he could even think twice, irrationally angered by her lack of care for herself. "Like hell you're going to the East End to look at some hovel with only an old biddy for protection."

She raised an imperious brow. "I'm sure it isn't any of your concern, Mr. Storm."

Ah, so he was back to being Mr. Storm now, was he? Here was the termagant he'd met in his offices once more, daring and brash and altogether exasperating. "And I'm sure it is, my lady. I'll not allow you to put yourself in danger again."

"There will be no danger." She sniffed. "We take the brawniest footmen we can find, and they do nicely."

Good God. The woman was going to make him go mad. One moment, he wanted to make love to her and the next he longed to throttle some sense into her. "The East End is no place for a lady. You and I both know that."

"And you and I both know that I'm no lady," she said quietly.

"You are the finest lady I know," he countered. "Don't do that, Helen."

She searched his gaze, her expression pensive, troubled. "Don't do what?"

"Don't tarnish what we shared, damn it."

"I only speak the truth." She shrugged out of his grasp and turned to take up a corset and slip the closures into their moorings. It was violet satin, trimmed in bits of black lace, and he wanted nothing more than to peel her back out of it. "Now if you don't mind, I would appreciate it greatly if you would return to your own chamber before someone catches you in mine."

She was right, of course. He needed to leave. He had no right tarrying here, worrying about what she planned to do with her day. He had his work waiting for him, the endless machine of business, the comfort and simplicity of his routine. But he couldn't bear the thought of something happening to her, some harm befalling her. To know she had been hurt in the past and there wasn't a damn thing he could do about it was torture enough.

"Find a house in a decent part of London," he urged her. "Don't go to the East End." He was a man of the world. He knew what lurked in the dark corners of every city. He had seen and heard it all before as a boy. It wasn't something he wanted her exposed to.

She pursed her lips, reaching behind her back to tug her laces. "I'm afraid we don't have the luxury of finding a Mayfair mansion. You see, a miserable cad bought the newspaper that was our primary method of raising funds to aid our cause. Our articles brought us the attention of benevolent benefactors."

Well, now they truly had come full circle once more. But he had been inside her, had tasted the most delicate and sensitive part of her, and his world as he knew it was beginning to shift in a way he couldn't comprehend. He tired of watching her struggle with her laces and went to her, shooing her hands away as he performed the task as efficiently as any lady's maid could. He'd fastened his fair share of corsets over the years, but never had the task affected him the way tightening up the laces for Helen did.

Even if she had called him a cad. He deserved that, and more than she knew.

"You didn't think me so very miserable last night," he reminded her softly as he finished her laces and tied a perfect knot. "Why not have your father, the earl, fund your efforts? Surely he can afford to offer aid?"

"He doesn't approve of my work because the ladies come from houses of ill repute. He gives me my pin money and little else." She spun about to face him, looking like a goddess in her half dress, her breasts threatening to spill over the top of her corset. "You really must go, Levi."

Yes. The light filtering through the curtains grew stronger. Servants would most certainly be about now, and he gambled with scandal and fate by tarrying. "Promise me you won't risk your fool neck by going to the East End today."

"Why do you care when you'll never see me again?" she demanded.

He could no more refrain from seeing her again than he could stop breathing. He didn't know what that meant for him. Not yet. But all he did know in that moment was that he had to see her again. Had to touch her again. Once was not enough.

"I will see you again, sweetheart," he promised her, unable to resist tracing her full lower lip with his thumb. And then he laid claim to her in the only way he knew how, by sweeping her into his arms and kissing the hell out of her.

When he finally withdrew, her mouth was red and swollen with his kisses, her eyes dazed. "Don't go to the East End today, Helen," he ordered.

He slipped on his trousers and his shirt from the night before, not bothering with the buttons. At the moment, he didn't give a damn who saw him in *dishabille*. He felt like a grizzly bear who'd just gotten a rude awakening during hibernation. He took one last look at her to find her standing precisely where he'd left her, watching him with wide eyes.

"For the first time in your life, listen to reason and do as I say, woman." With that, he stalked from her chamber and into the hall.

He had gone.

Helen raised a hand to her tingling mouth, still feeling the possessive kisses he had given her. The arrogance of the man. He thought he could order her about because she'd allowed him into her bed? He thought he could

121

commandeer her reform journal and turn it into a business paper and then demand that she stay away from the East End? Of course she was going with Gussie in spite of what he'd said. Perhaps because of it.

Do as I say, woman.

Obviously, Mr. Storm had no idea that those were the last words he should have uttered to a proud Harrington sister. Now she was more determined than ever. The intimacies between them did not mean he had any right to decree what she could and could not do.

But the thought of what they had shared heated her body all over. Good heavens, the things he had done. He'd brought out sensations she hadn't even known existed, had made her aware of her body and all its longings. Part of her had been shocked when she'd woken nude to find him still sharing her bed. Part of her had wanted more. And yet another part of her had been embarrassed, feeling hopelessly gauche. She had no idea what to do, what to say, how to act.

So she had resorted to distance. Perhaps it had been enough. Perhaps it hadn't been.

I will see you again, sweetheart.

The words, half promise and half sensual threat, sent a frisson of desire down her spine. Oh dear. It wouldn't do to stand about daydreaming as if she were a lovelorn girl straight from the schoolroom. She wasn't a girl. And she most assuredly was not lovelorn.

She rang for her lady's maid and finished dressing. If Willet was surprised to find her mistress partially dressed and already laced in her corset, her expression didn't reflect it. Helen didn't say a word, simply thanked the loyal retainer and went to breakfast as though she hadn't spent half the night in wicked abandon with the most handsome and thoroughly maddening man she'd ever known.

Of course he was not at breakfast, but Helen was pleasantly surprised to find her hostess already seated. They completed their morning greetings and as Helen settled in, she couldn't help but notice how lovely Bella looked. From her lustrous dark hair to her stunning, blue morning gown, she was perfection, as though she had spent all night in restful slumber rather than hosting a crush of a ball. Helen felt a bit bedraggled by comparison. Levi had kept her up very late and had woken her quite early. A slow knot of desire unfurled in her belly at the reminder, but she tamped it down. She would not allow him to barge in on her every thought.

"You are certainly the picture of sunshine for one who was up all night dancing away," Helen pointed out good-naturedly. "Indeed, I'm shocked you're up so early."

"My darling little Virginia decided that I must wake at the first light of dawn this morning. She was most insistent about it, so here I am. Anyway, my dear, I might say the same of you." Her friend delivered the kind of searching look one of Helen's own dear sisters would surely give her. An honorary Harrington sister Bella was indeed. "I saw you dancing with Mr. Storm."

Despite herself, she flushed. Dear heavens. She hoped she didn't appear half as guilty as she felt. "I danced with a number of gentlemen," she offered in a noncommittal tone before taking a sip of tea.

"I daresay you did." Bella's arch tone made it clear that she was not fooled.

Helen remained undeterred. "It was so nice to see an old family friend like Lord Denbigh again."

Bella dismissed the servants before turning back to her with a conspiratorial air when they were alone. "You didn't have eyes for Denbigh, and you know it."

Helen sighed, wishing Bella hadn't taken lessons in prying from Cleo. "Did my sister train you or have you always been this thoroughly invasive?"

Her friend laughed. "I believe I've always been this way, but I do confess that having you Harrington girls about has taught me a thing or two."

"Lovely," Helen gritted.

"Dearest, if I'm prying it's only because I care about you and because Cleo has ordered me to watch over you in her stead." Bella took a demure sip from her cup.

"Watch over *me*?" Helen sniffed at that. "I'm your elder, you ninny. I'm her elder too, for that matter."

"By a scarce few number of years."

"A good six years," she pointed out.

"Cleo would have my head if anyone broke your heart," Bella blurted.

"The Earl of Denbigh won't break my heart." Helen gave her friend and hostess her most forbidding frown.

"Oh, pish. You know very well I'm not speaking of Denbigh. I'm talking about Mr. Storm." She paused. "I could have sworn I saw you on his arm, and then you both seemed to disappear from the ballroom. Please tell me nothing untoward occurred, dear."

Oh drat it all. Levi had been wrong. Someone *had* seen, or at the very least she had noticed their absence long enough to question it. Helen didn't relish the prospect of misleading her friend, but neither did she wish to reveal the raw truth to her.

"Nothing untoward occurred," she lied, redirecting her gaze to the bounty of food upon her plate and treating it as if it were the most intriguing sight she'd beheld all morning. Not true, for the most intriguing sight she'd beheld all morning had been Levi's lean body without a stitch of clothing to hide it.

Bella gave a small harrumph reminiscent of her formidable mother, the dowager marchioness. "Something tells me not to believe you, Helen."

"Perhaps you ought to inform whatever that something is to mind its own business," she suggested with a sunny smile.

"I'll send it a letter posthaste." Bella grinned at that. "You're quite a curmudgeon when your heart is in peril, you know."

"My heart is not in peril."

"Better your heart than your virtue," her friend said primly. "If so much as a breath of scandal should find its way to your sister, she'll leave her lying in and swoop down upon us all like an avenging angel."

"More like a scandalous angel," Helen grumbled. "It's rich indeed for Cleo to be so protective when she created the scandal of the century herself. I'm hardly the sister to be worrying over. We won't even get into how Tia wound up wedding Devonshire."

"Be that as it may, I've been charged with your wellbeing, dearest Helen," Bella said. "I would be remiss if I didn't warn you I'm not entirely certain Mr. Storm's intentions are honorable. My husband counts him a true friend, but the man is something of an enigma. I cannot quite figure him out just yet."

Of course his intentions weren't honorable. They were passionate and sinful and altogether wrong yet altogether wonderful. But it was too late for Bella's sermon and concern both. The dye had been cast. Maybe she'd made a mistake. By the grim light of day, it certainly seemed that she may have. Still, she didn't regret a moment of their time together. Not one single moment.

She wasn't sure what that meant, any of it, and for the nonce, she didn't care to examine it any further. Helen stood. "I appreciate your concern, truly I do, however it is quite misplaced. I'm a spinster firmly and happily on the shelf. Now, if you'll excuse me, Lady Bella, I have an important call I must make to Gussie at the House of Rest."

Without waiting for her friend's reply, she sailed from the room and from Bella's unnerving observations both. By the time she reached her waiting carriage, her emotions were as jumbled and messy as a bag of yarn scraps that had been savaged by a kitten. As a servant handed her up into the carriage, she was so caught up in her thoughts that it took her by complete surprise when she realized she wasn't alone.

"Levi." She almost turned around and left the conveyance. Didn't he realize he couldn't simply ride in an enclosed carriage with her? It wasn't done. Belatedly, she observed that this carriage did not belong to the Whitneys. It must be his.

He caught her elbow and pulled her the rest of the way inside, unsmiling. The door closed behind her. "Sit."

Helen seated herself on the bench beside him, wishing the carriage was not so cramped. Her skirts brushed his muscled thigh and when she faced him, they were nearly nose to nose. The urge to kiss him was strong but she would not, could not give in.

"Have you gone mad? What are you doing in this carriage?" she demanded.

His expression remained impassive as ever. "I expect I have. Lord knows there are a hundred things I'd be better served by doing this morning than playing guardian angel."

The nerve of the man would never cease to amaze—or vex—her. "Then why are you not off doing those hundred things instead of importuning me in my carriage?"

"Because I cannot in good conscience allow you to go traipsing about the rookeries where anything can happen to you. And also because this is not, in fact, your carriage. It is mine."

Oh, blast him. He had a point there. And he had known she wouldn't listen to his high-handed decree. "You haven't the right to allow me to do anything, Mr. Storm."

He flashed her a thin smile that showed his even, white teeth. "We will have to disagree on that count, my dear."

But Helen wasn't done. "The servants will talk belowstairs. Everyone will know that I've been spirited away with you."

"I'm not spiriting you anywhere, and the servants will not talk. They're my men, and they're loyal to a fault. A decent wage will do that for a man."

Perhaps his servants were loyal, but she knew the rules. It was one thing to sneak about in the darkness and quite another to flagrantly travel the streets of London alone with him. "Have you any idea of how improper it is for you to ride in this carriage with me?"

"Surely not any more improper than traipsing about brothels with your reformer friend," he drawled. "Or inviting me into your bed."

His blunt observation had her flushing. "You came to my chamber."

"You didn't turn me away."

No, she hadn't. Nor would she if he somehow turned up at her door again tonight. How deflating. When it came to this man, she possessed not a jot of resolve. He had invaded her life and her senses just as surely as he'd invaded the carriage. Like a plundering army, taking all her defenses with him.

"Why are you really here?" she asked instead of responding to his observation. "Aren't you ordinarily at your offices by now, busy turning the *Beacon* into a glowing beast?"

"Someone has to protect you from your foolishness," he snapped.

Her foolishness indeed. The greatest foolishness in which she was currently engaged involved him, not any trip to the East End with Gussie. "No one has been protecting me for thirty years and I've managed just fine."

"Someone damn well should have." His tone was clipped. "Your brother ought to be dragged behind the nearest carriage for failing you the way he did."

She stiffened. "I prefer not to speak of it, if you don't mind. Besides, I don't wish anything ill of Bingley." Well, perhaps that was doing it a bit brown. What she truly meant to say was that she didn't wish anything painful and potentially life-threatening to happen to her brother. But if in one of his drunken stupors he accidentally received a sound knock to the head or fist to the jaw, she may have deemed it fitting.

"Helen, I'm trying to keep you from getting hurt," Levi said, sounding much aggrieved. He took her hand firmly in his. "I cannot right the wrongs done to you in your past, but

I'll be damned if I stand idly by while you put yourself in danger."

Somehow, the mere squeeze of his large hand around hers, burrowed in the pleats of her serviceable visiting gown, melted some of the ice she'd built around her heart. Emotions she'd been doing her utmost to repress all morning rushed over her.

She swallowed, wishing very much that she hadn't donned gloves, and clasped his hand as if it were a lifeline. He may be arrogant, but he cared. He cared or he would not have eschewed his plans for the day to accompany her. Perhaps she had melted some of his ice in return.

"Thank you," she said softly.

He appeared surprised by her capitulation. "Am I hearing right? Gratitude instead of a thorough dressing down?"

Helen smiled at last. "I can deliver a stinging dressing down if you'd prefer it."

"I can think of better uses for your mouth, sweetheart." With his free hand, he cupped her face. His thumb swept over her lower lip in a broad stroke.

In an instant, the air between them changed. She kissed his thumb, gazing boldly into his eyes. Every part of her rational mind knew she shouldn't very well be sitting so near to him in an enclosed carriage, let alone allowing him to touch her so freely. But hadn't they already gone far beyond the lines of propriety? wondered a wicked inner voice. Yes, they had. His body had claimed hers. What could be the harm in one more kiss? One more embrace? A slow, pulsing yearning began at the juncture of her thighs and radiated outward, over her entire body.

His mouth slanted over hers and she gave in to what they both so desperately wanted. More of the forbidden. She opened for him and his questing tongue. He tasted of coffee. The kiss deepened.

The carriage stopped.

They sprang apart just as the door opened to reveal they

had arrived at Gussie's House of Rest for women in need of shelter. Perhaps it was a fortuitous interruption, but Helen dearly wished she could've gone on kissing him for just a few moments more. Their arrival reminded her that there was work to be done. If nothing else could come of the day, she hoped that at the very least she might convince Levi to assist them in their efforts. He was not an unkind man. After he met the women and girls, she had no doubt that he would understand why she felt so strongly about their cause.

She descended from the carriage and took his arm in silence as they climbed the stairs to the front door. It was not an imposing edifice. Indeed, it was small and nondescript, though tucked into a decent neighborhood far enough from the brothels the women had once called home. Gussie herself greeted them at the door.

"Helen dear, do come in." Smiling, she stepped back so that Helen and Levi could enter. She wore an apron and her hair had been wound in a serviceable bun. "Forgive me my appearance. I'm afraid I was helping in the kitchens this morning."

Although Gussie had been born a lady, she was not afraid to roll up her sleeves and work alongside anyone, and it was one of the many traits Helen admired about her friend. "Gussie, may I introduce you to Mr. Storm? He is the new owner of the *Beacon*. Mr. Storm, this is Mrs. Augusta Bennington."

"I'm sure I'm pleased to make your acquaintance, sir," Gussie said with considerably less enthusiasm and warmth than she had previously displayed.

If Levi noticed, he didn't show it. "The pleasure is mine, Mrs. Bennington. I hope you don't mind the intrusion. Lady Helen has convinced me to assist you and your cause in any way that I may."

She had? Helen looked at him askance. He ignored her, imperturbable as always.

Gussie beamed once more. "Oh, how wonderful. Our Helen is an angel on Earth, and I just knew that if anyone could persuade you how important our mission is, it would be sweet Lady Helen."

"Yes," Levi agreed solemnly, sending Helen a meaningful look. "It would be sweet Lady Helen indeed."

Chapter Nine

"WHY HAVE YOU BROUGHT ME HERE?" Helen asked Levi much later that day as they stood alone in the entryway of a nicely appointed but empty house not far from Gussie's House of Rest.

She had accompanied him against her better judgment. But he had been startlingly kind and helpful at Gussie's despite his insistence that they refrain from visiting the property in the East End. He'd repaired a broken door lock and carried supplies into the kitchens as if he were a man of all work. He had taken interest in the stories of the women he met. He had assured Gussie before their departure that he would aid the cause however he could.

And Helen believed him, which was why she found herself in a large home in a good, middle class neighborhood, trying to tamp down the troubling stirrings of her heart. The more time she spent in Levi's company, the more her admiration for him grew. He possessed a keen intelligence and sharp wit, and beneath his arrogant, cool exterior there lurked a compassionate man. He wasn't all business, the enigmatic American before her.

"I own this property, along with a number of others here in London," he told her. "I was planning to use this particular building as lodgings for my engineers."

Helen wasn't accustomed to men who spoke so bluntly of trade, but rather than finding it tedious, she was interested. His mind was ever spinning, and it appeared that he had laid the groundwork for his business very carefully. "You provide your employees with lodging?"

"I provide them with *affordable* lodging," he explained. "If they need loans for homes, I provide them as well."

He cared about the people in his employ. She recalled his heated words in the library. *Hundreds of families put bread on their table through me, and I take that responsibility seriously.* "That is very good of you," she said softly. Oh yes, there was so much more to him than she had supposed.

He flashed her a self-mocking smile. "Not so good, I'm afraid. I merely know how to judge what is in my best interest and what isn't. A happy and comforting home environment is excellent for business. Well-treated employees are loyal employees, and loyal employees are productive and motivated. Productivity and self-motivation earn me money. Ultimately, it's a small thing that reaps great rewards for me."

Although he attempted to dismiss his actions as mere selfishness, she wasn't fooled. Providing employees with well-appointed and affordable lodgings was virtually unheard of. She may be a privileged member of the Upper Ten Thousand, but she had a reformer's heart, and she had made it her business to acquaint herself with the ways of the world.

"Employees need to earn a living," she pointed out. "Most employers know this, and they know that regardless of the treatment they receive, those in their employ will continue coming to work every day to feed their families."

Levi ran a finger down her cheek, the simple touch making heat snake through her veins. "You are surprisingly sympathetic to the plight of the classes beneath you, my lady."

"Do you think that because I'm the daughter of an earl I ought not to care about the world around me?" she asked with a wry smile of her own.

"To be candid, I don't know what I think about you any longer." He withdrew his touch and turned on his heel to pace.

"I daresay the feeling is mutual." Helen tried not to admire the sinewy grace of his body as he pivoted to face her, but she failed dismally.

Their gazes caught and held. "This home will be yours."

She stared at him, dumfounded by his abrupt pronouncement. "What do you mean it will be mine?"

"Precisely what I just said. I'll see that everything is properly drawn up so that you are the owner." He spoke in an impersonal tone, as though they were conducting business.

But they most certainly were not.

Her mouth went dry as myriad emotions flitted through her. She was equally aghast and excited at the implications. A large, fine home such as this one was what they so desperately needed, not only to help the women already crowded in Gussie's House of Rest but also to free others from London's wretched brothels. However, she had certainly not expected him to unceremoniously drop one into her lap as though it were of no greater import than a letter from her aunt in the Lake District.

"Mr. Storm, you cannot give me a home," she protested. Like spending time alone with him, it simply wasn't done. She was an unmarried lady. He was...well, she didn't precisely know what he was to her now. Her lover? Her friend? Neither? Both?

Everything, came the unwanted answer. He was everything to her.

"Of course I can." He frowned at her. "All it requires is some attention to legal formalities."

Was he being deliberately obtuse? She sighed, just as tempted to accept his offer as she was to refuse it and run out the door as fast as she could. They had entered dangerous territories. Her heart was more hopelessly entangled by the minute.

She closed the distance between them, crossing the freshly shined floors to him. "What I mean to say is that one cannot simply give property to an unmarried lady. It is not just unseemly, it implies a rather sordid understanding between the two of us."

"There is nothing sordid about either the gift of this home or what we've shared together." His countenance was composed as ever. "You are in need of additional lodgings to help the less fortunate creatures who have become your cause. I wish to help you, and as I cannot risk publishing your scandalous article, this seems the most expedient solution. That is all."

She touched his sleeve, not intending for the gesture to be as intimate as it suddenly felt. Helen snatched back her fingers before the heat of him scorched her and tempted her to do far more than stand too near to him. "Thank you for wanting to help. It is beyond kind."

"I'm not a kind man," he interrupted.

"You are," she insisted, undeterred, "despite your continued use of the word 'creatures' in reference to the ladies."

"I'm not sure the word 'ladies' is apt either."

It was her turn to frown. "Do be quiet. Must you forever interrupt me when I'm trying to speak?"

"I live to irritate you, my dear." He gave her a slow grin, and the force of it turned her insides molten. Ah, those dimples.

"Well you're quite adroit at it, that much I'll admit." She sighed, recalling the original subject of their conversation. The man had her forever at sixes and sevens. "But none of that is the point. Your offer is very generous and much appreciated. But I cannot receive property from you as it will seem as though I'm your mistress and the house my payment."

His gaze was hot upon her, and she flushed, horridly embarrassed to even utter such a thing to him. It brought far too many wicked images to her mind, images of what he'd done to her the night before. "But you are not my mistress. This is merely my gift to you."

It was surely the most extravagant gift that had ever been bestowed upon her. Helen knew that despite his words, there was more to his generosity than he implied. She imagined he could likely buy the entire neighborhood of homes and still have plenty of money to spare. In a financial sense, at least, the gift was a paltry one to a man of his great wealth.

But there was something deeply personal about such a gift that both warmed and disturbed her all at once. He was moved to help the women he had met today, but he had gone to the House of Rest because of her and stayed by her side there all morning when he need not have. He had yet to even go to his offices, which he had done each day prior with regimental precision.

"Give the home to Gussie if you must," she said. After all, Gussie was a married woman, and she already ran one such establishment. There would be nothing untoward in a transaction with Gussie.

He shook his head. "I want you to have it."

"Do you often gift houses to women?" she asked quietly.

"Only you, Lady Helen."

The words spoke volumes, said what neither of them could or should. Her heart seemed to beat faster than a hummingbird's wings. She stared at him as a truth as terrifying as it was unwanted crashed into her.

Sweet heavens, she was falling in love with Mr. Storm. She didn't know when or how it had begun, and she most assuredly had never intended to feel a tender emotion for any man. Especially not the man before her, tall and forbidding and arrogant and so handsome her heart ached just looking at him. He was a confusing man, at turns equally harsh and soft. He cared about the women whose lives she wanted to better. And unless she was mistaken, he cared about her as well.

"Mr. Storm," she began, forcing herself to speak lest she lose her wits and throw herself into his arms once more, "I thank you for the house, but you must see that I cannot accept it."

He slid an arm around her waist, bringing her solidly up against him. He caressed her cheek, his touch warm and reverent. She barely resisted turning and pressing a kiss to his palm.

"I grow weary of hearing you refer to me as Mr. Storm again," he said. "We are well beyond playing at being proper after last night. Call me Levi."

"Levi." She was trapped in his gaze, trapped by her realization and the sensation of his skin upon hers. "I won't accept the house." Her hands flitted to his chest, tantalized by the delicious masculine strength beneath his waistcoat and shirt.

"It's yours, sweetheart."

Helen knew she should not accept his offer of the house just as surely as she knew that Levi Storm was not a man who often revealed the warmth beneath his icy exterior. But he had given her glimpses, rare moments when his guard had lowered and he was open with her. It was those tender moments that wound through the briars and thickets guarding her heart, easily circumventing all obstacles.

The realization she had feelings for him terrified her. It made no sense. She was a confirmed spinster and he was wed to his businesses and his electricity. He had told her there would be no marriage, and she could not become his mistress for as many reasons as she could not publish her article. Scandal. Reputation. No, there was no future for them. They were altogether wrong for each other. And falling for him was altogether irrational and naïve. She had to stop these inconvenient emotions before they propelled her any further down the path leading to ruin.

"Why would you give me a house that you've clearly already gone to great expense to furnish and prepare for your employees?" she asked. "Why give it away to a woman you scarcely know for a cause you seem barely touched by?"

His fingers slid into her hair now, threatening to undo the pinning her lady's maid had done hours before. "The why doesn't matter. All that does matter is that this home as it stands would cost more than you could purchase by raising funds in a little-known newspaper for the next ten years. It will be yours, unencumbered, at no cost to you. Think of all the women you'll be able to help. If you must, consider it my formal apology for buying the *Beacon*."

He was right, of course, about all of it, drat him. Except for the first bit. The why really did matter, to her anyway. But perhaps harping upon the matter would reveal more to him than she preferred. She forced herself to think of what had become the most important part of her life over the last few years, her reform work. "You told me you would print my articles. Have you changed your mind?"

"I told you I would print reasonable articles, not articles with lurid details that would not only break the law but scandalize all of London and tarnish the good name of my business as well. You have my word that there will always be a place in my journal for any articles I can publish in good conscience."

Yes, she had known the facts she had written about had been too detailed, too shocking, too ugly and raw to be printed. She'd put pen to paper with more than just an inkling that he would never allow the piece to run. But perhaps she had in some sense accomplished what she'd set out to do after all, for now here she stood, in a house that was larger and finer than any she and Gussie could have imagined for their ladies, and it could be theirs. How could she be so selfish to shillyshally over accepting it? What was more important, her pride or her ability to give shelter to more women who so desperately needed it?

"Very well," she said at last. "If you see fit to give this house to our cause, I won't try to dissuade you any longer."

"Good." Some of her hairpins fell to the floor. Her serviceable updo became loose. His gaze strayed from her face to her hair, then to her mouth. "Finally sweet Lady Helen has agreed to see reason."

"I'm not sweet."

"Oh but you are. Every part of you is sweet." His tone was low and sensual, bringing an instant reminder of just where he had tasted her and how incredibly good it had felt.

A few long locks of hair fell onto her shoulder. Desire slowly spread through her. "You're ruining my coiffure."

"I'd say I'm sorry, but I only give apologies that are genuine," he said without a hint of contrition. "It's a damn sin to hide your beautiful hair away in a schoolmarm's bun."

Helen laughed as more pins fell to the floor. He was blunt and brash and thoroughly American, but she found his brutal honesty rather refreshing. When Levi wanted his thoughts known, there was no doubt about it. And she enjoyed the comfortable rapport that had settled between them. Being with him felt oddly familiar, as if they had known each other for ages rather than the admittedly scarce time since they'd first met. No other man had made her feel so at ease. Perhaps it was that so much time had passed since that painful day in the woods. Perhaps it was just something that was thoroughly, innately *him*.

Her laughter ceased as she saw the naked desire reflected in his gaze. How had she thought she could only share one night with him? The notion of never again lying with him, kissing him, touching him, and feeling him inside her was too much to bear. What had he said to her? Dear heavens, her emotions were in a muddle. Her brain an utter disaster. Her ability to resist him nonexistent.

"This is most certainly not a schoolmarm's bun," she protested softly.

The last of her pins dropped until all of her hair cascaded in long waves down her back and shoulders. "It's a moot point, sweetheart."

She ought to care about how much time she'd been gone, about the fact that his servants were aware of the time they'd been spending alone together, first in the carriage and now here. She certainly should worry about how she'd manage to sneak back into the Whitney household undetected with her hair and toilette tellingly disheveled. And she most definitely ought to worry that her heart, already thoroughly involved, would only become more attached to this dashing man than it already was.

But perhaps rational Helen had fallen asleep in the driver's seat of the runaway carriage that had suddenly become her life. "Levi," she forced herself to protest. "We cannot."

"There is cannot and there is ought not," he said lowly before lowering his lips to hers for a slow, delicious kiss at last. "We ought not, but we can. There is no one here but the two of us."

She twined her arms around his neck, her body giving her away. This heady desire would always spark between them. She knew it as instinctively as she knew there would be a tomorrow, and just as surely, she knew that she wanted him to be in it. Oh dear. Surely this was folly. Surely she should not act with such flagrant disregard for propriety. Last night had been a wild aberration from her uneventful life of Lady Helen the reformer. But to allow him to bed her again, and in the middle of the day...the part of her who had obeyed the rules all these years tried one more time. She was the daughter of an earl. She could bring great shame upon the sisters she loved by acting so recklessly.

"Bella will wonder where I've gone. Your servants are awaiting us outside."

"You've been with your paragon friend. She'll think nothing of it," he countered. "And I've already told you that my servants are loyal, generously compensated, and above all, silent when it matters most. But the choice is yours, as always. Tell me no, and we'll walk out to the carriage together right now."

She couldn't tell him no. Didn't want to.

And that was really the crux of the matter now, wasn't it? Lady Helen Harrington, spinster, who had watched her sisters fall in love with a jaundiced eye, who had been happy to exchange pleasantries with men and stay on the periphery, who had sworn to focus only on her reform work and her beloved sisters and their growing families—that selfsame Lady Helen Harrington was at the mercy of an American businessman who had tossed her over his shoulder the first time she'd met him. However, at the moment, she didn't really care. At the moment, she was Helen, and he was Levi, and she didn't give a fig for anything or anyone else.

So she rose to her tiptoes and did the only thing she could do in that moment. She kissed him with every bit of longing simmering within her.

"Yes?"

"Yes," she sighed. A hundred times yes. For him, it would always be yes. She could no more resist him than deny that she was a Harrington through and through.

Levi led Helen to the largest, nicest chamber in the house. He knew its location by heart, for he had overseen the renovation and furnishing of each of the eight properties he had purchased for employee housing. And it was because of his admittedly obsessive attention to every detail of his business that he had realized what he must do as he'd watched Helen move with such gentle care amongst the women at the House of Rest.

Some of them had been disturbingly young, and it had put him in mind of his childhood. Of his ma returning to their squalid rented room sporting a purple bruise and claiming she'd merely been clumsy. Of the girls he had seen, some nearly his own age, working alongside ma. Of the helplessness and hopelessness of it all. Today he had basked in the goodness, the pureness, and the beauty of Lady Helen, and he had known three things. He would give her this house. He would love her once more. And then he would let her go.

The first two were easy. The last would prove damn near impossible. He wanted her every way he could have her. He wanted to taste her and pleasure her and drive into her slowly on a thousand different days in a thousand different ways, and even that would never be enough. But he could not continue this madness, for she was not his. Nor was he hers.

Into the simple chamber, his hand in hers, his entire being on fire for her. All his life, he had forced himself to be as emotionless as a block of winter's ice. Ma had died when he was nine. He'd had nothing and no one, had begged and thieved to survive until he enlisted in the war a few years later with false papers. He'd been far too young. No one had noticed or cared, and he had grown up in gun smoke and carnage, in cannon fire and blood and death. He hadn't felt a goddamn thing in twenty years or more, and yet as he stood with her in the golden afternoon light, his heart thudded in his chest. He felt as though he were seeing a woman for the first time. Or maybe as though he were seeing the only woman he'd ever want.

Goddamn, but it scared him. Helen turned her face up to him, her blonde hair fallen in heavy ringlets over her shoulders, her creamy skin tinged with pink. She was shy, but she wanted him. The most angelic and loveliest woman he'd ever met, a blue-blooded daughter to a bona fide earl, wanted him, Levi Storm, son of a whore and whatever devil had paid to have her for the night.

Oh, she wasn't the first woman to have wanted him, not by a long stretch. But she was the first woman who wanted *him*, not the trappings of money and success. To the

VanHorns, he was only worthy for the wealth he'd built. Other women had wanted him for his money, for his fame, for the pleasure he could bring them. None had looked at him the way Lady Helen did now, as though…good Christ, as though he were someone worthy of her esteem, someone she cared about.

Hang it, if she kept on looking at him that way, he would take her right there on the floor like the base miscreant he truly was instead of wooing her as was his intention. So he cupped her face in his hands and took her mouth with his. She tasted of the sweetness of the tea she'd had before they left the House of Rest and something else that was indefinably her. She sighed and he pressed his advantage, his tongue sliding inside. Her hands fluttered to his shoulders, clutching at his jacket. He raised a handful of her fragrant hair and dragged his kisses to her ear, tasting her there, licking her lobe and the sensitive place behind it.

A low moan rose from her and he continued working this secret place with his tongue, reveling in her reaction. She was so responsive, his Helen. Made for pleasure. Made for him. If only he could have her forever. But that wasn't meant to be. All that could be for them was now, this stolen afternoon with no one the wiser. The Whitneys would think Helen at her reform work and him at his offices. His staff had been informed not to expect him. He breathed deeply of the sweet, seductive scent of her. Rose. Bergamot. Divine.

His mouth was on her neck now, feasting, licking, sucking. He should take care not to leave a mark, but his need for her was like a locomotive barreling through him and he couldn't control it.

"Helen," he said her name against her skin, a benediction. "Sweet Helen."

There were surely a hundred tiny buttons on her utilitarian gown, beginning at the hollow of her throat and ending at the nip of her waist. His fingers found the first button, the second, the third. He peeled away her layers.

"Please," she said softly.

He knew what she pleaded for. His own body thundered with the same need for completion. Had it been only last night that he had been inside her? It felt somehow a lifetime ago for the way it affected him. More buttons opened. He took care not to rip them away no matter how much he longed to. She could not return to the Whitney household with so much as a hair out of place. He would not bring shame upon her, not for the world.

Which made him feel the heavy weight of dread now mingling with desire. Wasn't he shaming her now, by keeping the truth from her? By taking what he wanted, what he needed, and leaving her behind? The devil inside him silenced his conscience for lust was a more powerful motivator than good had ever been straight from the days of Adam and Eve.

This was, after all, a mutual desire between them. They were equal partners. Her hands skimmed down his back to his buttocks and squeezed. He groaned, angling his rigid cock into her skirts, the only barrier keeping him from where he so desperately wanted to be. It was all the prodding he required to push past any lingering misgivings and go the rest of the way.

One more time, he told himself as they moved as one to remove each other's clothes, the trappings of their civility. Beneath the starch and stays, they were animals starving for the decadence of pleasure, the fulfillment of completion. He wanted her so badly that he would do anything to have her. Anything. To hell with honor. Most of the civilized world believed it impossible for a bastard to possess it anyway.

His jacket, waistcoat, and shirt fell to the floor. Her dress puddled around her on the carpet. He made short work of her petticoat, corset cover, drawers, and corset. Her chemise was nearly transparent. The lush peaks of her breasts were discernible, the hardened pebbles of her nipples poking the thin fabric. He took fistfuls of it and hauled it over her head until it too was gone and she stood before him gloriously naked but for stockings.

His breathing shallow, cock as hard as coal, he stood back to gaze upon her, committing each gorgeous curve to memory. She was tall though not nearly as tall as he, with long, tapered legs, full hips that led to a narrow waist and large, full breasts. More than a handful. With her hair trailing down her back and over her shoulders, she looked like Venus rising from the sea, only more breathtaking.

On a low, primitive growl, he caught her up in his arms and carried her to the bed. *Mine*, was all he could think. He deposited her with care and shucked the rest of his clothes before lowering himself onto her. Her skin was smooth and hot where they touched. He skimmed her calves with his palms, untied her stockings, and then traced higher, over her knees to her softly rounded hips.

"Open for me, sweetheart," he commanded. And she did without hesitation, her legs falling apart so that he could see the sweet pink center of her. If this was to be their last time, he couldn't deny either of them the pleasure of his tongue on her, inside her.

He lowered his head and licked. She cried out, fingers threading through his hair. He cupped her bottom and angled her to him, sucking on the tender little pearl there. He used his teeth and she jerked. Ah, that was what she liked. How she liked it. He wanted her to come undone for him, again and again. She was already incredibly slick. As he sucked, he sank a finger deep inside her tight sheath and she bucked against him.

This was what he wanted, her unravelling, losing all sense of inhibition, of time and place. He listened to her breathing, her cries, learning her. Just where to stroke with his tongue and his touch. She climaxed against him, her body shuddering with honeyed release, a soft rush of warm wetness on his fingers. He drew himself up and stared at her, her beautiful body flushed with pleasure, breasts full and high, head tilted back, lips open.

An odd sensation rushed through him. Something

unfamiliar. Heady as lust, potent as pleasure. But somehow foreign. *Mine*, he thought again as he drank in the sight of her, drank in the sight because it was the best goddamn thing he'd ever seen. How could he let her go after this? How could he ever let her go? He lowered his head like a supplicant and pressed reverent kisses to her mound, the jut of her hip bone, her belly's curve, her nipple. He could spend the rest of his life learning her, inside and out, and still not be satisfied.

He kissed his way back up to her waiting mouth and then there wasn't space in his mind left for any more thought. All he could do was act. He thrust inside her as slowly as he could, mindful that just the day before had been her first time. But the moment she hooked her legs around his hips and brought him deeper inside her wet heat, he was lost. He pumped into her, his lips never leaving hers, his fingers between their bodies stimulating the pearl he had so recently sucked. She came hard and fast, tightening on him with so much intensity that he lost control. Before he could withdraw, he exploded, spending himself deep inside her.

Damn it all, he thought as the world returned to him and he was once more aware of the light in the room, the sparse furnishings, the inferior quality of the bed linens. He had never spent himself inside a woman, not once. As a bastard, he took great care not to visit the same fate upon any innocent child. And yet he had done so with Helen twice. He rolled off her and lay on his side, disgusted with himself and yet also filled with a vast sense of...contentment. Yes, that was it. That was the strange sensation unfurling in his chest.

Helen smiled softly up at him and caressed his jaw. "Thank you, Levi. For everything."

He caught her hand and pressed a kiss to her fingers. He couldn't bring himself to respond past the twin knots of fear and self-loathing forming in his throat.

Helen must have fallen into a peaceful, sated doze, for she awoke with a start. Disoriented, she blinked and cast a glance about her unfamiliar surroundings. She was alone, she realized, in a rumpled bed. A bed that had been meant for Levi's employees. Oh dear heavens. She should be very ashamed of herself, she was sure, for what she had done. But as she lay there completely nude beneath nothing more than a sheet, her body humming with the aftereffects of the passion she was yet a novice to, she wasn't ashamed at all.

She felt, in a word, liberated. Yes, liberated. She felt free for the very first time in her life. There was no one to judge her, no one hovering over her shoulder to make certain that she observed all the proprieties and maintained her decorum. She had never, in thirty years of life, been beneath any roof other than that of family or family friend. She had never tasted independence. Had never owned anything of her own aside from the pin money her father bestowed upon her or the sometime payments she received from the *Beacon* for her articles, paltry funds she had instantly diverted to the cause. She had never even thought, having been born the daughter of an earl, that any other choices existed for her.

Now she wondered for the first time if there wasn't something more in store for her. Perhaps a little rebellion was in order. Lord knew her sisters had followed their hearts, and they had escaped relatively unscathed. Perhaps life wasn't meant to be lived the way she had lived it, watching everyone else pass her by. Had she been punishing herself without realizing it?

Being with Levi had made her aware of how she had allowed herself to be controlled by others for so many years. It had all begun with Wainross and Bingley that horrid day. Her brother had been disgusted to find his friend attempting to force relations upon her. But he had judged her, and in some small way, though she had not wanted it to, his judgment had affected her. She had felt shamed and less worthy. Even though she had known she hadn't done anything wrong, the scorn of her brother had made her feel as though she had. She'd lived her life in penance ever since.

Unnecessarily.

Making her own decisions, whether for good or ill, felt good. Felt right. Felt as if somehow, in some way, she was reclaiming the power and the decision that had been stolen from her.

The door to the chamber opened to reveal Levi, bearing a tray. He was so gorgeous her heart hurt just looking at him. She wondered, for a fraction of a moment, if it would be so very bad to live this way always? Then she dashed such horrid thoughts away. She would not become any man's kept woman. Not ever, regardless of the temptation he presented. It was only her own imperfect nature that made her entertain such an unworthy notion.

But she could still give him her body, partake in these wicked delights with him, until...until when? Until what? Until he grew bored of her and returned to America? Until she grew resentful of him and wanted more than he was willing to give?

She didn't wish to think about any of that now, for Levi was striding toward her bearing delicacies, and she was suddenly famished. He was properly buttoned up, looking every inch the gentleman. Only his hair was slightly mussed from her fingers having sifted through the glorious strands, the sole sign of their lovemaking.

He gave her a slow smile as he sat on the bed, the tray between them. "I thought you might be hungry."

Her stomach rumbled in a most undignified fashion just then. She pressed a hand to the bedclothes, flushing. "Perhaps some sustenance would be in order. Have you any idea of the time? It seems to me that it must be late and I do need to return to the Whitney residence before anyone grows suspicious about how long I've been gone."

Yes, for all that her body vibrated with pleasure and she lay abed entertaining fanciful notions about him, she was still Lady Helen, devoted spinster. She had sisters and parents and friends to answer for, people she loved who she dared not hurt. He had to return to America. His heart belonged to his business. This ill-fated idyll would necessarily come to an end.

"Half past four," he answered, sitting beside her on the bed, the tray of delicacies between them. Tiny sandwiches, tarts, and scones tempted her. Dear heavens, he even had lemonade, which would ever be one of her weaknesses. Everything looked delicious.

Half past four. They had time yet. She accepted a scone. "How did you get these?" It seemed an odd question to ask after all they had shared, but her heart and her mind were equally upended, and somehow focusing on the mundane seemed far easier than addressing anything else.

"I had my man get them." Levi frowned. "Do you not like them? I have it on good authority that the establishment selling them is one of the best here in London."

Helen took a bite. Heaven. It was fluffy and rich and everything a proper scone should be. "It is delicious. But your man, what must he think? Surely he cannot believe we are taking afternoon tea."

"He is paid handsomely not to think at all," Levi responded, his tone grim. "You needn't fear for your reputation. I will see to it that no one is the wiser. None of your fancy lords and ladies will ever know you've been sullied by the likes of me."

Was that what he thought of her? How could he, after their tender intimacies? She dropped the scone to the tray as though it were a hot coal. "You cannot sully the sullied," she said tartly.

He stroked her cheek then, his face unreadable. "You were never sullied, sweetheart. Never, do you understand?"

No, she hadn't been sullied by Wainross. But she had felt as though she had, had carried the weight and the guilt of it through her life for years. In that moment, bathed in sunshine and seated so near to Levi Storm, she felt completely free of her past. It hadn't brought her low, hadn't ruined her. It had shaped her, made her into herself. Imperfect and flawed, good and wicked, sister, daughter, lover, reformer. Stronger than she'd ever been.

"For so long I felt as if I had been," she said slowly, puzzling it out for him as much as for herself. "I thought I was to blame. I thought something must be wrong with me."

He bit out a curse. "Nothing is wrong with you, goddamn it. Nothing. You are pure and good and true." He caught her hand and raised it to his lips for a fervent kiss. "Give me his name. I'll hunt him down like the dog that he is."

"No." She didn't need a savior. She had been her own. "His name doesn't matter. *He* doesn't matter."

"Which is precisely why I'd like to gut him like a cod."

He was bloodthirsty, her brash American. She smiled. "No, thank you."

"Or beat him to death with a sack of his own shit."

His crudeness wrung a laugh from her. No one had ever dared to speak so openly in her presence, and she found his temerity equal parts refreshing and shocking. "Tempting offer sir, but no. I have a feeling that the procuring of the...material for the sack might prove troubling."

He shrugged. "It depends on who is doing the procuring. But have it your way for now."

He hadn't released her hand and his fingers tightened over hers. She didn't want him to let go. She'd never had a champion before, apart from her sisters. His concern touched her heart. He touched her heart, this strong, forbidding man who was not as hard and cold as he would have the world believe. He cared about what had happened to her, and he cared about what would happen to the ladies at the House of Rest.

"Stop looking at me that way," he broke into her thoughts. "Hang it, you're not wearing a stitch under there, and much as I would like to keep you here for the rest of this day and every day after, I can't."

No, he couldn't. And neither could she stay.

But it was only half past four, and they had time.

Chapter Ten

*J*UST AFTER DAWN, LEVI WAS BACK in his makeshift office at the *Beacon*. It was far smaller than the office that was still being stripped and repaired, but it suited him just fine nonetheless. He had always preferred, regardless of where in the world he happened to be, to rise before the sun and begin working in the peaceful solitude of the early morning before it sprung to life with his workers. He accomplished a great deal more when there was no one afoot to ask him questions. He disliked people requiring things of him, and it seemed they always did. Perhaps he was a solitary man, though he hadn't meant to be.

But this morning was different from most. This morning, he was poring over his business and engineering journals without even reading the words. This morning, there was an endless litany of questions raining down on him, and they all came from the same source.

His damned conscience.

What the hell was the matter with him? What the hell had he done?

He had bedded Lady Helen. Repeatedly. She was a virtuous lady, a guest beneath his friend's roof, and she could not have been further from the sort of woman one dallies with had she taken her vows and become a nun. He'd never intended for things to progress so far between them. The night of the ball had been madness. Yesterday had been... Christ, yesterday had been utter, selfish stupidity. And magnificent, but that was beside the point.

He'd begun the day intending to tell Helen about Miss VanHorn, knowing he needed to unburden himself to her. But his every good intention had been swept away when Helen stood in the sunlight and they were completely alone and he'd begun taking down her hair. From that moment on, he'd been lost. He was still lost this morning, trying to reconcile his actions with the man he'd believed himself to be. A man of reason, a man of honor. The last shred of decency he maintained had kept him from going to her chamber again last night. He had resisted, but only by dissecting two of Jesse's mantle clocks and then reassembling them.

There wasn't a doubt in his mind that he had to tell her the truth today. He'd hinted at his obligations to her, but somehow the word "betrothed" had never fallen from his lips. She deserved his honesty. He'd thought he could let her go, but after yesterday, he didn't know how. Didn't think it possible.

Damn it, he never should have touched Helen. Never should have read her article or accompanied her to the House of Rest or kept her hat that first day. He never should have slid inside her sweet body or seen her with her hair wild down her back or realized how kind and giving a heart she possessed.

But he had. And now, a decision loomed before him, vast and complex and with a complicated tangle of consequences. His impending marriage to Miss VanHorn was the equivalent of a pail of cold saltwater to the face. What once had seemed like an excellent idea, a facile way for him to cement his standing and enhance his business and wealth, now seemed as appealing as the open maw of a grave.

He didn't want to marry the girl, and yet her father was the largest investor in North Atlantic Electric. Breaking the engagement would undoubtedly deal a tremendous blow to his company. Perhaps even a death blow, unless he proved somehow able to free up enough of his own funds to pour into North Atlantic Electric's coffers.

And even if he should cry off, would Helen have him? She was far too good for him, that much was without question. It didn't matter where he went, how much money he earned, how many successes or accolades he achieved in business—he would always be Levi Storm, a man who didn't know his father, son of a whore. Even his surname was almost certainly not his, merely a whimsical notion that had taken his mother's fancy one day. Helen was a blue-blooded lady to her core.

But she was also compassionate, surprisingly so for a noblewoman of her station. Not only did she devote herself to the plight of London's denizens, but she also hadn't been shocked or repulsed by his revelation about his ma. Instead, she had been sweetly kind. Damn if it didn't make him want her all the more. There was the crux of the matter. He didn't just want Lady Helen in his bed. He respected her. Admired her mettle and her intelligence and her compassion even more than he appreciated her beauty. Lady Helen would be a fine wife, a woman he was more than proud to have by his side.

A knock sounded on his door then and he glanced up, half hoping and half expecting it to be her. "You may enter," he called, and was instantly disappointed when the portal opened to reveal not the object of his frustrated musings but his trusted man of business instead.

"Eddy," he greeted, and if he was less than cordial, it was owed to the tortured state of his mind more than to the appearance of the man himself. "Tell me, what brings you here at this time of the morning?"

It was a generally understood rule that no one, not even Eddy, not even the Lord himself, interrupted Levi before eight in the morning. He'd discovered long ago that the early morning quiet provided him the opportunity to puzzle out quandaries and solve problems without any outside interference, and when his businesses had grown large enough and his reputation important enough, he'd simply implemented the rule for all of his employees to observe. If they thought him eccentric or odd, he didn't give a damn. It kept him sane. Eddy's shamefaced expression said that he was well aware of the temerity of his early call.

"Please forgive me, sir." Eddy pushed his spectacles up the bridge of his nose, and Levi knew the visit was not a whim. Eddy typically never wore his optics in company unless his brain was too taxed to remind him of the necessity of removal. An odd compunction, Levi had always found it. What was the shame in something that aided a man to see, after all?

"You are, of course, already forgiven." He gestured for Eddy to sit. "Tell me, do I want to know what devil has brought you here for an interview at this ungodly hour, or do I want to remain blissfully ignorant until I've finished my first coffee of the day?"

Eddy winced, his expression akin to seasickness, as he folded his tall frame into the seat opposite Levi's desk. "You may want something stronger than coffee."

What was it with everyone wanting him to imbibe of late? He was beginning to think it a disturbing trend. "Coffee will suffice. Out with it, Eddy. I'm a man fully grown."

He prayed that no one had been harmed, none of his workers maimed or killed. It was a fear that weighed upon him. Electricity was a modern marvel capable of making everyone's lives infinitely better. But it could also, on rare occasion, pose a grave danger.

"The direct current generating station in Paris," Eddy

began.

"Damn it all to hell, Eddy," he interrupted. He didn't need to hear the rest of what Eddy had to say. His sinking heart already knew that it would be something he didn't want to hear.

"Yes, sir. I'm terribly sorry to report this, sir." Eddy swallowed, and for a brief moment Levi wondered just how bad it could possibly be for his man to be this shaken. "As you are undoubtedly aware, the grand ceremony was yesterday."

Of course he knew. His men had installed a system to operate electric lights at the *Gare de L'Est* in Paris, illuminating it in a way that had been previously impossible. Multiple test runs had proven that their equipment could run and power the hundreds of lights without fault. He had seen to it.

"What the hell happened at the grand ceremony?" Damn it, what did he have to do to get Eddy to tell him the awful truth? He felt as though he was dealing with a chicken who'd already had his head chopped off, its body spinning around in a dance, unaware it'd been dealt the death blow.

But that wasn't kind, neither to Eddy nor to chickens.

"You know that we tested. We tested many days without error or fault. It was fully operational, and everything should have progressed as perfectly as our trials." Eddy pulled his spectacles from his face and studiously wiped them with his handkerchief, looking down into his lap as he continued. "It would seem, however, that upon the ceremonial lighting yesterday, something occurred that unfortunately resulted in an explosion."

An explosion.

Hang it all.

First the lawsuit in America, and now this. When it rained, as a wiser man than he had once opined, it damn well poured.

"Damn it, Eddy, was anyone hurt?"

"That is the good news, if any, that is to be had from this

incident, sir. There were none injured. There was, however, a wall that I understand was blown out entirely."

"Jesus. A wall?" This was not good. Not good at all.

Eddy nodded. "A brick wall. Fortunately, the crowd that had gathered for the occasion stood on the opposite end of the station so that when the wall exploded, only small debris found its way to those in attendance. Half a brick, I'm given to understand, landed a mere foot from the President himself."

Of all the saints and by all that was holy.

If he'd thought he was having a hell of a day ten minutes before, he was most assuredly having the worst day of his life now. "You are telling me that the President of France nearly had his damned head taken off by half a brick during an explosion that was caused by our work and our design?"

Eddy was paler than a man who'd just witnessed his first hanging. "From the information I've been able to gather, the danger was averted thanks to the distance of the crowd from the explosion, as it were. A few inches would have been a different matter entirely."

"Good sweet God, man. This is an utter disaster. Why did you not make me aware of this sooner than this morning?"

And it was a disaster as surely as he possessed two hands and two feet. How the hell were they going to contend with the very stiff competition they faced when they were exploding brick walls near the goddamn President of the Republic of France? It would be a miracle if North Atlantic Electric wasn't somehow accused of treason. How would they convince a wary public that electricity was a safe and necessary technology when the very company providing it narrowly avoided assassinating a head of state?

"I'm sorry, sir. I should have informed you yesterday, but I only received word later in the evening and I hesitated to disturb you as you were…unavailable. Please know that I take responsibility for this failure." Eddy met his gaze stanchly. "I oversaw much of the field operations there myself. I read the test reports and I advised you to proceed. If anyone must be crucified for this, let it be me."

While he had been playing lovelorn suitor with Helen, all hell had broken loose. One day away from the office was all it had taken to threaten everything he'd been working so hard to build. He took a steadying sip of the strong coffee he drank each morning, brewed by his own hand without fail. "While I appreciate your noble offer, Eddy, no one will be nailing you to a cross today. I am at fault for this as much, if not more, than anyone else. Tell me, have we received any word from the French government?"

"They are refusing final payment of the system until it is safely running. I've received a telegram that is very succinct in its displeasure."

The French were not happy. This was to be expected. But North Atlantic Electric had already outlaid a tremendous amount of capital on the development and installation of the *Gare de l'Est* station with the expectation that they would be expediently repaid by the government of France.

Now, it seemed, that expectation was dashed to pieces the same way the damn brick wall had been. Here he sat, faced with the grim specter of failure. An explosion on their largest project couldn't have possibly happened at a worse time. If he wanted North Atlantic Electric to succeed, if Levi himself wanted to succeed at the levels he'd always dreamed he could, it was a grim possibility that he needed the support and influence of VanHorn. VanHorn just happened to be good friends with many well-placed men in the French government.

"Send my sincere apologies to Paris. Let them know that North Atlantic Electric is appalled by this situation and that we will do everything in our capability to set this matter to rights as quickly as possible." His mind spun with all that needed to be done and all that needed to be undone, both at home and abroad. "I need to go to Paris, Eddy, and investigate myself what went wrong. We will fix it, free of cost, no expense to be spared. We will not accept so much as a handshake from the French until the system we promised them is safe and fully operational. We must also rebuild the wall just as we must rebuild their trust in us. This matter is of the gravest import. I'll need you to run things here in my absence."

"Yes, sir." Eddy sprung to his feet, ever a man of action. "I will do my utmost, sir."

"I know," he said quietly. "Thank you."

Still looking shamefaced, Eddy beat a hasty retreat from his office.

"Jesus," Levi said again, staring unseeing at his cup of coffee, now beginning to cool. Hang it, how was he going to extricate himself from this awful, tangled mess? Was it even possible? He delighted in facts, in mechanics, in the way things worked, in trying to make them work *better*. He had been certain, so very certain, that he'd found the path he was meant to forge through life. He lived by certainties, damn it.

Suddenly, it seemed that he wasn't very certain of anything anymore, and that scared the hell out of him. He would go to Paris. First, however, he would see Helen one last time, tell her everything. He owed her that much. In fact, he owed her far, far more than he could ever begin to give her. But the truth would be a start.

Helen was still at the desk in her chamber, poring over letters from her sisters, when there was a scratch at the door. She paused in the act of reading a most amusing account of her younger sister Boadicea's adventures at finishing school and glanced to the door.

"Dear heart, it's Bella. May I come in?"

"Of course." Helen straightened her dressing gown as she rose from her seat.

Bella breezed in, resplendent in a green gown that set off

her raven hair and pale skin to perfection. Her face, however, was far from the cheerful perfection of her toilette. She carried a newspaper in her hands. "I hope you don't mind my intrusion. Were you at your correspondence then?"

"Yes." She waved a hand toward the stack of letters behind her. "It would seem that my darling sister Bo is getting on quite famously with one Miss Clara Whitney."

Her friend's smile didn't reach her eyes. "I'm so pleased if they are friends."

"You look positively bilious, Bella," Helen observed with a slowly blossoming sense of dread. "But of course you haven't come to me to discuss the contents of my epistles, however entertaining they may be."

Bella gripped the newspaper so tightly that it crumpled beneath the wrath of her fingers. She caught herself, glancing down to assess the damage and taking a noticeable breath before meeting Helen's gaze once more. "Very regretfully, there is something I must show you. Jesse has always had a habit of reading American papers, and I occasionally borrow them when he is finished with them. Today, I saw this. You must read it, Helen, though it pains me to show you."

She held out the newspaper as though it were as offensive as a pile of manure she'd been obliged to scoop up. The dread was like a rose inside her now, its tight bud opening to full bloom as she took the newspaper from Bella. Her eyes caught on an engraving of an undeniably attractive young lady. A Miss Constance VanHorn, to be precise. A wealthy heiress with a dowry of over fifteen million dollars, a waist of no greater than twenty inches, a *retroussé* nose, and hair like the finest sable.

And then, as if arriving to her from very, very far away, other words took command of her attention. Fiancée of Mr. Levi Storm. Their nuptials were to be the most anticipated wedding of New York City, just a few short months away now.

The *New York Times* fell from Helen's fingers, landing on the soft carpet with a whoosh of sound. She swallowed, clasped her hands at her waist, tried to calm her madly whirling thoughts. "Is this true, Bella?"

"I've asked Jesse, and he says it is so. Mr. Storm made no secret of it to him." Bella put a comforting arm around her shoulders. "I'm so very sorry, dearest friend. If I had known, I never would have encouraged you to set your cap for him."

Set her cap for him.

Dear God, if only that was all that she had done, this sudden revelation wouldn't be so horrible. So painful. So shocking. "He is going to wed this woman in a few months," she repeated dumbly, as though speaking the words aloud would render them any more comprehensible. "Yet he never breathed a word of it to me."

Bella's complexion went a shade paler than it naturally was. "Would he have had reason to tell you...or perhaps opportunity?"

Helen was dimly aware that her friend sought to assess just how badly the revelation of Levi's betrothed had hurt her. She could almost read Bella's tortured thoughts as she wondered if there had been some lapse on her part as hostess, if she'd been remiss in observing the proprieties. No, she had not. Helen's actions had been entirely her own. Her own mind, her own fault. Her own foolishness. How had he never told her that he planned to wed another woman? How had he kissed her, held her in his arms, taken her to bed?

He had lied to her, again and again. Perhaps not precisely with his words but with his actions. And she, good sweet Lord...she had fallen into his hands, headlong into ruin.

"Helen, darling," Bella's voice cut through the haze of confusion and betrayal fogging her mind. "If something untoward occurred between you and Mr. Storm, you need only tell me."

Something untoward. Such a tidy, passionless phrase to

describe all that had passed between them. "He has given me a house," she said, as though it made any sense at all in the context of their conversation. But to her overwrought brain it did, for she realized at last why he had been so generous. Surely the act had been an effort to assuage his guilty conscience rather than a gesture borne of true kindness and caring. After all, hadn't he proven himself to be a man who made decisions based on how they would benefit him? It would seem her lovelorn assessment of him had been far too generous. He didn't care. Not a bit.

Her friend blinked. "He's given you a house?"

"Yes." Helen smiled grimly. "A large one, already furnished. I was there, you see, with him. It will help to alleviate the crowding at Gussie's."

"Angels in heaven, Helen, you must tell me everything."

"Do you know where Mr. Storm can be found this morning?" she asked instead of answering Bella's demand. She felt oddly detached from everything now, almost as if she were another person entirely. Perhaps she would have to become one again. Lord knew she had in the past, reinventing herself to survive the pain. Helen the spinster reformer had risen from the ashes.

"I believe him to be at his office, but you cannot go there, Helen. Not alone and not in this state." Bella clutched at her arms as though she were a mad woman who had escaped from the asylum and needed convincing that returning would be in her best interest.

"I can, and I most assuredly will." Of this, Helen was quite adamant. Once, she had simply walked away and licked her wounds. But the woman she had become refused to wallow in silence.

"I won't allow it." Bella was equally adamant. "I insist that you tell me if Mr. Storm has paid you insult in any way. Jesse will make him answer for it. I'll make certain of it."

An odd calm overcame Helen then. She gently extricated herself from her friend's grasp. "Thank you, dearest Bella, but I don't need someone else to be my champion. *I* will make him answer for it."

She sank down to retrieve the fallen newspaper. Miss VanHorn's engraving taunted her. Oh yes, she would make him answer for it. And she was keeping the damned house too.

Helen stared down the fellow who was intent on keeping her from what she needed to do and the man she needed to see. She recognized him from the day she'd ventured into the offices of the *Beacon* and unwittingly into enemy territory. He was Levi's man of business.

"I'm sorry, my lady, but I cannot allow you to disturb Mr. Storm." He pushed his spectacles up the bridge of his nose. Fair-haired and slight of build, he was younger than she, unless she missed her guess. His accent gave him away as American as well.

"It is imperative that I see him at once," she hissed, giving the man the haughtiest façade she could manage given the turmoil rolling through her. The carriage ride to the offices had not done a whit to tone down her anger or her dread. She didn't want to believe that Levi could keep something as significant as a betrothed from her, but the facts were clamped firmly in her hand. She'd carried the paper with her the entire ride, alternating between torturing herself by re-reading the simpering article and fighting incredulous tears.

"Madam, he has given express orders not to be interrupted."

"Sir, I don't give a fig about his orders. Now, you can take me to his office, or I can simply go about looking for him." She intentionally knocked a sheaf of papers from a nearby desk, sending them flurrying to the floor. "But I warn you, I can be quite messy when I'm in high dudgeon."

The man pushed his spectacles again, looking rather as bilious as Bella had. She swung her reticule wide and knocked a stack of journals to the floor. He threw up his hands. "Very well, I'll take you to him. His office is not yet restored. It's this way, if you can only refrain from strewing about any more of our research."

Finally. She followed in the man's wake, dodging the same bustling hive of activity she recalled from her previous visit. The dynamo hummed loudly, and the place blazed with electric lights. She would have been impressed if she wasn't so distressed. Dear heavens, she had told herself that she had been allowing herself to enjoy the passion she'd long denied herself. But in truth, what she had come to feel for Levi was far stronger than she'd cared to admit. The haste with which it had occurred didn't render it any less valid. Or any less painful.

They stopped before a closed door and Levi's man of business knocked twice before announcing himself. "I'm sorry, sir. You have a guest."

The door swung open, and there he stood, as magnificent and handsome as ever. Their gazes clashed. Her heart was sick. The mere sight of him affected her, giving her a physical jolt. Electricity. How ironic. How pathetic.

"Lady Helen," he said softly before nodding to his man of business. "Thank you, Eddy, I will speak to my guest in private."

Eddy gestured for Helen to enter and disappeared without another word. She crossed the threshold with grim trepidation, prepared for a battle. How dare he play her for a fool? How *dare* he? The door closed at her back.

"You look troubled, Helen. What is it?" he asked, blunt as ever. No simile this time. Just an observation and a question.

"Mrs. Whitney shared a most interesting piece of reading with me this morning," she said, impressed by how calm she sounded. "American newspapers are so very quaint. Would you care to read it too, Mr. Storm?"

He glanced at the paper she held clutched tightly in her fist. "I reckon that I ought to read it, Lady Helen, if it has given you such grief."

Grief. Perhaps it was an apt word.

"Here you are." She held it out for him, keeping a safe distance between them as he took it. "I think you may be interested to hear of your impending nuptials, Mr. Storm, as surely they must be a surprise to you since you neglected to mention them to me during the course of any of our...conversations."

He didn't even look at the *Times*, merely kept his gaze trained to her face. "Helen."

"Who is Miss VanHorn?" she asked him, needing to hear him admit the truth aloud. Though her voice was quiet, it held an edge of steel.

He stiffened, his expression hardening, his sensual mouth tensing. His reaction told her all she needed to know. "She is the daughter to Elias VanHorn, one of the wealthiest men in America and the largest investor in my electric company."

Of course. Her father was an investor in his company. It all began to make perfect, heart-rending sense. He hadn't acknowledged that she was his betrothed, but he didn't need to. He had kept it from her. All the times they had been together, and he'd said not a word. Not in private. Certainly not in public. He had kissed her and loved every inch of her body, and yet he had never told her—had not so much as hinted—that he had another woman in New York City waiting for him. Had he touched his betrothed the way he'd touched Helen? Kissed and caressed and brought her passion the likes of which she'd never known? Helen refused to think of that now, for the thought made her ill. She had been foolish and reckless with him. Now she would pay the price.

The smile she gave him was equal parts bitter and wry. "I daresay you left out a rather important part of Miss VanHorn's story."

Levi crossed the office in two strides, a tall and imposing presence towering over her. He looked as grim as she felt.

"I am to marry her in the summer."

Despite the fact that she'd already known, his stark admission still cut her every bit as painfully and easily as if it had been the blade of a knife scoring her flesh. Or plunging deep into her heart. She met his gaze, unflinching, daring him to be the first to look away. "Did you plan to tell me that you had a betrothed, or were you simply going to disappear one day and sail back to America?"

"Helen, it's far more complicated than you realize." He tried to touch her and she shrugged him away.

Complicated. Surely there was nothing at all complicated about the matter of his having a beautiful heiress in America that he planned to wed. A woman he had never mentioned in all the days they had spent together, not when he'd kissed her, held her, made love to her. Not ever.

She didn't know whether to rail at him, strike him, or walk away. Perhaps she ought to do all three in that particular order. She was angry, hurt, and yet somehow oddly numb too. "It all seems rather straightforward to me."

"It is anything but straightforward, damn it." He touched her waist but she slipped from his grasp once more.

She would not make herself an easy target any longer by allowing her body's response to him to cloud her judgment. Rational Helen held the reins quite firmly. "Do keep your hands to yourself, Mr. Storm. I find the mere thought of you repulsive."

Of course it wasn't true. If only it were. Then this would be easier. Then she wouldn't have cared. If only she were the sort of woman who flirted and had affairs and never lost her heart. If only she'd spent the last decade of her life kissing and bedding whomever she'd liked. But she was not, and she had not, and she didn't want to bear the pain of it all. The abject humiliation of realizing that while he had come to mean so much to her, she had never meant anything at all to him. Not even enough to merit his honesty.

He stalked to his desk then and picked up a sheaf of

papers, thrusting them at her. "You needn't suffer my touch again, but at least take these documents I had drawn up for you. The house will officially be yours, whether I repulse you or not."

She clutched the documents to her bosom as though they were a shield. "I accept the house as payment for my services."

He caught her elbow and dragged her against him, his entire body radiating with raw anger. "Jesus, Helen. I'm not giving you the house because I fucked you."

The words were harsh, ugly. She flinched. "Please unhand me."

He released her. "You can be as angry with me as you please, but I won't let you diminish what is between us."

She scoffed. "Lies are between us. That is all now."

"I never lied to you. I told you I could not offer you marriage."

That much was true. He hadn't professed to love her. He hadn't proposed marriage. He hadn't made a single promise. But his omission had been a lie of its own, of dreadful and all-consuming proportions. What had his intentions been? Had he thought to make her his mistress? Had he believed she would follow at his heels like a puppy and travel across an ocean to happily watch him marry another woman?

"Do you love her?" she demanded, unable to keep herself from asking the question.

"Helen, I had every intention of explaining all to you this evening." He was solemn. "I agreed to the match back when her father invested a large sum of money in my company and proposed the idea. I was unencumbered at the time, and it seemed a wise decision given her family's wealth and influence. I've only met her twice, and I'll be damned if I can even remember what we said to each other. I'm given to understand there was some sort of scandal that made her father anxious to see her settled. The answer to your question is no, sweetheart. I do not love Miss VanHorn."

"Do not refer to me as your sweetheart. I'm Lady Helen to you now." The tremor in her voice betrayed her and irritated her at the same time. Oh how she didn't want to appear weak before him. She didn't want him to know just how much he had hurt her. If only she'd been as worldly as a woman of her years should have been. Thirty years old and she hadn't learned a blessed thing about men in all that time. Even now, he weakened her resolve.

Objectively, she could understand why he had agreed to the match. Subjectively, she could not comprehend why he would keep the knowledge from her. She supposed she should take comfort knowing he didn't love Miss VanHorn, but she found precious little solace in his admission. He quite obviously didn't love Helen either. She wasn't sure that he could love anyone more than he loved his business. Perhaps he was incapable of emotion. How could he have made love to her as he had, wooed her and won her, all while keeping the fact that he was going to marry another woman from her?

If only she had not fallen hopelessly, helplessly in love with him.

The thought, as unwelcome as it was startling, couldn't have hit her at a more vulnerable moment. Dear God, she feared that she did love him. Realization crashed down on her now as she stood staring at him, a complete stranger to her, this man who had made her body feel as though it was made for his. This man who had given her pleasure and stolen kisses and moments of the most intense bliss she'd ever known.

None of it mattered anyway, for it was too late, far too late, for love.

His jaw clenched and he caught her about the waist, hauling her back into his chest. "Damn it, Helen, listen to me. I'm leaving tomorrow for Paris. I haven't a choice—I must go. But let me explain. Please."

"No." She shook her head, forcing away the tears stinging her eyes. "Go to Paris then. Go back to New York

City and your life there. Go anywhere you please so long as it's away from me. I don't need or want any more explanation."

"Helen."

She pushed away from him, even as a traitorous part of her still longed to be in his arms. "I am deadly serious, Levi. I don't care. I don't give a damn about your betrothed or your electricity or your business. And I most certainly don't care about you. You never belonged here and you never will. I should not have lowered myself by being with you. Now I am well and truly ruined."

"I never lied to you, Helen," he said again, as if the distinction was somehow important to him. As if it would make a modicum of difference to her.

Whether he had lied or omitted the awful fact, he had broken her heart and she could not forgive him for that. Nor could she forgive herself for her naïveté. "No I suppose you didn't, did you? How gentlemanly of you. Thank you, Mr. Storm, for your kindness in only misleading me rather than lying to me, which I suppose is all one could expect from the bastard son of a New York City doxy."

He was as forbidding and cold as he'd ever been. "That is enough, madam."

Her words were intended to wound. Though it may be childish of her, she wanted to hurt him as he had hurt her. To make him feel the same bitter pain. "You warned me that I was too good for the likes of you, and you were right. You are nothing but a vile opportunist who cares only about your businesses and your money and your pleasure. You disgust me."

"You've gone too far, Helen," he warned, taking her arm in a punishing grip.

Good, she had angered him. "What do you intend to do, Mr. Storm? Punish me? Use me the way men used your own mother? You already have."

"Goddamn it, enough," he roared, releasing her as if she were a poisonous snake. "Enough, Helen."

"If hearing what you've done makes you angry, you need only look one place to lay the blame. The mirror." She shook like a tree in a violent winter wind, so furious was the torrent of emotion coursing through her. "Goodbye, Levi. I never want to see you again."

With tears blurring her vision, she turned and practically fled out the door. He didn't follow, nor did he call after her. It was all done now, and Helen had never felt more hollow or more alone.

Part Two

Chapter Eleven

London, One Year Later

$\mathcal{I}$T HAD BEEN A HELL OF A LONG TIME, but Levi had finally made his return to England. As he cooled his heels in Jesse's stately townhome and waited for the butler to come back, he reached inside his waistcoat pocket for the folded sheet of paper holding his reason for leaving New York City. There it was, right next to his watch, the same place it had been ever since he'd received it though he had extracted it at least a hundred-odd times to read its contents again, always first in disbelief. Then in sheer, unadulterated anger.

Yes, the disbelief had come as his eyes had caught upon one word. *Son.*

Not far behind in its wake had been anger, a deep, scoring blade of righteous rage. *Son.* He could still recall the precise moment he'd read the sentence that had changed his life forever. He'd been at the desk in his study on Fifth Avenue, the bustle and noise of the city he loved humming outside, a cup of coffee steaming at his right hand, a Waterman pen half deconstructed to his left alongside a

171

stack of engineering journals awaiting his keen eye.

And there it had been, the letter from London. The cup of coffee, the pen, and the journals would never be the same. Nor would he.

The dour-faced butler reappeared. "Mr. Whitney will see you now."

Levi hadn't forgotten the man from his time spent as a guest here, but apparently *he* had been forgotten. No matter. He would reacquaint himself with everyone soon. And with one woman in particular, the very woman who, at their last meeting, had sworn she never wanted to lay eyes on him again. She was about to be vastly disappointed.

He followed the butler to Jesse's study and crossed the threshold, his memories inevitably stirred by the familiar chamber. Jesse stood upon his entrance, but there was no warm smile. No friendly handshake. The discreet butler closed the door at Levi's back. He tucked the letter into his pocket once more, realizing he'd been carrying it still, his thumb worrying the fraying fold.

"Damn it, Levi, I'm not sure if I should shake your hand or give you a sound beating," his friend said, his Virginia drawl all the more pronounced in his ire.

Levi inclined his head in acknowledgment. "I wouldn't recommend a beating, however well-deserved. Don't forget what happens when Johnny Rebs tangle with Yanks."

Jesse's grim expression cracked for an instant, and he grinned. "I'm not likely to forget, sir. Though we did hand you a crushing defeat at Manassas upon two separate occasions."

Levi clasped his hands behind his back. "Need I remind you of Richmond?"

"Hell." Jesse skirted his desk and clapped him on the back, perhaps against his best intentions. "It's good to see you again, old friend, in spite of the bind you've put me in."

They shook hands, and for a moment, Levi could almost forget the seriousness of his visit. Almost. "It's damn good to see you as well, Jesse." Since his abrupt departure for

Paris last year, he'd had little time for anything other than business. He'd thrown himself headlong into his work, in rebuilding North Atlantic Electric's reputation, fighting Edison's patent-infringement lawsuit, gaining his freedom. "Thank you for writing me."

"No need for gratitude. Your making things right will be my ultimate thanks," Jesse said pointedly.

Ah, there was the censure he'd been expecting. "Damn it, if I'd had even the slightest inkling, I wouldn't have left. She was very angry with me after she found out about Miss VanHorn, and there'd been the explosion in France that I had to answer for. I did and said things I regret, Jesse, but I sure as hell never would have left her behind knowing she carried my child."

Inevitably, his mind traveled to her. Lady Helen. Beautiful, sweet, good Lady Helen. Perhaps not so good nor so sweet after all, even if she continued to pen her fiery reform articles and he'd been fool enough to seek them out and read them all, just for the reminder it gave him of the sound of her voice, the passion of her convictions. She had refused to see him before he'd gone to Paris or to answer his letters later, and he didn't entirely blame her for that. He should have been open with her about his engagement from the start, but things between them had progressed so rapidly and unexpectedly. He'd been selfish and careless.

He did, however, blame her for not telling him about their son, goddamn it. An entire year had passed, and she'd made no effort to contact him. Hell yes, he blamed her for that crippling omission.

He had tried, over the last year, to tell himself that their end would have been inexorable anyhow. And that their two worlds, while they had overlapped for a charmed sliver of time, could never coexist for a lifetime. But a day had not gone by, in all the days since she'd stormed out of his office, when he hadn't thought of her. When he hadn't read her words from another continent and wondered at what might have been, and that was the bitter truth of it.

"I know you're a fine man, and I'm inclined to believe you," Jesse said then. "But Lady Helen is as dear as a sister to me, and she deserves to be treated with utmost care."

Levi didn't know about the utmost care bit of his friend's statement. He hadn't ever been as enraged as he was when he'd discovered that she had kept their child from him. He wasn't sure that he could handle her civilly, but he also wasn't about to waste any more time without seeing his son. "She kept my son a secret from me, and she'll have to pay the price for that. All I need is for you to tell me where to find her, and the rest is not your concern."

Jesse's countenance grew grim. "It became my concern when you got an innocent woman with child beneath my goddamn roof. My wife is already angry enough with me for interfering in her friend's personal matters and informing you of the babe. If you do anything to upset Lady Helen in any way, there will be hell to pay, as much as from Mrs. Whitney as from myself."

Anything to upset Lady Helen. The rage inside him continued to fester. She damn well could have answered his letters. She could have written him, sent him a telegram, anything for Christ's sake, and he would have come running to her. It would have been so very easy for her to find him. Instead, she hadn't done a thing. She'd had his son. And she had said nothing.

"Tell me where she is, Jesse."

Jesse gritted his teeth. "I don't like this, Levi. Not one damn bit."

"Nor do I. But I've come an awful long way from New York City, and I'll be damned if I have to go one more hour without seeing my son."

His friend sighed. "My wife will box my ears for this, but very well. Lady Helen can be found at the House of Rest, the one she and Mrs. Bennington opened not long after you left for Paris. Lady Helen runs the place now. She's living quite a different life these days."

The House of Rest. Of course. He should've known. If

she'd been trying to hide from him, she hadn't made it very difficult to find her. He knew the way by heart. "Thank you, old friend."

And without another word, he turned on his heel and stalked out the door.

"B-o-y," sounded out one of Helen's latest protégés at the House of Rest, slowly and painstakingly. "Boy."

"Excellent progress, Ruby," Helen encouraged, a warm surge of pride welling up within her. "Now try this one." She pointed to the next word in the primer. Teaching the ladies was one of her greatest enjoyments. Although education was compulsory until age ten, many of the women and girls they aided had scarcely attended schools at all, caught up as they'd become in the underworld of London's vices. Between running the house and spending time with her sweet little Theo, her days were full and long, arduous but also satisfying.

"G-i-r-l," Ruby said slowly. "Girl."

"Wonderful." She and Gussie made every effort to help the women build a foundation from which they could eventually flourish on their own. Many of the ladies had few hopes of bettering themselves without assistance. At the Houses of Rest she and Gussie operated, women could learn to read and write and train for positions at shops and in service. They could learn history, arithmetic, and science.

Ruby gave her a gamine grin. She was younger than Helen, and far too young to have endured what she'd gone through at her tender age. "I reckon I'm getting quite good at this, my lady. What d'you think?" Her accent gave her away for the East End girl that she was.

Helen smiled. "Yes you are, my dear. Before you know it, you'll be borrowing all my books."

"You'd loan me your books, my lady?" Ruby appeared suitably impressed by the prospect.

"Of course I would, dear." Her books were one of the few material possessions she had held on to.

Her new life was much less fussy. She'd rather grown to relish it. She was infinitely grateful to Gussie for not shunning her following the revelation that she was with child without the benefit of marriage and without prospect or desire to acquire a husband. Gussie had proven a true friend, taking all in stride.

Now, Helen had her routine, each day a rhythm of teaching, tending, watching. Yes, she was happy here. Happy with her life. Happy with her son. Theo gave her the greatest sense of accomplishment she'd ever known, greater even than the reward of helping women like Ruby. The love a mother had for her child was different than the love she could experience for any other.

She supposed she could thank Levi for that much, for giving her the wonderful gift of her son. As determined as she'd been to remain a lifelong spinster, she never would have known the joys of motherhood without him. Oh, it wasn't all rosebuds and rainbows, to be sure, especially since she was without the trappings of the fine life she'd been accustomed to. When she had initially realized she was with child, she had been devastated. She'd gone to her sister Tia in tears, not knowing what to do next.

But she was a Harrington woman, and Harringtons always found their feet when it was time to land. The tears had dried, and she'd realized what she must do. She moved everything she could call her own into the House of Rest, which was sadly little for a woman of her years. She'd sold off gowns and jewels, cut ties with her old life. No more balls. No more Lady Helen. She'd reinvented herself, and she rather found that, free of all societal encumbrances, she could embrace life in its rawest and realest sense. She worked for her dinner. She relied upon herself now. It had made her stronger, even if she'd never particularly considered herself weak. Perhaps she had Levi Storm to thank for that too, for learning that there was no shame in working and providing for one's self.

As for the heartache he'd left her with, she could not thank him for that. She did her best to keep him from her mind, but she could see so much of him in sweet Theo's tiny face that it was impossible to force him from her thoughts altogether. Not a day passed that she didn't think of him, wonder at what might have been.

"Lady Helen?" Maeve's voice pierced Helen's musings then, sounding unusually troubled.

Helen glanced up from Ruby's laborious studies to find Maeve in the doorway. Small and spritely with her halo of golden ringlets, Maeve was as darling on the inside as she looked on the outside. She had come a long way since that awful day Helen had first come upon her at Madame Violette's. "Whatever can be the matter, Maeve?"

"There's a man here to see you, my lady. A tall gent, handsome and well-dressed. Says he won't leave till he sees you." Maeve worried the skirt of her plain gray dress as she spoke. In general, unexpected male visitors made all the residents uneasy.

But Maeve's description of this particular visitor made Helen uneasy. He had asked for her specifically. Tall, handsome, well-dressed. But, no. Surely it couldn't be Levi. Surely he had long forgotten all about her. A year had passed, after all, and for Helen, so much had come to pass in that year that it may well have been a lifetime instead.

Helen stood, pasting a reassuring smile on her lips that she didn't feel. "Don't fret, Maeve. I'll see what the gentleman wants."

Maeve frowned. "Are you sure, my lady?"

"Of course," she said mildly, crossing the room to give Maeve a comforting pat on the arm. "Would you go see to Theo for me, please? I'm sure he must nearly be done with his nap."

"Yes, ma'am." Maeve dipped into a curtsy and hurried away.

"Carry on with your reading, Ruby," she called over her

shoulder. "I shall be back in a trice."

Of course it wasn't Levi, Helen reassured herself again as she hastened to the front room where visitors were received. She was simply allowing her wayward thoughts to get the best of her. No indeed, Levi Storm was an ocean away, married to the ethereal heiress whose engraving she'd never forget. Miss VanHorn. She'd be Mrs. Storm now, likely heavy with child herself.

The notion shouldn't make her queasy with jealousy, but somehow it nevertheless did. Helen stepped over the threshold, disgusted with herself, and then froze.

He stood at the large windows overlooking the street, his back to her. The man had dark hair, broad shoulders, long legs. Everything about the cut of his clothing spoke of wealth. The air around her seemed to hum with awareness. His hands were clasped behind his back. She'd recognize those long, capable fingers anywhere. Those hands, that sinewy form. Impossible to forget. Even more impossible still that he stood before her, conjured like a wraith.

Impossible, yes, but dear God, it was him.

Levi.

She didn't know if she gasped or if he had simply heard her footfalls. But either way, he spun about, his gaze snapping into hers. He was every bit as fine-looking as she had recalled, though he appeared leaner and a thicker beard shadowed his strong jaw line. Every bit as forbidding too. Her traitorous heart gave a pang at the sight of him.

She hadn't expected to ever see him again. After he'd left for France, he had sent her letters. Half a dozen or so. She'd read each one against her better judgment, but she'd never allowed herself to send a reply. Right about the time she'd discovered she was with child, the letters stopped.

"Mr. Storm," she said, forcing herself to be polite. To appear unaffected. "What brings you to London?"

He smiled, but it was not a pleasant one. The first words to emerge from his beautiful mouth, the same mouth that had once kissed her so tenderly, were clipped and cold, hard as the frigid ground in winter. "Where is my son?"

He knew.

Her mind grappled, struggling to comprehend how it was that he stood before her, issuing a demand to see their son. He had returned to his life in America. A year had passed. She had purposefully withdrawn from public life, both to protect her family from scandal and to keep Theo her precious secret. She had been so careful.

Yet, here he was before her, as though resurrected from the memories that were never far from her thoughts. And his hard expression, his distant tone, his stiff bearing, all told her the same story. He was angry. He knew about Theo, and he was very, very angry.

Helen felt as if the breath had been robbed from her lungs. Icy dread spread through her but just as quickly, her instincts prodded her into action. It wouldn't do to allow him to scare her into wavering. "I know not what you speak of, Mr. Storm," she told him in a tone that was surprisingly unruffled.

He closed the distance between them in three irate strides, not stopping until he was so near she could see the rigid set of his jaw and the dark, furious blue of his eyes. "Do you truly think now is the time to prevaricate, madam?"

She was briefly taken back to the day they'd first met, when she'd stepped over the threshold of the *Beacon* offices and into his world. He had won that day. He would not win this time. "I'm not prevaricating, sir. If you have a son, he must be with his mother, your wife."

It pained her to say the word *wife*, to think again of the girl he'd married. The young, lovely heiress who would have helped him to broaden his empire in ways she, the spinster daughter of an earl, could not.

He gripped her arms and pulled her body flush to his. The rage emanating from him was potent, almost tangible. "I'm speaking of the son you bore. My son. Take me to him. Now."

Fear crept into her heart then, for she knew him well enough to know that there would be no dissuading him. Her dissembling was a means to an end, and he already knew he was right about the precious babe napping upstairs. She could read it quite plainly in his immovable expression.

"No," she denied just the same, her voice almost foreign to her own ears, as tinged as it was by trepidation.

How could he know? It hardly made sense. She had not imagined this day would ever come. She had not envisioned that he would hunt her down and invade the sanctuary she'd created for herself on a drizzling morning, demanding to see his son. She felt unutterably helpless in that moment.

"Why have you come here?" she asked him instead of heeding his command. "What purpose does this visit serve?"

"Come now, Helen. You're no fool. I've come for him."

He wanted to take her son from her. Of all the thoughts that had been galloping about in her mind, she'd never once considered he would try to take Theo. He had obligations in New York City, a wife. Certainly he had his businesses. What need did he have of her sweet boy?

Her response was instantaneous and vehement. "No."

"What you want is immaterial." He was unyielding as ever. "He belongs with me, in my household, not here in London, living as though he has no father."

"He's not yours," she denied, even though she knew the attempt at further subterfuge was futile.

"Indeed?" Another tight smile molded his lips, and she didn't mistake it for kindness or amusement for one instant. "Tell me whose bed you shared other than mine."

She said the first name that came to her mind. "The Earl of Denbigh."

Her quick response gave him pause. But he hadn't amassed his fortune without being shrewd. His eyes narrowed, his gaze probing in that unrelenting way only he possessed. "You're lying."

"I'm not." Perhaps it was an ill-advised strategy to

attempt to make him believe Theo was not his, but at the moment it seemed the only tactic left to her. "If you wish to claim another man's bastard as your own, you may gladly have my son," she lied, though it hurt her heart to do so.

"Look me in the eye and tell me that he isn't mine," he demanded, his tone low and tinged with rage. "Tell me you welcomed Denbigh into your bed. Tell me that he fucked you. Go on, my lady. Do it."

His coarse, ugly words and visceral response shocked her. Her lips were numb, her body trembling. She stared at him, her mouth going dry. She had always known he was no gentleman. Never had that been more apparent than now.

"Say the words, Lady Helen." He spoke her name and title as thought it were an epithet, his countenance deadly grim. "Tell me."

She was weak, and she couldn't bear to lie to him. It was too much. "You cannot have my son," she said instead, half denial, half plea.

"He's mine. My blood, my heir. You know as well as I that you never warmed Denbigh's bed."

"Who told you?" She had to know. There was no way he could have suspected unless someone within her circle had informed him. She had taken every precaution to disappear from society before there was even a hint of scandal swirling about her.

"Jesse."

Damn Jesse Whitney for his interference. She supposed she shouldn't be surprised at the revelation. He and Levi were old friends, after all. Still, she hadn't expected anyone she'd trusted to betray her. And betray her he had, for now all her chickens had come home to roost in the form of one very angry and very imposing man. A man who was threatening to take her son away and leave her with nothing.

She nearly wilted as her Herculean efforts came crumbling down around her and the ugly realities of her situation hit her all at once. "He had no right. How dare he?"

"How dare he inform me of the fact that I have a child? He had every right. *I* had every right to know, damn you." His grip on her grew almost punishing. "What the hell was going through that misguided head of yours? Did you think you could just bear my son without me knowing? Did you truly believe I'd never find out?"

"What does it matter now?" She couldn't contain the edge of bitterness lacing her voice. "Nothing here is your concern any longer. Indeed, I doubt that it ever was."

"Of course my son is my concern," he bit out. "Why did you not write me yourself? You had an entire year to inform me, and yet you chose to keep him from me."

She had thought of writing him. Indeed, she'd scratched out a letter more than once only to think better of it and toss it into the dustbin each time. "I did what I thought best."

In truth, she hadn't told him because of her pride. She refused to be a burden to anyone. Not to her family, and not to the man before her. What would he have done? Rushed from his new bride's side? Sent her money she didn't want? No, she couldn't have stood that, and so she had simply decided to keep Theo to herself.

"What you thought best." His lip curled in sneer. "Forgive me if I find your judgment sorely lacking, madam."

"For once, we are in complete agreement, Mr. Storm. My judgment is sorely lacking indeed," she said pointedly. "I trusted you, for instance."

Her barb hit its mark. He stiffened and released her arms but made no move to put distance between them. "I made you no promises, Helen."

She'd been foolish. Careless. She had allowed her always reliable mind to be governed by her wild and fanciful heart. The devil of it was that even as he stood before her, as aloof and cool as ever, threatening to take the one joy he'd given her away, she loved him still. The realization made her tremble. She didn't like feeling so helpless. She didn't like the power he had over her, the power to make her hurt.

"Nor did I make promises to you," she managed to say. "We have no need of you here. I absolve you of any foolish notions you have concerning the welfare of my son. He is well cared for. You may return to America with a clear conscience."

"I'll return to New York City with my son," he countered. "You may come along if you wish, or you may choose to remain."

As if she would permit him to uproot Theo and spirit him off to New York City alone. Some things, it seemed, didn't change. The man still had more audacity than anyone she'd ever met. "You can go to hell for all I care, but I won't be going with you and neither will Theo."

He stared down at her, surprised, she supposed, that she would contradict him. "Unfortunately for you, my dear, you've forfeited your rights to the boy by keeping him from me. Therefore, he goes where I say from this moment forward. And he's going to New York City, with or without you."

"You're mad. I haven't forfeited a thing. I'm his mother, and any court would rule in my favor." Did he truly think she hadn't an inkling of a woman's rights when it came to her child? The laws were not so much in favor of the husband or father of the child as they once had been. Woman was no longer merely man's chattel.

"My lawyers will eat yours for breakfast." His tone was dismissive, matter of fact. "No court will give custody of an infant to a woman who has deceived the father and intentionally withheld the boy from him. A woman who is living in a home filled with ladies of the night, no less. I have an endless well of funds and the best law men that money can buy."

His words shook her, but she was determined not to let it show. She would fight him tooth and nail. "I won't let you take my son from me," she vowed. "I don't care if you have all the blood money in the world and a legion of law men at the ready."

"Then you had best pack your bags, madam," he commanded icily, "for you're America bound."

"No." She was not about to allow him to cow her, to make her bend to his wishes merely because he was a man and he was accustomed to getting his own way. "You cannot buy Theo, and you cannot buy me. Nor do you own us. We are staying right here in our home, and there isn't a thing that you can do about it."

"You don't understand, do you? I can do whatever the hell I please." He was angrier than she'd ever seen him and it almost frightened her. He gripped her shoulders now, his palms like hot brands even through the fabric of her dress and undergarments. "Damn you, Helen. Why did you keep him from me?"

Perhaps it had been wrong of her not to tell him about Theo, she acknowledged inwardly. He did have a right to know he had a son. But that certainly didn't mean he had a right to try to take Theo away from her. "I understood that you had returned to America to wed your heiress. I didn't wish to disrupt your life. What good would it have done?"

"There would have been no disruption. He's my son and he belongs with me."

Her mind whirled, trying to find ways of dissuading him from the road he was hell-bent upon charging down. "You aren't thinking about this properly. When your anger cools, you'll see that there is no need for anyone to ever be the wiser that Theo is yours. Your bride will not want a bastard beneath her roof."

His jaw clenched again. "He's not a bastard. He is my son. Take me to him now, Helen. I want to see him."

"He is napping," she protested, partly because the mother's instinct in her feared that he would snatch Theo away and ride off with him and partly because she didn't think her heart could bear the sight of him holding their son in his arms at last.

"Wake him. I've traveled an ocean to see him."

There was an undercurrent of emotion in his voice,

something more than mere anger. And it fractured her. She closed her eyes, steeling herself. "Please don't try to take him from me, Levi. I couldn't bear it." Her voice broke on the last words as tears threatened to overtake her. She wasn't too proud to beg, not for the sake of her son. Everything had changed from the moment she'd first looked upon his tiny, precious face. Theo was her world now.

"Wake him." He was unrelenting as ever.

Had she expected him to crumble in the face of her tears? He was the same man he'd always been. Harsh. Immovable. "Very well." They were at an impasse, but now that he was here, she would no longer deny him. "Follow me."

She turned and hurried down the hall, Levi close behind. Maeve descended the steps ahead of her, Theo in her arms. "Oh my lady, I was just coming to get you, I was. The little lord woke with a hungry belly."

Theo wailed into the silence. Helen hastened to take him from Maeve, patting his bum and cooing to him softly. "Thank you, Maeve," she said.

Maeve eyed Levi, clearly not sure if he was a welcome visitor or an unwelcome one. Helen wasn't sure either.

But Levi had eyes only for his son. His hard expression softened to one of awe. Helen fought the urge to cry anew at the sight. There was no denying the truth in the way he looked upon Theo. The little life they had created together was the one thing that could crack his seemingly impenetrable shell. Mayhap Levi Storm had a heart after all.

He closed the distance between them, reaching out to gently cup Theo's cap-covered head. "He isn't a lord. He is a commoner, like his father. He is a Storm, and he can wear that mantle with greater pride than any title in the land."

Theo let out another shrill wail in response, his face crumpling. He turned toward her, seeking sustenance, rooting against her bosom. She flushed, meeting Levi's gaze. "I must feed him." Oh dear. Surely he didn't mean to hover over her while she nursed Theo.

"Feed him then," he said, relieving her for the moment. "You needn't look at me as if I'm a complete ogre. I well understand that a babe has needs."

At least she could retreat from him, attempt to gather her wits and her emotions both. "Maeve will prepare you some tea while you wait."

This was a brief reprieve and she knew it. The battle between them had just begun. Helen turned and ascended the stairs before she embarrassed herself by bursting into tears before him.

Chapter Twelve

"**D**O YOU WISH TO HOLD HIM?"

Levi stared at the babe Helen held against her bosom as though she were protecting the child from the devil himself. And maybe she was. If ever Levi had felt weaker or more low in his entire life, incontestably it was now, looking upon his son. How could he ever be worthy of such a pure, innocent life? How could he, who had never known a father, now be one?

Levi hesitated, uncertain of what to do next. He wanted to hold his son, of course he did. He never wanted to let him go. He would raise him with love, in a happy home where he never need fear where his next meal would be coming from or whether or not he'd have a roof above him. The emotion bursting in his chest was almost too much to comprehend. He was simultaneously elated and terrified of the tiny being before him.

The tiny being had a name, he'd discovered. Theo.

"Go on, Levi." Helen's voice was gentle yet urging. She held the baby out, it seemed, with the greatest of reluctance. But she offered him nonetheless, a living, breathing olive branch between them.

He was not ready to forgive her for keeping Theo from him. But he reached out and took the beloved bundle from her, cradling his son against his chest in an awkward pose. "Hello there, son." He met eyes the same startling blue as his own. Theo grinned up at him as if to return his greeting.

Helen hovered close, her beautiful face etched with worry. They were well and truly alone now, closed off in a formal parlor away from the prying eyes and ears of the home's other residents, with nothing but their ghosts and their son between them. He glanced briefly back up at her, feeling equal parts fury and desire for her. It had been so long since he'd seen her, touched her, kissed her soft pink lips, and breathed in the fine scent of bergamot and rose. God in heaven, he'd missed her. He'd missed her every day since she'd walked away from him, and Jesse's letter had given him the reason he needed to cast his pride aside and bring her back to him where she belonged.

That didn't mean he wasn't still furious with her, for he was. But everything had changed when he saw Theo for the first time. All of his righteous indignation had been vanquished by a towheaded baby with Helen's nose and cherubic cheeks. Had she truly expected to keep their child a secret forever? Had she meant for him to never know his own flesh and blood? She had much to answer for, but there remained something he must do above all else. Jesse had told him to make it right, and so he would.

"He will have my name, Helen," he said firmly.

"He has my family name, which is a good and proud name," she protested.

"It will be changed." In this, he would not waiver. His son would be a bastard no more. "As will yours."

Her eyes widened. "That isn't possible. Perhaps for Theo, but not for me."

His mind whirred ahead, undeterred by her lack of enthusiasm. Levi didn't have a habit of leaving anything to chance. Not any longer. "Of course it is. I'll make it known that we were wed in secret before Theo's birth. I can make certain that no one will ever be the wiser." Theo babbled happily then, stealing Levi's attention again. It would seem that he had his son's approval at least. "I'll not have it be said that my son is a bastard."

He had been a bastard. An unwanted child with no name, no home, and no father he'd ever known. He'd been a burden to his ma, who had loved him in spite of the grief he must have caused her as an extra mouth to fret over feeding. It would be different for his son. He was bound and determined to make it so. He owed that to Theo and to himself.

"Have you gone utterly mad? You cannot be married to two women at once, Levi, no matter how much money you possess." Helen was in high dudgeon now, twin dots of scarlet anger on her high cheekbones, her hands planted firmly on her hips. She was every bit as stunning as ever, damn her, and he wanted her every bit as much as he ever had. More, even.

"I'm not married, Helen."

Her expression turned to one of shock. "What of Miss VanHorn?"

"I didn't wed her."

"But you returned to America to do so."

No, he had not, but he wasn't prepared to discuss that with her just now. There wasn't a need for it as nothing would change the straits in which they found themselves, two people hopelessly at odds with each other. "I didn't wed her," he repeated.

She searched his gaze. "You cannot mean to marry me."

He did and he would. Once his course of action was planned, he never strayed from it. Not ever.

"You're the mother of my son. We will wed as quickly and quietly as possible."

"You *are* mad."

"Not any more than I've ever been. This is what needs to be done, Helen."

"What needs to be done according to you?" she scoffed. "I don't need you and neither does Theo. We have been getting on fine in your absence and will continue to do so when you leave."

"I'm not leaving," he countered. "Not without you both. I'll not have my son be known as a bastard. You needn't be stubborn about this, Helen. Can you not see what is best for the child?"

"Of course I can, and it isn't my being trapped into a loveless marriage with a tyrant. Give him back to me now," she demanded. "Please."

Theo had fallen asleep, his sweet face nestled trustingly against Levi's waistcoat. He wasn't about to relinquish his son so quickly, tyrant that he was. Hang it, but she knew how to goad him. "He's sleeping. There's no need to disturb him."

"Please, Levi. Give me Theo and leave us alone."

Helen stared at him, her worry evident. Did she fear that he would simply take Theo and ride into the sunset, never to be seen again? She loved the boy, that much was apparent. But she was thoroughly wrong-headed when it came to deciding what was in the boy's best interest and what was obviously not. Because *he* was in Theo's best interest, damn it, and he was in Helen's best interest too, if she'd only take the time to consider it.

He ruthlessly tamped down a surge of sympathy that rose within him. She had kept their son from him, had denied him of the most basic right of even knowing of Theo's existence. He must not forget that.

"I'll decide what is best for son from now on," he told her curtly. "You're both coming with me. You had best accustom yourself to the idea of marrying this tyrant, for if I have my way, it'll be done as soon as I can obtain a license."

There truly was no other way to extricate themselves from this tangled mess of scandal and lies. He would have Theo legitimate. It was of the utmost importance to him. As for Helen, she would have to accustom herself to the reality that it was what was best for her son as well. And Levi would have to acquaint himself with the idea that Helen would finally be his.

The thought gave him little comfort at the moment.

"I'm not marrying you, Levi." His wife-to-be was not precisely ready to give in. "You may be a part of Theo's life as his father, but you can't force me to bend to your whims."

Damn her, why did she insist on being so stubborn? He clenched his jaw, willing his rising temper to abate. "I'm not forcing you. I'm informing you that you will marry me as soon as possible as it's what must be done for our son."

"I'm not certain that it is. And forgive me if your informing me seems rather a lot like forcing me. I confess I cannot see the difference." Her supple lips flattened into a thin, grim line. He wanted to kiss her anyway, kiss her senseless, kiss her until the protest was gone from her and they both forgot all the reasons why they were at odds. He would have were he not cradling their sleeping baby.

"Marry me and give our son what is rightfully his, my name and my fortune one day at his disposal. As my wife, you'll have the best of everything. I'll see to it that you have all the funds you need for whatever you like. Build homes for East End doxies and orphans. Pursue your causes to your heart's content. Buy all the baubles and fripperies you'd like."

She shook her head in denial. "Your money doesn't mean anything to me."

"Perhaps not to you, but this is not about you or I. No one will ever turn down our son. He will have the finest education, all the opportunities I was denied. One day, he'll run my business should he wish it, and the world will be in his palm." He paused, allowing her mind to digest the gravity of her decision. "We cannot afford to be selfish in this, Helen. You are accustomed to wealth and privilege as the daughter of an earl. Bastard children aren't so blessed. No one knows that better than I do."

Her resolve was weakening at last, he could read it in her eyes. He was right and she knew it. Theo had to be put before the both of them, before their separate wants and hopes. He had changed their lives forever.

"You must accept this, Helen. He will be an outcast. Your family will never be able to acknowledge him without courting scandal. There's only one way for you to protect him from that."

"If I wed you, it will be a marriage of convenience only." She hesitated. "I will not share your bed."

His blood went cold. She didn't want him. The confirmation shouldn't cut him straight down to the bone, but somehow it did. Her words that day rushed back to him. *You never belonged here and you never will. You disgust me.* Those words had kept him from her in London on his way back to New York City. As time went on and the distance and silence between them stretched, he'd been forced to admit that she'd finally realized what he'd known all along. Helen was a lady to her core, her blood bluer than the sky. Too good for the likes of him. He knew what he was and who he was. It would never matter how much money he amassed or how great the company he built became. He would always be the bastard son of a whore.

"It will be as you wish. I wouldn't want to sully you with my common touch, my lady." The last he said with a mocking air, unable to help himself.

But she wasn't finished with her demands. "I want to keep my funds to dispense with as I like, and I want to retain ownership and control of this home."

He nodded. He had no need for any of her possessions. "It's yours and more. I'll see to it that you're kept in the greatest comfort."

She wrung her hands now, obviously distraught. "We will live here in England, Theo and I. You may visit as you please."

There he drew the line. "Theo will travel with me. I'll not be separated from my son ever again. You may accompany us or choose to remain here. I don't give a damn either way."

"I won't be without Theo."

"Then you will travel where we go." On this, he was firm. She could have her house and her funds and her empty bed, but by God, she couldn't have their son.

He could plainly see that she was not pleased but neither did she have room to make further mandates. When she had decided to keep Theo a secret from him, she had chosen the path of enmity upon which they now found themselves.

She closed her eyes for a moment. "Very well."

"What are you agreeing to, my lady?" he pressed.

"I will marry you." Her eyes opened, brilliant and glistening with tears. "You've gotten what you wanted. Now may I have him?"

Good Christ. Did she really despise him so much that the fate of wedding him brought her to tears? With great reluctance, he passed the still sweetly sleeping babe to her. She pressed a kiss to Theo's forehead and held him close, as though she'd just rescued him from the seething maws of a dragon.

He was disgusted. Disgusted with himself, with Helen. Angry too, and he clung to that anger, let it seep down deep into his soul before he made a fool of himself again over her. He wanted her so much he ached with it. He couldn't have her. It would seem they were both doomed to a life of misery.

"It would seem I'm getting married," Helen announced baldly later that afternoon.

The faces of her three dear sisters mirrored their shock. Bo looked intrigued, Tia puzzled, Cleo bemused. The equally lovely face of her honorary sister, Bella, reflected contrition mixed with guilt. Helen had asked all four to assemble at Cleo's townhouse after Levi's departure that morning to discuss a matter of supreme urgency.

And they had loyally come together for her, awaiting her late arrival in the sun-streaked drawing room. Late because the horse of Helen's hired hack had gone lame. Late because she and Theo had suffered a miserable ride thereafter, trundling into another rickety hack in the chill torrent of an early spring downpour. She was soaked. Theo was soaked. She had the remnants of horse offal on her left shoe, and she'd never been more tired or more miserable.

They stood practically in unison and rushed to greet her, ringing her in a half circle of sisterly support.

"You're getting married?" Tia echoed. "Good heavens, to whom?"

"Lord, you're drenched," Cleo noted with a frown of disapproval, ever the mothering hen even though Helen was the eldest of them all. "Your dress is quite ruined, though I daresay it didn't look its best to begin with. What is that on your hem, dearest?"

"Whoever can it be? Is he horribly dashing?" Bo asked, clapping her hands. Finishing school hadn't done the minx a bit of good.

"I'm so very sorry, Helen," Bella offered with a wince.

Helen glanced down at her hem to discover that the horse dung wasn't limited to just her left shoe. A whiff of stables made its way to her nose. Could the day get any worse?

Theo cried then, as if on cue.

She was tempted to join him.

"I'll answer your questions in the order in which they were received," she announced instead, looking to Tia first. "I'm marrying Levi Storm. I'm drenched because my hired hack went lame, the offensive smear on my hem is horse manure, and it's also on my left shoe if you must know. Bo, he is horribly dashing and horribly arrogant and at the moment, altogether horrible in general. And Bella, you needn't be sorry. You aren't responsible for your husband. He, however, will be on the receiving end of a lengthy harangue from me at the first opportunity."

She sighed. Theo continued wailing. "He is soaked, Cleo. Can we have him changed into a dry gown and blankets?"

Cleo was mother to two boys, her youngest less than a year older than Theo, and from the looks of things, she appeared to be breeding yet again. There had to be scads of baby necessities tucked away.

"Of course!" Cleo rang for a servant and requested her sons' nurse be brought round to take temporary custody of Theo and make him warm, dry, and happy once more.

"Helen darling, I thought the roué was marrying that horse-faced heiress?" Tia put a sisterly arm around her shoulder. She and her husband, the Duke of Devonshire, had offered to take Helen in when she'd turned to them for aid, telling them everything. Well, almost everything. Helen would always be grateful to them for their kindness that day and in the days that followed.

"He was, and both you and I know that she wasn't horse-faced in the slightest," Helen admonished, thinking again of Miss VanHorn's engraving. She had been unmistakably lovely, and Helen was fiercely glad that Miss VanHorn had not become Mrs. Storm in the wedding of the century after all. "But he didn't wed her. Perhaps Bella knows more than I, since Mr. Whitney is such dear friends with Mr. Storm?"

If she said the last with a trace of bitterness, well, it couldn't be helped. Bella appeared to take it in stride as any proper honorary sister would.

"I'm sorry to say I know very little on the matter." Bella's tone was contrite. "My husband and Mr. Storm weren't corresponding regularly after…well, anyway, all I know is what I read in one of Jesse's papers. Miss VanHorn broke the engagement and married another. I wanted to tell you, Helen, but I didn't know if the information would be welcome to you or not."

Ah, so it had not been Levi's doing, then, but his betrothed's. Helen begrudged the stab of disappointment that sliced through her. Of course he would have married Miss VanHorn and her millions and her heart-shaped face and her twenty-inch waist. How foolish, how silly, how unutterably stupid for a tiny part of her heart to have hoped that Levi had somehow cried off because of her. No, the news that he had been thrown over by beautiful, rich, wasp-waisted Miss VanHorn would not have been welcome. Not at all.

Tia sniffed the air then. "Lud, but you smell foul, Helen. Perhaps someone ought to change you as well. Cleo is right. Where *did* you find that dreadful gown?"

"One of the ladies made it for me." She gave Tia her most severe look. "You ought to be ashamed, calling it dreadful." She had sold every last one of her fine dresses, and in addition to being a budding reader, Ruby was also a dab hand with needle and thread. Helen knew her dress didn't compare to the gowns she'd once donned without a second thought, but Ruby had worked very hard on it for her.

"I'm ashamed alright," Tia drawled, "but only that my sister is gadding about wearing a sack lined in donkey manure."

"It isn't a sack, and I'm quite sure the manure in question came from a horse." Helen stared down her sister. Tia was like a butterfly, beautiful and bold, but Helen was the eldest, and even if her circumstances had been dramatically reduced by her own poor decision-making, it didn't mean that she couldn't still browbeat her younger sibling. Even if said sibling was a duchess who outranked them all.

"You know Heath and I would give you anything," Tia returned. "You needn't live as a pauper and an outcast."

It was true that Tia, Cleo, and Bella had all offered Helen assistance. They had offered to help her with money, shelter, whatever she needed, and regardless of the potential scandal she could bring upon them. She had refused them all in the end, choosing to live her life on her terms. She'd discovered a great deal about herself in the last year. She'd realized that she was capable of surviving on her own, and she was fiercely proud of that.

The nurse arrived to take Theo from Helen, a stout woman with steel-gray hair and a kind smile, and Helen relinquished her son with great reluctance. She'd entrusted his care only to herself or Maeve thus far, and being separated from him at all induced a strong sense of anxiety. If she held on to him a moment longer than necessary or polite, she couldn't be blamed. She turned to watch Theo's little white cap and gown disappearing out the drawing room door in the arms of someone else.

"You needn't be so territorial," Cleo admonished when the door closed once again. "Evans is the finest nurse to be had, I assure you. Theo is in wonderful hands." She caught Helen's elbow and dragged her to the ornate settees and *Louis Quinze* table laid out with an impressive array of tea, muffins, and scones. "Do sit. You look as if you require sustenance. Do you wish for something stronger than tea? Wine? Whisky? Thornton has an excellent stock."

Helen didn't know what she required. Whisky was tempting indeed. Anything to calm the jagged edges of her nerves. She sat dutifully, the odor of her befouled hem and shoe wafting up to her. She wrinkled her nose in distaste. Perhaps Tia wasn't that far off the mark with her suggestion.

Cleo, Tia, Bo, and Bella all sat as well. With their grand gowns and elaborate coiffures, Helen felt as out of place as a goose in a pond filled with gorgeous swans. She hadn't allowed herself to venture to any of her sisters' homes after her pregnancy had become evident for fear of tainting them with her scandal. She had to admit that she had missed this, not the finery but the camaraderie, the sisterhood. Sisters spoke to each other's souls. They understood each other in a way no one else ever could.

"Tell us everything," Bo ordered. With her vibrant auburn hair and flashing blue eyes, Bo was a true original. Though her outer beauty was undeniable, it was her vivacious personality that made her blindingly beautiful. She was giving, loving, naïve to a fault, and never failed to make Helen laugh. "Helen, dearest, you don't look happy. Is he not a fluent kisser?"

Cleo spit the sip of tea she'd just taken all over her cup and saucer. "Boadicea," she sputtered, indignant.

"It *is* a valid question," Tia pointed out with a wicked grin.

"Quite," Bella agreed, her cheeks pink. "Kissing is most important."

Dear, sweet heavens. This lot was going to be no help to her whatsoever. Three of them were hopelessly in love with their husbands and the fourth was a rapscallion in skirts.

"Boadicea, what do you know of kissing anyway?" Helen demanded, because she was oldest and she felt responsible. She was certainly no model for her youngest sister to pattern herself after, though that didn't seem to matter in the moment. Yes, Levi was a fluent kisser. *Everywhere.* Helen was very wisely inclined to keep that knowledge to herself.

Bo blinked and attempted to school her features into an expression of demure innocence. "I'm sure I don't know a thing, sister dearest."

"Clearly, I'll have to tell our mother to do a more thorough job of scrutinizing your suitors," Helen said, her brow raised.

They all knew quite well that their parents were a bit unorthodox. Well, perhaps very much so. Mother hadn't blinked an eye when Helen had delivered the news of her pregnancy. She'd simply asked her if she wished to go abroad or send her maid to the pharmacy. *Don't be silly*, the countess had said, waving a careless hand in the air. *You can't believe you're the first to ever require such a solution?* Helen, of course, had chosen neither the former nor the latter.

"Angels in heaven, he isn't attempting to force you into this, is he?" Cleo asked suddenly, her gaze far too shrewd as it narrowed upon Helen. "You needn't go through with it, you know. Thornton would gladly take up the cudgels for you if need be."

Somehow, Helen doubted that even Thornton, solid example of English masculinity that he was, could best Levi in a fight. Levi was taller, for one. And his muscles...she had forgotten how splendid and strong he was beneath his waistcoat and shirt. But when he'd held her against him earlier, she had remembered. She had remembered everything.

Much to her shame.

Cleo's offer was appreciated nonetheless. Was Levi forcing her? He had been very angry with her, yes. He had threatened. He had raged. And yet, she knew that he would never hurt her, not physically. And she knew, too, that much of what he'd said had been the product of his anger. He would never make her wed him. Nor would she allow him to force her into a union that was unwanted. She was strong enough to stand on her own. She'd been doing so for a year and could continue for the rest of her life. No, then, he was not forcing her. Nor, if she was brutally honest with herself, was the union entirely unwanted.

The thought gave her pause.

Still, that didn't mean that she was going to simply take up where they had left off. She wasn't a meek and mild miss easily influenced by a handsome face and a wicked mouth. She'd been very careful to enumerate all of her requirements prior to agreeing to the marriage. Now that she'd had her taste of freedom, she found that she didn't wish to lose it, even while she knew that protecting Theo by marrying Levi was the right thing to do. She was marrying Levi because she *chose* to, plain and simple.

"He isn't forcing me." She took a sip of her tea at last and wished it was far stronger, perhaps with a dram of the whisky Cleo had so recently extolled. "He was rather irate with me for not informing him about Theo. We had quite a row, and he threatened to take Theo back to New York City without me. But in the end, I suppose he calmed down enough to reason with me. And I realized that it isn't fair to punish Theo with a life of shame because of my own foolish actions. He can't help the circumstance of his birth, but I can do my best to rectify it for him. I *will* rectify it. I owe him that as his mother."

"Oh my," Tia said. "Mr. Storm sounds like a veritable beast."

"He's not a beast," Helen defended quickly. Too quickly, for she caught her sisters' knowing smiles.

"You care for him," Cleo observed.

"You love him," Tia chimed in, smiling gaily. She and Devonshire were almost sickeningly in love, and so of course she assumed everyone else must also be suffering from the selfsame malaise.

"Oh dear, I think this is all my fault," said Bella.

"Old Helen has finally met her match," crowed Bo.

Helen glowered at the four miscreants before her, all of them beloved, all of them irksome indeed. "I am not old, you incorrigible minx. And I do not care for him or love him. But Bella, I must confess that you are, in part, responsible for the sad state in which I find myself, for Mr. Storm was your guest."

"Of course you're not old." Bo blinked, the picture of innocence yet again.

"Of course you don't love him," Tia added, rolling her eyes skyward.

Oh, they were too much, these sisters of hers. They saw too much. They knew too much. They said too much. Helen's shoulders sagged.

"Perhaps I do care," she acknowledged. "Just a bit."

"Only a small bit, I'm sure," Cleo said agreeably. "You know, dearest, men are a most exasperating species. Ingratiating themselves to us in one deed and vexing us in the next."

"But they aren't ever vexing for long," said Bella.

"Oh no," agreed Tia with a secretive smile. "Not for long."

"How can they be exasperating when they kiss so wonderfully?" Bo asked.

Helen, Tia, Bella, and Cleo all groaned.

Perhaps, Helen thought, she wouldn't be the most scandalous of all her sisters after all. What *had* they taught Bo in finishing school, anyway? That she ought to be kissing every suitor who came across her path? Surely not. Helen sniffed the sour air once more. Oh, fiddle. Mayhap she would need to change anyway. That horse dung was proving most unshakeable.

Most unshakeable indeed.

Chapter Thirteen

$\mathcal{S}$HE HADN'T ALLOWED HIM TO KISS HER on the mouth, and it rankled Levi even now as their carriage hurried through the streets of London, taking them back to Helen's House of Rest to gather her belongings and little Theo. The ceremony had been succinct. A far cry from the lavish affair that would have brought the cream of elite New York City society together to watch him wed Miss VanHorn. Helen had deserved such a splendid and ostentatious showing. She deserved orchids and roses and an orchestra and a blue-blooded prince among men. She'd gotten instead a hasty marriage, no flowers, no sweeping orchestral accompaniment, and a commoner who had bribed the Registrar to record their marriage with the wrong date after wedding them by License.

That part didn't sit well with him, but he'd had little choice. He didn't consider himself an unethical man, had never succumbed to the temptations of Tammany Hall corruption like some of his contemporaries. In his youth, he had stolen, sometimes to feed himself and other times simply because he could. In war, he had wounded and killed, bound by his oath as a soldier.

It had been during that very war, the war that had torn apart a nation and ravaged his youth, that he'd realized the true meaning of honor. He could take pride in knowing he had never committed another crime since his time in the Army of the Potomac until today. But for Helen and his son, he was more than willing to take that black mark against his soul. He wanted the Marriage Notice Books to reflect the story he would tell the world hereafter, that Theo had been born after his parents' marriage and not before. He'd pay any price to protect his wife and his son.

Wife. Strange word, foreign word to tie to the woman he'd wed. A title, a benediction. For a year, he had thought of her with longing and bitterness, with regret and anger and the driving fear that he'd made the greatest mistake of his life in letting her slip through his fingers. He'd kept her hat, had carried it with him to Paris and then on the long journey back to New York City. An albatross indeed. Now, their time apart was almost as if it hadn't been. The annals of history, certainly, would never know otherwise.

"Happy anniversary, Mrs. Storm," he told her drily, watching her on the well-appointed bench opposite him. She held herself stiffly, even in the swaying conveyance. Her gown was simple and plain beneath her equally plain redingote. She, however, was not. Her golden hair had been wound into a heavy knot of basket plaits at her nape, putting the elegant beauty of her features on display. Mrs. Storm. She was his wife now, and the knowledge sent a sudden surge of something strong and sharp straight through him. Something he couldn't define.

"We haven't been married for a year, and it was wrong of you to lead a man into sin merely to absolve ours." Her gaze, trained to the small window to her right, swung to his at last.

His eyes slipped to her lush mouth, the mouth she had denied him. "If he was that easily led into sin, I'm afraid this isn't the first time he's danced with the devil, my dear."

The good man suffered from a gambling addiction. Levi didn't make a practice of underhanded business dealings. But he wasn't a fool. He had always been adept at finding his opponent's weaknesses and using them against him however he could. However he must. And in this instance, his desire to protect had been tantamount. Theo would never be known as a bastard now, and that was all that mattered.

"I hadn't realized the two of you were old friends," she said pointedly, and then looked out the window once more.

She could imply he was the devil all she liked, but it wouldn't change a damn thing that had happened this day. They were married in the eyes of God and man now. And regardless of how angry he was with her for keeping Theo from him, regardless of her insistence that their union be in name only, and regardless of the murky circumstances surrounding their abrupt nuptials, taking Helen as his wife felt right all the way to his bones.

"You married this devil," he reminded her, wanting to needle her a bit, to rattle her out of the frigid poise she'd displayed since she had stepped into his carriage earlier that day.

"For the sake of my son," she retorted.

"Our son," he corrected.

"For the sake of Theo," she amended, "that he be afforded the life he deserves."

"Our son." He wanted to hear her say it. "Our son, Helen."

"Very well, *our son*." She turned to him once more, her eyes flashing with fire. "You win, Levi. There, are you happy now? You always win."

"No," he said slowly. "I don't."

No indeed, he did not always win, else he wouldn't be in a carriage with the only woman in the world that he wanted, a woman who was his wife, goddamn it, and who didn't want him to touch her.

"Perhaps you're right," she said quietly. "You didn't win

your heiress after all, did you? I understand she jilted you. That must have been quite a blow to your pride."

"There was no blow to my pride. I didn't wish to marry her, nor did she wish to marry me. We parted ways with a great deal of mutual relief." By the time he'd returned to New York City after overseeing repairs on the Paris station, he'd had just enough time to undo the damage he'd done the day he'd accepted VanHorn's investment and his daughter's hand both. The VanHorn money and power weren't worth a cold union to a woman he scarcely knew. He wasn't willing to sacrifice himself for the sake of his business, regardless of the cost.

And so, he'd arranged a meeting with Miss VanHorn, who had tearfully revealed to him that she loved another and wouldn't be heartbroken in the least if their engagement were to end. Her father, however, had been another matter. VanHorn had been enraged. He'd pulled his funds and his support of North Atlantic Electric, and Levi had spent the last few months working as hard as he possibly could to keep his business afloat after such a crippling blow.

It hadn't been easy, but he'd managed by selling off some of his stocks and nearly all of his real estate. Everything but the Fifth Avenue and Belgravia homes was gone, but North Atlantic Electric had withstood, and it had begun venturing into a new form of power generation that Levi felt was far more promising than the geographically limited direct current method they had previously used. He'd made it all happen the way he'd made everything happen, with his own hard work and determination.

"Why didn't you wish to marry her?" Helen asked then.

Because she wasn't you.

Levi cursed himself inwardly for the wayward thought. But it was true. Something within him had changed during his time in London. Helen had changed him. He'd realized he'd turned into a man who was willing to sell himself for greater riches, a man who no longer recognized what he had become. Her angry words to him at their last parting had stung, and they had stung because they had been true.

He held her gaze. "Someone once told me that I was a vile opportunist who cared only about my businesses, money, and pleasure. I sought to prove her wrong."

If hearing her own words unnerved her, it didn't show on her face. She remained implacable. "I daresay you'll have to do quite a bit more than that to prove her wrong."

"I have a lifetime in which to do it, Mrs. Storm."

His less-than-subtle reminder of their recent marriage gave her even more starch in her posture. She frowned at him, but not even a ferocious moue of disapproval could dim her beauty. "I don't require you to prove anything to me, *Mr. Storm*. You've upended my life. Let that be enough."

"As you have upended mine," he said grimly. "Had you simply responded to any one of my letters, had you simply sent word to me that you were carrying my child, I would have come for you without delay."

"Had you not already possessed a betrothed you kept secret from me, I would have."

Damn it, they were always talking in circles. He leaned across the carriage, bringing their faces temptingly close as he bracketed her skirts with his hands. "You too are guilty of the sin of omission, my dear, and don't you forget it."

"That was different," she protested, twin flags of color appearing in her cheeks.

His nearness flustered her. Good. His gaze lowered to her mouth again. Just a dip of his head or a bump in the road, and their lips would meet. She smelled sweetly of rose and bergamot, and it was nearly his undoing. His body reminded him that it had been a year since he'd last had a woman. Since he'd last had *her*.

A marriage in name only was going to be goddamn impossible.

But he wasn't going to kiss her, not now, not yet, because he was still angry with her. Damned angry. "It was no different," he countered, recalling how she tasted, how much he had loved kissing her. Everywhere.

She drew back into the carriage squab as far as she could go. "You never told me you were marrying another woman."

No. He had been too caught up in Helen to do so. Somehow, it hadn't mattered until it had *mattered*. And by then, the damage had already been done. He should have told her. He should have charged back to London the moment he'd rectified matters in Paris, back to Helen's side. But he couldn't atone for things he should have done. He couldn't rewrite their past and neither could she.

He leaned closer. "You never told me I had a son."

They had each wronged the other, wounded each other. They bore equal guilt in their mutual state of distrust. But some of his fury had already dissipated.

She worried her lower lip and the urge to kiss her had never been stronger. "You should have told me, Levi."

"Yes, I should have," he agreed, because it was true. He could own his faults. "I'm sorry for that. I intended to tell you before I left for Paris, but you found out on your own before I could. Believe me, it was never my intention to hurt you."

"I wish I could." Sadness darkened her eyes. Sadness that he had caused.

He hated that he'd been the source of any of her pain. "As I said, I have a lifetime to prove you wrong in your opinion of me."

"But you also have a lifetime to prove me right, and that is what I fear most," she said softly.

She looked incredibly vulnerable in that moment, and he thought of how changed her circumstances had become. When he had left her, she had been every inch the earl's daughter, draped in silk and jewels. But now her dresses were cotton, unadorned. She wore no jewels. She had been an unwed mother living in a small room alongside the women she was attempting to help. He was responsible for that. He had not been careful with her. He had been reckless and foolish and too filled with pride, and he had been wrong. Part of him didn't blame her for keeping Theo from him. What an ass he'd been.

He drew the backs of his fingers across her cheek, unable to stop himself. How had he ever imagined he could live the rest of his life without seeing her again? Without touching her again? Without her?

"Helen, from this moment forward, you needn't fear anything. You're under my protection now, you and Theo both. You'll have the best of everything." And they would, by God. His business was intact and so were his funds. He hadn't needed VanHorn wealth after all. He'd damn well made his own.

She didn't flinch away from him, simply held still as he traced a path down her cheek to her creamy throat and then slid his hand back to cup the base of her skull. She was so soft. So warm. "I don't need anything from you," she said, stubborn as ever.

He stroked the tense cords of her neck, worked them with his thumb and forefinger. "Perhaps not, but I will give freely anyway, beginning with a new wardrobe. What happened to your fine silk gowns?"

"Someone else is enjoying them." She leaned into his ministrations ever so slightly, giving in despite herself it seemed. "I sold them all. We needed the funds to help start our endeavors at the House of Rest."

She'd sold her dresses. Hell. He wondered what else she had sold, how far she would have gone to refrain from asking him for help. "Surely Jesse and Bella would have aided you. Would not anyone in your family?"

"They all offered but I refused."

Obdurate, willful woman.

"Why would you refuse?" His fingers slid into her silken hair, finding a bevy of pins that begged to be removed.

"I wanted to rely on myself alone." Finally, she swatted at his hand, keeping him from taking down her hair as he so longed. "For my entire life, I have lived beneath someone else's roof, depending on the mercies of my father or a family friend or a sister. I wanted to prove to myself that I could manage on my own."

And she had more than managed. The house was thriving from the looks of things. In the week since his arrival, he'd learned from the girls that Helen was teaching them valuable skills that they could use to better themselves. They were learning to read, write, sew, and cook from Helen and from each other. It was all rather enterprising of her.

He should have retreated back to his side of the carriage, but he couldn't seem to force himself to move away. "That's admirable of you. Foolish and stubborn, but also admirable."

She smiled then as the vehicle came to a halt. Just a curve of her lips but enough to make him realize it was the first genuine smile she'd bestowed upon him since his return. Perhaps he was thawing her ice the same way she was steadily melting his. "Thank you. For the first and the last part of what you said, though most assuredly not the middle bits."

He found himself smiling back at her in spite of everything. It had only required one year, bribing a Registrar, some meddling, and a few ocean crossings, but she was finally, at long last, his wife. As she should be, and as she should've been this long year past. That same, odd sensation he'd felt once before settled in the vicinity of his chest for a lingering moment.

Contentment.

Mrs. Levi Storm.

How many nights had she lain awake, staring into the inky darkness of the ceiling in her little bedchamber at the House of Rest, thinking about Levi's wife? How envious she had been of the tiny-waisted girl who would have taken his name and shared his bed. She hadn't wanted to be of course, but the thought of Levi with another woman had cut in a way nothing else could. All those nights when she had fed Theo and rocked him back to sleep, her mind churning, how could she have known that she would be here in this moment?

Now, it was Helen who sat before a mirror in the dressing room of her sumptuous new chamber in Levi's Belgravia home. It was Helen who stared at her reflection, wondering how the events of the last week had possibly come to pass. The deed had been done in a quiet ceremony by a beleaguered Registrar of Marriages, recorded for posterity with the wrong year to cleverly mask the truth of their scandal. Yes, she was well and truly Levi's wife.

In name only, she reminded herself with equal parts sadness and sternness. While she hadn't forgiven him for keeping the knowledge of his betrothed from her, neither was her heart perfectly guarded against him. Earlier that morning, on their carriage ride, she had very nearly given in to temptation and tipped her head forward so that their lips would seal. She hadn't forgotten what it felt like to be in his arms. She hadn't forgotten a moment of his kisses or the wicked things he'd done to her.

And she hadn't forgotten that she loved him.

She had tried, very hard, to stop. But she'd discovered that love was a most persistent and vexing emotion. It didn't simply cease to exist because of a betrayal or time or distance. Love was always there, a pulsing, vibrant, and terrible thing that merely waited beneath the surface of every hour to let its steadfast presence be known.

A knock sounded at the door that adjoined her chamber to Levi's, giving her a start. She'd reluctantly put Theo down to sleep beneath the watchful eye of his new nurse, a woman who came highly recommended and seemed more than capable but who Helen had yet to completely trust. Her lady's maid had been dismissed. There was only one person who could be on the other side of the door, in Levi's very own chamber.

Dread settled in her stomach now, for she was about to

face a most uncomfortable dinner with him. At last, her sisters and their husbands and Bella and Jesse had left them after a celebratory breakfast that had spilled well into the afternoon. She'd been grateful for the company, a way to put some much-needed distance between herself and her husband after that carriage ride. Indeed, she didn't think they'd even spoken more than a handful of words to each other during the festivities.

Another knock came, this one a bit more firm and insistent than the last. If she ignored him, would he simply go away? She very much doubted it, and rose to her feet, ready to do battle.

"Enter," she called.

Of course it was he, effortlessly handsome in his evening finery. His long legs ate up the distance between them. His black jacket and gray waistcoat set off the crisp white of his shirt, and it all had been lovingly tailored to fit his tall, lean form to perfection. But it was his face, and not his body that stole her breath.

A shadow of dark whiskers shaded his strong jaw, and his lips were meant for sinning. They quirked into a smile that didn't reach his gaze. "Mrs. Storm." He stopped an arm's length from her and bowed as if they were in court and she was his queen. "You are lovely as an angel this evening, even though you've chosen to eschew the gowns I purchased for you."

She wore an artless day gown that Ruby had made, plain pink cotton, rather poorly fitted. No décolletage to speak of. He'd somehow filled her wardrobe with a small fortune in beautiful gowns since that morning, assuming she would be more than happy to don whatever he'd chosen for her. "I've made it plain to you that I don't want your money."

"You accepted the house," he pointed out, his tone harsh.

Yes, she had, but for a greater good, and at the time she'd believed he had given it from a decent place in his heart. Now, she was fairly certain he didn't possess a heart. "That was not for me."

"Yet you lived there while hiding my son from me." He took a step closer.

Helen was determined not to take a step back in retreat, no matter how tempting it would be. "I wasn't hiding Theo. You were in America. I had nowhere else to go. What would you have had me do? Take some female pills to cure my troubles? Go abroad until Theo was born and then give him away to another family? That is what my mother recommended, you know."

"That isn't what I would have wanted, and you damn well know that." His jaw went rigid. "Jesus, Helen, is that truly what she told you?"

"Yes." And it still cut as deeply as it had the first time she'd heard the words. "Those were my choices. I chose the only path I could envision myself upon. I chose my son."

"Our son," he corrected again as he had earlier. "I would have been here for you had I known. You denied me that right."

"I wasn't going to beg a man who was already married to another for his aid," she said coolly.

"Ah, but I wasn't married to another, was I?" He flashed a grim, self-deprecating smile. "And if you had but listened that day before I left for Paris, you would've known I had no intention of following through with the wedding."

His statement gave her pause, for it implied that she had been as complicit in the tangled muddle of their situation as he was. But she had listened to him, hadn't she? He had said he didn't love his betrothed, but he most certainly had never said he wasn't going to marry her. *It's complicated*, he had said. Complicated, her foot. How dare he try to turn the tables on her now, after all she had endured?

This time, it was she who took a step in his direction. She poked him in the chest with her finger. "You said nothing that day to leave me with the impression that you were crying off your nuptials. Not a single, bloody word."

Oh dear, she never swore. But she supposed she had

done a great deal of things in the last year that she'd never done before.

He caught her finger in his grasp, stilling her angry jabs and eliciting an unwanted frisson of desire deep within her. "Hang it, woman, don't poke me."

"I will poke you," she said mulishly, demonstrating by getting in another solid prod with her free index finger. "You had ample time to tell me everything before you were leaving for France and I had just discovered you had a beautiful betrothed from a newspaper article."

He caught her other hand too, and the contact sent the same unwelcome heat through her body. Gently, he pulled her into him, his hands still holding hers. Her breasts brushed his hard chest. His eyes bored into hers. "I own that I didn't tell you when I should have. But I had a great deal on my shoulders then. My company was being sued, we'd just blown up a damn wall and nearly assassinated the President of France in the process, we were short on funds, and I had begged Miss VanHorn's father for a greater investment. And in the midst of all that, was you."

She hadn't known any of those things. None of them. It occurred to her then that she scarcely knew anything about his business other than his belief that his employees should have quality living arrangements. She knew nothing about electricity, how it worked, or how his mind worked beyond his propensity for dissecting pocket watches.

"You could have told me all of those things," she said fiercely, "or any one of those things. I would've understood, Levi. And yet you did not. You didn't say a word about your business being short on funds. Heavens, I don't even know anything about your business, and I scarcely know anything about you. I suppose you simply didn't care for me enough to share anything with me other than your bed."

"Of course I cared for you," he bit out. "How can you doubt it?"

"You cared for me," she repeated bitterly, noting his use of the past tense.

"Damn it, what do you want from me?"

He was angry again, but so was she. How could he not see what was so obviously before him? "I don't know what I want from you now." She shook her head. "Nothing. I want nothing from you. I don't want your dresses or your money. I don't even want this chamber or this house or your name. Those are all just trappings, easily given or taken away."

"Trappings," he echoed, his voice cool. "You ought to be well accustomed to trappings as the daughter of an earl."

"I was," she corrected. "I have changed. *You* changed me."

Levi's countenance remained forbidding. "As you have changed me, madam, and yet it would seem we are destined to be forever at odds."

"Yes," she agreed. "And I hope you can see it is for the best if I do not join you tonight for dinner. I ought to check on Theo in his nursery."

"Theo is being well cared for," he said, unyielding. "We will have dinner together."

At the moment, there was nothing she wanted more than to go to bed after this exhausting day. Alone. "No," she said.

"Yes." He tilted his head, considering her in a way she mistrusted. "The first day I met you, I discovered there was only one way to win an argument with you."

Her eyes went wide. He wasn't about to throw her over his shoulder again, was he? The Philistine! He released her hands, took a step away, and then in one deft movement, hooked her round the waist and hauled her over his shoulder as if she weighed no more than a feather. The breath left her in a swift whoosh, which was fortunate for him indeed since it rendered her momentarily incapable of blistering him with a few choice words.

She thumped on his back and struggled to regain her breath. Her corset made it nearly impossible, but she somehow managed. "Let me down, you oaf."

"No," he said slowly, pivoting and heading toward the door. "I don't think that I will, Lady Helen."

"What in heaven's name do you think you're doing?" The blood rushed to her head, making her quite dizzy.

"I formally request the honor of your presence at dinner," He opened her chamber door and breezed out into the hallway, still carrying her over his shoulder as though he were a pagan and she his spoils of war. "Will you join me of your own free will, Mrs. Storm, or must I carry you the whole way to the dining room?"

"If I say yes, will you put me back on my feet?"

"Perhaps," came his cryptic reply.

"I will join you," she said as primly as she could while hanging upside down, "as it seems I must one way or the other. Now do put me down, if you please."

He did, and she reluctantly took his proffered arm, allowing him to escort her to dinner.

Levi believed himself to be a man of reason, which was why he stood silently, hands clasped behind his back, as his new wife wandered through his private workroom. When he'd overseen the new design of this elegant old edifice, he had taken great care to make it have as much of the same feel as his Fifth Avenue home as possible. Of course, there was no denying that his home in Manhattan was far larger, far more encompassing and grand than his Belgravia house. But London had always been meant to be his second home, the helm from which he managed the European arm of North Atlantic Electric. He wanted to feel at home wherever he lived, damn it. And so he'd taken a drawing room and the study, removed part of a wall, and fashioned a workroom instead.

This workroom was not nearly as brimming with projects as the one in his Fifth Avenue house, but he hadn't known how long his stay in London would last when he'd left, and he'd brought as many of his projects as possible with him. He had a habit of deconstructing the works of others and rebuilding them into improved versions. There wasn't a thing on earth that couldn't be somehow reworked into something better.

She bent down to examine a contraption he'd dissected, fingering a foil-wrapped cylinder. He itched to say something. To explain to her precisely how the parts all came together to be one working machine. But he had decided to permit her to look her fill and to hold his tongue. He owed her that. So he waited and he watched.

As a general rule, he didn't allow anyone into his workroom. Not even servants, for a careless maid could do a great deal of harm, whether by unintentionally dislodging a component or by revealing his prototypes to someone else. No, a man didn't share his works-in-progress with anyone.

Unless a man had a glorious, blonde-haired goddess of a wife who was as stubborn as she was regal, even in her shapeless sack of a pink gown. A wife who was the father of his precious son. A wife who had recently pointed out to him that he'd shared very little with her other than his body.

Hang it, she wasn't far off the mark.

Helen stopped at another version of the same contraption, this one fully assembled and in working order. "What is this?"

He stalked forward at last, approaching her from behind and standing near enough to her to touch both the machine and her. Near enough to smell her and experience an aching surge of desire. He was tempted, so tempted, to sink his fingers into the silken web of her hair, pull out the pins keeping her long wavy locks tucked away. To undo the row of buttons fastening the front of her gown. To take the kiss she'd denied him earlier. But she had asked him a question, this alluring wife of his.

He cleared his throat and touched a finger to the handle on the side of the machine. "This is an Edison speaking phonograph. Have you heard of it?"

"I have, though I've never seen one myself." She turned to him, her eyes bright with excitement. "Will you show me how it works?"

The urge to kiss her grew even stronger. He forced himself to think of the machine, an inanimate object, its components. Crank and needles and diaphragm. Anything but her mouth, a sweeter color pink than her gown could ever hope to match. He fitted the conical horn to the mouthpiece on the machine, holding it in place for her. "Speak into this part here, and I will record you."

"Truly?"

He nodded, enjoying her enthusiasm even as he knew a spear of jealousy that it wasn't directed at his own work but of that of one of his greatest competitors. "Truly. Speak into the machine, and I'll play your words back for you."

Her eyes went even wider, fixated back upon him. "What shall I say?"

He could think of more than a few things, none of which seemed likely to spill from the luscious lips he couldn't stop admiring. "You may say anything at all."

"But will it be recorded forever? If it is, I'll want to say something grand. Something that isn't silly."

Maddening woman. He sighed. "Mrs. Storm, you may say anything you damn well like so long as you don't stand here all night fretting over the words without actually saying them."

Her expression changed, going mulish once more. "I've got just the thing now," she announced. "Tell me when I should begin."

He waited until she had positioned her face in the wide, open end of the horn as he'd demonstrated before turning the handle. "Be sure to say it loudly and clearly." He began turning the handle. "Now."

"Mr. Storm is the most stubborn, vexing, thoroughly arrogant man I've ever met, and his disposition is worse than a surly bear's." she announced loudly into the machine.

A startled laugh almost burst from him, but he managed to restrain himself, focusing on the task at hand. He stopped turning the crank as she stepped back, throwing him a look of sheer defiance. He might have said the same about Mrs. Storm. Indeed, he had surely thought it on more than one occasion. Perhaps they would make a fine match for each other after all, given time.

Carefully, he lifted the needle away from the tin-foil-wrapped mandrel on the machine, readjusted the cylinder back to the indentations marking the beginning of the recording, and lowered the needle into place before turning the handle once again.

"Mr. Storm is the most stubborn, vexing, thoroughly arrogant man I've ever met, and his disposition is worse than a surly bear's," her words echoed back through the workroom from the horn, in a voice that, while slightly altered by the recording medium, was undeniably hers.

"Dear heavens." She pressed a hand to her mouth and stared, first at the phonograph and then at him. "It's amazing! I daresay it's the oddest thing imaginable to have one's own words spoken again in one's own voice."

"Amazing," he agreed in a dry tone, "other than that the delicate tin foil upon which the speech is recorded doesn't withstand much repetition. If I were to replay your recording more than a handful of times, it would no longer be intelligible. I believe that a better version of this machine can be created, one with a more durable medium of recording. I've been experimenting but have yet to discover the solution."

"This is a phonograph that you've taken apart," she observed, turning back to the machine he had dismantled and running a finger down the mandrel. "Is that why you dissect things? To find out how something works so that you can improve upon it?"

How easily she read him. "I like to know how everything works. It's an odd but inescapable habit of mine. At some point, I realized that just because something already exists doesn't inherently mean that a superior version of it cannot be made. In fact, nearly everything that exists can be improved upon."

Except for her. No improvements necessary in that regard.

"At what point did you realize that?" she asked quietly.

He thought for a moment, surprised by the question. "To be honest, I'm not even certain when I first started taking things apart. There was a time when my mother had found a patron willing to give us a small rented flat to live in. I was a lad no older than five, and I found his pocket watch while he and my mother were...otherwise engaged. I had it in pieces by the time he came out of her chamber. That was the worst backhand I've ever received in my life." He rubbed his jaw, recalling all too well the shock and the pain, some thirty years later as a man fully grown with a wife and son of his own and more money than that sad son-of-a-bitch had earned in his lifetime.

"How dare he hit a small boy?" Helen's hand settled lightly over his, just for a moment, as if she could somehow lift away the pain and the memory. Apparently thinking better of it, she snatched her hand back. "Someone ought to have hit him. A man of his own size."

"It wasn't the last time a man hit me, not by a long shot." One of his mother's customers had found pleasure in abusing women. Levi had rushed to defend her after hearing her pained cries and had promptly received the worst caning of his life. Only his mother's begging and pleading had tempered the man's rage. He'd been seven then. Two years later, his mother was dead.

"I wish I could go back and find the people who would hurt a child," his wife said then, her gaze steady and searching. "I would give them an earful. Why, if someone were to abuse Theo, I'd want to see him run over by the nearest carriage."

"I'm sure they've all found their own reckoning by now anyhow." He worked very hard to keep his voice even. In truth, he never spoke of his past, and he rarely even visited it in his own mind any longer. When he did, the anxiety and the anger inevitably settled in, and there he was again, a helpless boy who loved his woefully imperfect mother, ready to take any of the pain and weight off her shoulders that he could. "That was all many years ago. My mother is long dead, God rest her soul, and I'm not that boy anymore."

Helen turned back to the table then, tracing her fingers lightly over the parts and pieces assembled there. "How old were you when your mother died?"

"I was nine," he said roughly. "Consumption took her." His relationship with his mother had never been easy. But he had loved her, and she had loved him in her way. She'd done the best she could've done for him, considering. "She's buried in a pauper's grave on Ward's Island. I tried to find her when I was older, when I had the means. I was never able. I was too naïve to realize that they don't give paupers the dignity of individual graves. They dig a trench and lay in as many bodies as they can. She has no stone, and I have nothing to remember her by, not even a lock of hair."

He didn't know why he'd confessed that to Helen just now. It was something he'd never said aloud. Not to anyone. His mother and his past were closed books, slid onto a shelf to molder into oblivion. He didn't care to take them down off the shelf, blow off the dust, re-read them.

Helen laid her hand on his arm, and it wasn't a pitying touch but one borne of compassion. "Levi, I'm so very sorry."

The fury he'd felt toward her for keeping Theo from him drifted completely away then, as a thundercloud might flit into the horizon after a brooding summer storm. Slowly, but leaving a brilliant sun in its wake. He closed his hand over hers, and the contact brought the same sensual fire to life that had always blazed between them. She sensed it too. He could see it in the way her eyes darkened, the way she tensed as though ready for flight.

Something within him shifted. Perhaps it was the glass of wine he'd had with dinner or perhaps it was her, but suddenly, the thought of her withdrawing from him seemed unbearable. He had to do something, say something, to preserve the tentative link between them.

"If I hadn't lived the life I did as a boy, I never would've been driven to be the man I am today. Having nothing makes you want something, makes you want to become someone." His thumb rubbed a lazy circle over the top of her hand, savoring even this smallest of connections. "What do you wish to know, Helen? Earlier, you accused me of only sharing my bed with you and not telling you anything of import. Ask what you want of me now, and I'll tell you."

Her expression remained guarded but also became pensive. She tilted her head, considering him for a moment in that patent way she had, seeing—so he thought—all of him, even the parts he would prefer to hide. "What is your middle given name?" she asked.

Levi almost laughed. He hadn't expected a question so simplistic. "Zachary. I was born in an election year, and my mother wasn't very original. What is your middle name?" Zachary Taylor, a national war hero, had been elected president in the year of his birth. Levi had not lived up to his namesake, though he'd done his duty.

"I thought you were the one answering questions." She gave no quarter, even if she hadn't yet pulled away from him.

His thumb traveled to the delicate bones of her wrist, tracing with the lightest touch to the stitches on her sleeve. Damnation, he had missed her. Her skin felt like heaven to him. "Forgive me, Mrs. Storm. Continue your interview."

Her pulse beat fast against his thumb, indicating she was not as calm as she appeared, but she nevertheless didn't move away from him. "You told me before that Miss VanHorn's father was your greatest investor. Did he withdraw his investment from your business when you didn't marry his daughter?"

He shouldn't have been surprised that her sharp wit had made the connection. "Yes, he did. Our agreement was not contingent upon my marrying his daughter, but it did contain a clause allowing him to withdraw his investment whether or not the withdrawal was for cause."

"And yet you also said that your company was in need of funds before you went to Paris, and you were still engaged to Miss VanHorn at that time. How did you manage?"

He was well aware that most men in his acquaintance—Jesse Whitney being perhaps the only exception—would not allow their wives to pry into their affairs or question their business. Most men didn't think it a woman's place. But Levi had been raised by a strong woman, a woman who had earned a living in one of the worst ways imaginable to try to keep him from the poorhouse, who had tried to take the caning for him that long ago day. He wasn't most men, and neither was he afraid of a strong woman.

His thumb slid beneath the thick cuff of her sleeve now, his fingers in a loose grasp on her wrist, holding her to him as long as she allowed it. "I sold nearly all of my real estate holdings. Everything but this house and my house on Fifth Avenue in Manhattan. I decided that risking just about everything I possess on a business I know will succeed was worth more to me than the price I had to pay for the VanHorn money."

"Yet you married me so easily, with nothing to gain except Theo's legitimacy."

"With everything to gain," he corrected before he could think better of his words.

She withdrew her hand at last. He had pressed his luck too far. "What is everything?"

"You and Theo." The answer was instant, straight from the very depths of his admittedly black soul. She thought his money and his business were all he cared for, but she couldn't be more wrong. "The both of you are everything to me, and the rest of it, all of this—" he waved his hand to encompass his workshop, its contents, and the entire house—"could disappear tomorrow for all I care. I'd start again, rebuild everything, with my wife and my son by my side."

Helen stared at him, and he wished to God that he could see inside her in that instant, read her thoughts. She shook her head slowly. "You don't mean that."

But he did. He meant it more than he'd ever meant anything in his life. He hadn't understood just how powerful their bond was until that moment when he realized that everything he had worked a lifetime to achieve—the wealth, the standing in elite New York City society, the patents, the businesses, the homes—it all paled in comparison to the sensation of at last being anchored in the world, of belonging. He was an orphan no more. He had a wife, a son. A family. Money couldn't buy something so precious. Shouldn't buy something so precious.

"I mean it, Helen." He stepped toward her. "Hang it, I mean it as surely as I stand before you."

"What has changed for you so suddenly?" Her brow furrowed. "How can you make such protestations when only a week ago, you threatened to take him from me and leave me here alone?"

"I was angry," he admitted. Angry, and too thick-headed to think straight. He might be adept at learning the inner workings of all manner of machines, but he sure as hell didn't know what to do with finer emotions.

"Victoria," she said suddenly. "My middle given name is Victoria, after the queen." She skirted a table, putting a wooden expanse cluttered with components and half-deconstructed objects between them. The electric lights bathed her in an otherworldly glow. "Thank you for the demonstration. It's been most edifying, but I fear I've been away from Theo too long. He's likely quite hungry and I daresay I ought to go."

He'd offered to hire a wet nurse and she had refused. She was fierce and protective when it came to Theo, and he hadn't a doubt as to how much she loved their son. While he was loath to see her go, Theo came first, even if Levi suspected Helen's urge to flee was more inspired by the direction of their conversation than by her need to return to their son's cradle. It hadn't even been two hours since they'd first gone down to dinner.

Edifying, she had said. Yes indeed, their time had proven most edifying, but not in the detached, passionless manner she suggested. She had burned for him once, and she would again, he vowed.

First, however, he would allow her to retreat, for now. He inclined his head to her. "Should you ever want another demonstration, you know where to find me."

But he wasn't just talking about phonograph demonstrations, and they both knew it.

Chapter Fourteen

ELEN WOKE TO THE URGENT CRIES of her hungry son. She rose from bed in the chill night air wearing nothing but her nightgown before scooping him up into her arms. Levi had seen to every detail of Theo's nursery, but Helen had not been able to leave him in another chamber for the night just yet. For all his life, he had lain in a crib by her bedside. She could hear his breathing and rustling and rest easy in the knowledge that he was always within reach.

Theo continued to wail as she struggled to find her way in the darkness of her new surroundings. Levi's dynamo was shut down for the evening, meaning his hundreds of bright electric lights wouldn't work again until tomorrow. The convenience was a novel one, but perhaps needed some refining. What had Levi said? *Nearly everything that exists can be improved upon.*

Yes, so too his electricity. Not that she missed the odorous gaslights, but she'd always had a dreadful time seeing in the dark. She had an oil lamp somewhere at hand, but of course she couldn't find it now when she needed it most.

"Drat," she muttered, feeling blindly for the table. Her toe connected solidly with another piece of furniture and she cried out, which startled Theo enough to make him keen even more vehemently. Perhaps she ought to simply toe her way back to the bed and burrow into the warm cocoon of blankets to feed him rather than sit in her customary chair.

Suddenly, the door connecting her chamber to Levi's was thrown open. The warm glow of a hand lamp filtered into the murky chamber as her husband strode into the room, his expression one of alarm.

"What are you doing in here?" she demanded, at once painfully aware that he wore nothing more than a pair of drawers he'd slapped on in a hurry. The placket was unbuttoned at his waist, and his taut abdomen and muscled chest were stunning in the soft light. His body was every bit as strong and rigidly defined as she'd recalled. For a moment she couldn't help but stare, drinking in the sight of him, masculine and glorious, his battle scar dark and proud on his arm. An answering ache blossomed deep within her, undeterred by the wailing infant in her arms and the fact that she had insisted their marriage be chaste.

"The baby is crying," he said, sounding concerned. "What is amiss? Where the hell is his nurse?"

"His nurse is dismissed for the evening. I've no need of her, and nothing is amiss." Levi was plainly unaccustomed to hungry babies who woke in the night. Helen hadn't had a good night of rest in months. "Theo's hungry, that is all, and he's possessed of a rather foul humor when he's suffering from an empty belly." She offered their wailing son to him. "Take him, would you please, until I get settled?"

He took Theo into the crook of his open arm without hesitating before setting his lamp on a table and patting their wailing son's bottom. She stared for a moment at the intimate picture he presented, bareback and cradling their child. Some men wanted precious little to do with their children, believing they belonged in the nursery or with their mothers or nurses at all times. Not Levi. He had taken to being a father with an instant ease that didn't fail to touch her heart. Theo calmed down in his arms, his cries subsiding.

How had she ever thought to keep father and son from knowing each other? From this special bond they already shared? She had been wrong not to tell him, she acknowledged to herself. She should have sent word to him, regardless of her pride.

"You're a good father, Levi." The words tumbled from her mouth before she could think better of them. It was late, she was tired, and their earlier camaraderie was doing odd things to her senses, she was sure of it.

He looked up at her, seemingly startled by her praise. "Thank you."

She felt suddenly awkward, standing there with empty arms as he deftly coddled their son in his swaddling. The cold evening air made her shiver. Levi's eyes trapped hers, bringing back a flood of unwelcome memories and feelings. She turned away from him and retrieved a dressing gown, stuffing her arms into the sleeves with precious little grace.

"You're a good mother as well, Helen." His voice was low, scarcely audible above the rustling of fabric.

She stilled, her back to him, her defenses against him sagging. It was her lack of sleep, she told herself, coupled with the newness of her situation. She'd lived a quiet life for nearly a year, working alongside the ladies at her House of Rest, learning a deep appreciation for the mass of servants she'd spent her life taking for granted as they toiled below stairs. There had been no electric lights, no lovely ceramic water closets. There had been chamber pots, tapers and oil, scrubbing with the cheapest soap to be had until her hands turned raw and red, cracked open and bleeding. There had been cold nights with no fire in the grate, stand-up washes rather than tub baths, there'd been learning to cook and clean and black a range.

And yes, there had been nights when she'd asked herself if she hadn't made the greatest mistake of her life, choosing to raise her beloved son on her own. He had deserved more than she'd been able to provide him. But she loved him, loved him with a ferocity that she'd never before experienced. Loved him so much she would do anything, even sacrifice her pride and her future, binding herself forever to a man who didn't love her. She mustn't mistake Levi's fatherly doting for anything more than what it was.

"I try to be a good mother." She wasn't sure she could express her gratitude to him, not now for fear of breaking down before him. Her emotions were still in a jumble. Cleo and Tia had told her it was common for a woman to feel at sixes and sevens after childbirth. But these days, she nearly turned into a watering pot at the slightest provocation. She hardly knew what was wrong with her. "I'm not sure that I always have been."

"I'm sure you have. I don't doubt that for an instant."

She turned back to him, wanting to be at odds, to create conflict so that she wouldn't long for him quite so much. "I kept him from you."

"I can't say I blame you," he shocked her by admitting. "In your shoes, I think I may well have done the same. I'm not perfect, Helen. Sometimes, I'm wrong. Sometimes, I make mistakes. I'm only a man, humble before you, hoping for a second chance."

A second chance? Dear God, where had that come from? He'd said nothing of it before now. He'd agreed to a chaste union, a marriage in name only, and he had seemed more than willing to comply. He hadn't even tried to kiss her when they married. She wouldn't say she was disappointed he hadn't, not even in her own mind. And the mere thought of opening her heart to him again, of allowing him back into her life as he'd been before, back into her bed…it was enough to make her dizzy.

She didn't know how to respond to him, so she decided to leave his words hanging in the air as she sat in a plush, upholstered chair and propped a pillow in her lap. She simply didn't say anything at all. She made a great show of arranging everything properly, feeling his hot stare upon her with each move she made. He expected something from her, though just what that was, she couldn't determine. Indeed, she didn't know if she had aught to give anyway.

"There now," she said at last, her throat thick with an emotion she didn't care to examine. "I'm ready for him."

Levi brought Theo to her, relinquishing him gently to her waiting arms. Theo turned his head toward her, instantly rooting. Her cheeks went hot as she met Levi's gaze. "Some privacy, Mr. Storm?" She adopted a deliberately formal air to combat their partial state of undress and his presence in her chamber this late at night. There had been an unmistakable air of change between them earlier in his workshop, and it remained there now, lingering as surely as his touch had branded her wrist. It made her terribly uneasy. She couldn't deny that she was as drawn to him as ever. His mere touch had set her pulse racing earlier. In the warm glow of light now, his body was a sleek reminder of how much pleasure he could bring her. How much she had missed him. How much, even now, she loved and wanted him.

"Please," she forced herself to say when he remained, allowing her to gawp her fill, as though she'd never see a man before, as though she'd never seen him before. But she had, and all she needed to do was close her eyes to remember every gorgeous bit of him.

He gave her a formal half bow then, his gaze boring into hers. "Mrs. Storm, forgive me for the intrusion. Good night." As though they were strangers, or mere acquaintances meeting in a drawing room. As though they'd never shared a smoldering passion that had changed everything for the both of them and redefined who and what they were.

But perhaps it was for the best.

She watched him go, the light he'd left behind for her

use casting its golden radiance over the hard planes of his back. Desire stirred through her again, thick and jarring and most unwelcome. The moment the door closed, she unfastened her robe and nightdress brought Theo to her breast, effectively quashing any such feelings.

It was certainly better that they remain polite and aloof to each other. There could be nothing more for them. She was too fearful to go back down that road with Levi ever again. The last time had nearly been her undoing. She couldn't trust him, she reminded herself. He was yet a stranger to her in so many ways, a stranger who dissected watches and machines, and was at turns cool and angry and forbidding, who had deceived her and broken her heart.

But another voice inside her reminded her that he had also once brought her scones in bed and kissed her senseless during a ball. He was also the man who held their son as though he was the most precious and wondrous being he had ever beheld. He was the man who had worked hard to achieve success and wealth after beginning his life in poverty, who had never known a father and yet bestowed unparalleled adoration upon Theo, who had been beaten as a child and still touched her with reverence. He was also the man who believed that everything could be made better. The man who probably believed that *they* could somehow be made better, their jagged pieces fitting back together again.

But she was too afraid to hope for that. Reasonable Helen had been at the reins for quite some time, and she wasn't ready to relinquish her place. So she promptly told the other, far too persistent voice—foolish Helen—to go to the devil.

He wanted his wife with a desperation that was fast becoming as pathetic as it was distracting. Levi had spent the night tossing and turning in his bed, thinking of Helen separated from him by nothing more than a door and a layer of cotton that was cheap as a Waterbury Watch. Of course she was still wearing her homespun weeds and not a stitch of the expensive French confections he'd provided her. She didn't want his money. She didn't want him.

Damn it all to hell.

He splashed water on his face and stared at his reflection in the mirror. Probably, he ought to shave today. But he'd had precious little sleep and if he looked the part of the barbarian he was beginning to feel he was on the inside, perhaps she'd take pity on him. Or perhaps she'd continue to keep her cool, polite distance. And it wasn't her charity he wanted after all, was it?

Either way, he was still a businessman, and he had work to do while he remained in London. He finished his morning ablutions and began dressing. As he buttoned up his waistcoat, a thought struck him. He strode to the door connecting his chamber to Helen's and rapped upon it, barely waiting to hear her bid him entry before sweeping inside.

Early morning light sluiced into the large windows where Helen sat at a desk, taking tea and reading her correspondence. Her eyes were upon him, homing in with an intensity that cut him straight to the bone. Her curls were pinned up, and she was buttoned to the throat in one of her plain gowns—this one an unsightly gray—but the force of her loveliness hit him square in the chest just the same. He almost stopped to stare, drink her in, this deity he had somehow wed.

"Good morning, Mrs. Storm," he said instead, not halting until he was at her side and the faint scent of her teased him. "How did you find your sleep?"

She stood, her expression wary and otherwise unreadable. How he longed to pull her against him, to kiss the soft skin of her neck above that stiff collar, to catch the luscious lobe of her ear between his teeth and bite.

As if she could sense the base direction of his thoughts,

she clasped her hands firmly together at her waist, a shield of sorts. "Good morning to you, Mr. Storm. I slept very well, thank you."

She waited politely for him to reveal the reason for his abrupt invasion of her territory. Perhaps she was that eager for him to leave her to her letters and her cooling tea. Very well. He had earned her aloofness, her disdain, her mistrust. But he would earn back everything he'd lost. He would peel away the layers she'd built in his absence and find the Helen he'd known before. That Helen was still there, beating within her like a heart.

He clenched his fingers at his sides to keep from touching her. "I have a meeting scheduled for this morning, a very important meeting that I believe will change a great deal for North Atlantic Electric. It will change a great deal for all the world, in time."

"Oh? That sounds like a very important meeting indeed." Her tone was noncommittal.

"I want you to attend the meeting," he announced, then thought better of his delivery. "If it would please you." Somewhere along the way, he'd grown unaccustomed to asking permission. For her, he would relearn it.

Her surprise reflected on her suddenly expressive face. "You wish me to attend?"

He smiled. "Yes." And he did. He wasn't merely inviting her because he wanted to win back her trust and respect. He was including her because she was intelligent and interested, and because it had occurred to him that she wasn't so very different from him. *I wanted to rely on myself alone*, she'd said to him. And she had done so. She was not just good and kind, his Helen. She was also capable and brave and daring, and those were all qualities he sought from the people he chose to employ. Brave and daring people changed the world. They always had, and they always would.

"Why should you want me there?" she asked, her clasped hands tightening until her knuckles turned white.

He couldn't resist catching those linked hands in his

then, raising them to his lips for a kiss. Just one, and fleeting. "I believe you might find it interesting. I respect your opinion, Helen. You have a keen mind."

Her cheeks warmed. A small smile tipped the corners of her mouth before she pressed her lips together to stop it from blooming in full. She didn't tug her hands away from him, however, and he noted that small victory with satisfaction.

"Won't your business associates find it odd to have a woman in their midst?"

Perhaps, but if he spent much time fretting over the opinions of others, he wouldn't even walk out the door in the mornings. He certainly never would have pursued electricity, a concept that the masses had initially found as perplexing and foreign as Greek gods. "Hang them. I don't care if they do. I want you there, if you want to be there, that is."

For Helen's sake, he was making an effort to be less demanding. Arrogant, she had called him. With a temperament worse than a surly bear. Like the machines he dissected and reassembled, her opinion of him too could be made better. He was doing his damnedest.

"Very well," she agreed. "I will join you, Mr. Storm."

Theo began rustling and cooing in his bassinet, announcing that he'd risen from his morning nap. Levi kissed Helen's hands again. "Thank you, Mrs. Storm."

While he was tempted to linger, draw her close, nibble her ear, lick the pulse beating at her throat, he did not. He wouldn't press her. He had a lifetime to do penance, to make her realize he was worthy enough to be her husband, to be by her side. So instead, he crossed the room to pick up his son, who blinked up at him like an owl. His cherubic cheeks gave him the look of a Renaissance angel.

"Good morning to you, Mr. Storm," he said to Theo, staring down proudly into blue eyes that matched his own. His chest felt full. Near to bursting. This was what he'd been missing his entire life, what he'd been pursuing in every business deal and real estate purchase, in every invention he'd chased, every technology he'd attempted to recreate, every machine he'd tried to understand. It had been this feeling of humbling, all-encompassing…love.

Levi stilled, looking at his son, this miniature version of himself and Helen melded into one. Yes, damn it, love. He'd been wrong about what he'd felt before, when he'd made love with Helen, and yesterday on the carriage ride following their marriage. It hadn't been contentment at all. It had been love. Pure and true. Genuine and real. Jesus, how had he failed to realize it? How had he failed them all so utterly?

If he hadn't been so damn stupid, so blind, he would have never let Helen walk out of his office and out of his life that day. He would have ignored his pride and followed her to the bowels of hell to convince her to marry him. He wouldn't have learned of his son's existence from a letter. Helen wouldn't have lived a year in hiding, working her fingers raw and selling off her belongings. She wouldn't have had to be alone. Hang it, he had wronged her. Badly.

I'll make it up to her and you both, he promised his son with his eyes as he ran a finger down his plump cheek, not daring to say the words aloud. *I'll make this right.*

Theo rewarded him with a large, toothless grin, and that was all the endorsement he needed.

"This, Mr. Storm, Mr. Stillwell, my lady, is our secondary generator," announced the well-dressed, bearded man before her in a German-tinged accent. If either Mr. Gebhart or his confederate, the taller and slightly built Mr. Young, found her presence at their meeting with her husband odd, they hadn't indicated. Not even a flaring of the eyes, no protestation. These were men of science, she supposed, so excited by their work that they cared not who their audience may be. Either that or they were intelligent enough to realize that a woman's mind was worthy of respect and attention.

Preferably the latter.

Mr. Stillwell, Levi's man of business, was also present for the congregation being held in the workroom where Levi had recently demonstrated the phonograph for her. Helen had spent so much of her life being excluded that it rather startled her to find herself being spoken to directly, to be not just present at this meeting but included. As if she—her opinion—mattered. It was gratifying.

Helen stared at the contraption laid out on the table before her. Mounted to mahogany wood, it appeared to be little more than a lump of metal coils and rods with wires springing from it. The idea that this object could somehow perform feats beyond her ken fascinated her. "What does it do?"

"It transforms electrical voltage by stepping it up or stepping it down," Levi told her. "This will make it possible to transmit power a great distance by stepping down high voltages before they reach their end user. No longer will our ability to electrify homes and factories and train stations be reliant upon individual dynamos as they are now. With the secondary generator, one powerful station can do the work of many."

Electricity, like her husband, remained a bewitching mystery to Helen. How could a conglomeration of metal and wood propose to change the world? She looked from the second generator to Levi. His gaze was upon her, unflinching and so warm that she had to look away. He had looked at her as if…as if she were someone precious to him. As if she were someone he cared for deeply.

Impossible. Silliness on her part. Foolish Helen attempting to retake control. She turned her attention back to the safety of the inventors and their wood and metal machine.

Mr. Gebhart nodded, his mustache twitching. "Just so, Mr. Storm. While our secondary generator is by no means the first of its kind, we are certain that it is the best. Moreover, it's the first that will make it possible to distribute electricity for industrial use. The secondary generator allows us to harness the power of alternating current and step it down before use, which in turn renders alternating current the ideal form of electricity. With the secondary generator, direct current method will be replaced by alternating current in very little time. Mr. Edison's machines will become a thing of the past."

"And North Atlantic Electric will make all of that possible, once you grant us your patent rights," Levi concluded.

Mr. Stillwell didn't appear quite as enthused as the other occupants of the room. He pushed his spectacles up the bridge of his nose, fidgeted with them a moment, before removing them altogether and frowning. "But there is inherent danger in the use of alternating current. What were to happen if the consumer touched the wrong component? Would he not be electrocuted?"

"I'm pleased you asked," chimed in Mr. Young. "The principle circuit that supplies the secondary generator is closed at the limits, meaning that any component the consumer might touch would not possess enough volts to be a danger."

"Just last year, our secondary generator featured in an exhibition using alternating current at the London Aquarium," Mr. Gebhart added. "We powered over a thousand Swan lamps."

"I saw the exhibition," Mr. Stillwell said simply in a tone that made it clear he hadn't been impressed.

"Eddy requires some convincing, I'm afraid, gentlemen," Levi said easily. "I see the potential for your secondary generator with some adaptation on our part."

Mr. Stillwell removed his spectacles and blinked. "Convincing is not quite apt. I'm not sure I can be convinced."

"Surely you can see the benefit?" Mr. Young asked. "The greatest hindrance to electricity is the question of transmission to a great distance. With this issue effectively minimalized, electricity will flourish so that one day, every dwelling in England and indeed all the world will be electrified."

Electrified. Helen liked that word. It was the way Levi made her feel. Then and now.

"What say you, Mrs. Storm?" Levi asked, startling her out of her reverie.

She stared at her husband, not sure what he was asking her, if his question was as simple as it pretended to be or if a deeper meaning dwelled within it. She thought carefully for a moment. "I've always believed that potential is a worthy investment, Mr. Storm. I don't pretend to know all there is to know about electricity. Indeed, I daresay I find electricity a rather baffling conundrum. However, it seems to me that if this secondary generator does what Mr. Gebhart and Mr. Young propose it does, it would indeed create the opportunity for exponential growth, not only for you and your business, but for the entire world."

He smiled, his gaze even warmer than before. It did things to her, that gaze. He did things to her. Wilted her resistance. But she must not allow him to do that.

"Well, gentlemen," he turned his attention to Gebhart and Young. "It seems my wife is a believer, and I trust her judgment above all else. Do you know there isn't currently an alternating current machine being built in America at all?"

"None?" Mr. Gebhart seemed baffled by this revelation.

"Not one," Levi answered, sounding rather pleased. "We will be the first to revolutionize the field there. I've been reading a great deal about the alternating current machines designed and tested both here and abroad, and I'm convinced this is the future of our industry. Eddy, what do you say?"

Mr. Stillwell made a great show of extracting a handkerchief from his waistcoat and polishing his spectacles before answering. "I remain unconvinced."

"Unconvinced? Sir, there can be no question of the

validity of our secondary generator. Direct current will find its replacement in alternating current, given time." Mr. Young was passionate in his belief, his entire being radiating as he spoke, with vehement sentiment. Rather like a leaf in a violent spring wind.

"Eddy is my chief engineer," Levi told Young and Gebhart in a conciliatory fashion. "A genius among men. We will win him over, gentlemen. Thank you for this presentation today. Please, think about what you'd be willing to accept for American patent rights and have your attorney convey the offer to mine."

Eddy smiled thinly. "I trust your price will be commensurate with the amount of work that will need to go into this on our part. As constructed, this secondary generator cannot be mass produced. It will require a great deal of modifications and experimentation on the part of North Atlantic Electric."

Helen wondered for a moment if Eddy was intentionally acting as a counterbalance to Levi so that together they could manage a fair price for the American patent rights. This was the first time she had ever witnessed Levi truly in his element. Even at the *Beacon* offices, he had not been so thoroughly in command, so incorruptibly powerful. Witnessing him in action, she couldn't help but to be impressed. He was not only incredibly intelligent but he was also persuasive. He had something…not the polished wax of charm but an undeniable pull that was as indefinable as it was infectious. He came to life. And she could well understand how he had been so successful, how he had amassed so much at such a relatively young age.

It occurred to her then that she didn't even know how old he was. Five-and-thirty? Six-and-thirty? He was the father of her child. Her husband. And how little, still, she knew of him. She yearned to know more.

"We will confer and have our lawyer contact yours," Mr. Gebhart said.

"Thank you," Young added, looking a bit awestruck as

he shook Levi's hand. "It's an honor, sir, for you to consider our work. I've long been a student of your innovations, and I'm a humble admirer."

Levi gave the younger man a half smile. "Thank you, Mr. Young. I trust I will hear from you soon?"

"Yes, indeed." Mr. Young nodded. "Yes, indeed, Mr. Storm."

Chapter Fifteen

ELEN FIDDLED WITH THE SOUP COURSE, doing her best to look anywhere but upon her husband. They were seated uncomfortably near to each other, the only two at the dining table and indeed, in the very room, now that he had just dismissed the attending servants.

"You don't care for the soup, Mrs. Storm?" he asked idly, his deep voice cutting through the heavy silence that reigned following the departing servants.

She dragged her gaze to meet his with reluctance. Looking at him was dangerous. Looking at him tested her resolve. He was dressed as impeccably as ever. He had treated her as politely as ever on their way down to dinner. And he radiated the same magnetism as ever. One could not look upon him in his black evening clothes, his hair a bit too long for fashion, his whiskers darkening his strong jaw, those molded lips that called for sin—*Helen* could not look upon him, drat it—without wanting him and wishing that their marriage could be different.

"I can call for the next course," he added. His gaze warm

and unsettling, burning into her. "I stole Chef Dubois from the Duke of Something, reckoning that he ought to have the best. But perhaps not?"

Helen almost smiled at his revelation. "I'm afraid I'm unfamiliar with the Duke of Something, so I cannot speak for the quality of his retainers."

Levi gave her one of his rare grins that put his dimples on full display, and a familiar feeling of longing unfurled in her stomach. His charm was downright diabolical when he chose to apply it. "Forgive me. As an untutored American, I find your English ways perplexing at times. But it stands to reason that a duke ought to have the best chef money can afford, does it not?"

Her lips twitched and she forced herself to look back at her soup. "I suppose it depends upon the duke in question. I daresay the Duke of Something might not necessarily have the finest meals awaiting him at table."

"I'll consult my *Debrett's* at the next opportunity." His tone was wry. "To hell with *The Electrical World* and *Engineering.*"

A chuckle escaped her. She pressed her fingers to her lips, silencing any further mirth. She didn't want to laugh with him. She didn't want to allow him to stalk through her defenses like some omnipotent, invading marauder. Most importantly, she didn't want to remember how much she had enjoyed his company, how much she had reveled in dueling wits with him. He had a sharp mind that she very much admired. But he had also hurt her, and she must not forget that. He'd been very good at making her forget these last few days, and she knew she needed to put an end to the thawing of their mutual ice. For her own sake.

"Perhaps it would do you good to expand your reading," she said lightly, plunking her spoon back into her soup with an appalling lack of grace. He was distracting her, making her clumsy. Rattling her.

"Undoubtedly." His tone remained warm, agreeable and intimate all at once. Dangerous. "Helen?"

She stilled, looking at her hand's tense clench upon her soup spoon. "Yes?"

"Will you not look at me?" Soft, this question, more dangerous than ever.

Helen bit her lip. "Shall I look at you whilst I eat my soup, Mr. Storm? Would you have me dribble it all over my bodice?"

"You aren't eating the damn soup, and don't think I haven't noticed. Besides, if you dribbled soup on your bodice, it would likely be looked upon as an improvement. An adornment, as it were, to that drab confection you've chosen to wear."

His criticism of her dress had her pinning him with a challenging stare. "There is nothing wrong with my dress. Ruby worked quite hard on it, I'll have you know."

"There is nothing wrong with that dress if a washerwoman were to wear it. But a gown that ugly on a woman as undeniably beautiful as you is a crime, particularly when you have a wardrobe overflowing with some of the finest gowns a man can readily acquire with little notice and vague measurements." His gaze slipped briefly to her mouth. "Do you not wear the dresses I bought you to spite me? Is it a show of pride, or is your disgust for me that great?"

Ha! If only she harbored disgust for him. But even her anger and disillusionment were beginning to fade. Even her hurt. Her traitorous heart had not stopped loving him, this ingenious man who had made millions from nothing, who reinvented the world around him, who took apart everything in an effort to make it better than it once had been. Who was so handsome, who kissed so wickedly, who had brought her body to life in ways she'd never dreamt possible. This man who had taught her that she was worthy, that she was strong, and that she deserved more from him than he'd once been willing to give.

He had given her something. She was his wife, and he treated her as an equal partner. But was it too late? Was a license and a ring enough to heal all that had happened between them? The woman she'd become in his absence couldn't be sure. And so she clung to this new identity she'd crafted for herself, the woman who didn't need silk Worth gowns or ballrooms or a title and servants. The woman who didn't need her husband to try to earn back her respect with his unimaginable wealth and charisma.

"I've told you already that I won't be bought," she told him curtly. "Dresses are not reparations."

His closed fist hit the table, rattling the silverware and the glasses. "What would be reparations, Helen? Tell me, damn it, and I'll do it. Whatever you need, whatever you want."

"I need and want nothing. The time has passed for what I needed and wanted." Bitterness laced her voice. "You cannot undo what has already been done."

"I'm not a god, Helen." He rubbed his jaw, gorgeous even in his anger. "I'm a man. I was wrong. Hang it, if I could travel back in time and heal these wounds between us, I damn well would."

"But you cannot, and so here we are, two strangers trapped in a room and a marriage both."

"You have that wrong, my dear." The charm had quite fled his features and now he looked hard, impassive as granite. "We aren't strangers, nor are we trapped. Maybe you've forgotten just how well I know you. I can remind you, if you'd like."

His suggestion shouldn't have sent a frisson of desire through her, but it did. She shook the feeling away. "I'm different now. I'm not the woman you knew before." Indeed, for all that the last year had been hard on her, she had also become a more potent version of herself. Perhaps she'd needed to do so, all along.

"I'm not the man you knew before either." His eyes were cutting in their brilliance. "You aren't the only one capable of change, of seeing wrong and attempting to make it right. Or are you so determined to cast me as the villain of this piece that you can't even for a moment see that I'm doing my best to atone for my sins?"

That was not fair. How did he think he could so easily erase the damage he'd done? "By buying me fripperies and demonstrating how to use a talking machine?"

"A phonograph." He stood so abruptly that his chair flew back. "No, Mrs. Storm." He stalked to her, catching her elbows and hauling her from her seat in one fluid motion until she was pressed against his chest. Their noses nearly brushed. The scent of him, soap and musk and so very masculine, teased her. His sensual mouth tightened in a grim line, his jaw rigid. His eyes snapped fire. "I bought you the dresses because you're wearing rags. I showed you how to use the phonograph because I thought you'd enjoy the novelty. And I'm exercising restraint right now because you required a chaste marriage. I could have denied your wishes, demanded my marital rights. What would you have done, Helen? Refused my hand and continued to live the life of penitential pauper?"

She cursed the heat that skipped through her at his touch and his proximity, at the sight of that tempting mouth so close to hers. "I was living the life you left me to live," she shot back at him.

"The life you chose," he countered, his hands traveling to her waist. "Don't pretend you didn't have a hand in any of this. You, my dear, are not a saint though it certainly pleases you to play one."

No, she was not a saint. He was right about that. Because a saint would not be so tempted. A saint would never have allowed him to kiss her the first time. A saint would never have welcomed him into her bed. Would not want him there even now. She was all too human.

"I never claimed to be a saint," she said coolly, maintaining her poise by sheer will as he trailed his fingers over her cheekbone then, the touch so light she wanted to lean into it, rub against him like a cat seeking to be pet.

Good God, she truly was pathetic.

"Not tonight." His voice was low, seducing as his touch. His hand stopped above her madly beating heart, a scant few layers of cotton keeping her bare skin from him. "Tonight, you are a witch rather than a saint."

He had touched her thus before, what seemed like forever ago now. That night, he had brought her body to life beneath his wicked mouth and knowing fingers. He had been tender and gentle, had shown her pleasure, had broken her free of the dark fears of her past.

It required a formidable amount of willpower not to arch her back and force her breast into his waiting palm. She would not bend, would not melt for him. Her heart remained too bruised and sore to trust him again. "What do you want, then, Levi? Will you atone for your sins by forcing me to give you your marital rights?"

He stiffened. "I would never force you."

She met his gaze, unflinching. "Then what is it you're seeking to do? You agreed to my terms."

Levi lowered his head, bringing them together so that his breath drew across her lips like a brand. Desire was a slow and steady wave, drowning her from the inside. He was going to take the kiss she'd denied him at their wedding. She longed to wind her arms around his neck, bring their mouths together, taste him on her tongue.

"We both know it wouldn't be force, Helen." He rubbed his thumb over her lower lip once, twice. "I could take you right now, here on this table, if I wanted." Three times. "And you'd beg me for it."

He was right, damn him. She wanted to hold on to her anger. She was clawing at it with desperation inside, a mantle that could protect her from further heartache at his skillful hands. But it was slipping away, sliding like a scrap of silk ribbon to the floor, leaving her vulnerable and exposed. Her lips parted. His hand cupped her jaw as though she were a delicate bloom, something to savor. His thumb traced her lip a fourth time, teasing, taunting. His other hand tightened on her waist, a possessive grip she liked far too much.

She gave in to her weakness and nipped at his thumb with her teeth before sucking the pad to quell the sting. He inhaled, his eyes darkening. He was not any more in control in this game they played than she. "I wouldn't have to beg," she whispered.

"No." His smile was forbidding, intense. "You wouldn't have to beg, sweetheart. But I would take great pleasure in making you."

His wicked words sent a thrill straight to her core. "You couldn't make me," she lied. Of course he could. One touch of his mouth to any part of her body, and she'd likely be hitching up her skirts. She had no control when it came to him, no hope to resist him. She never had.

"Shall we test that? Right here, Helen. Right now." His fingers sank into her hair then, sending pins raining to the floor. Curls slipped from the intricate coils her lady's maid had used to tame the unruly skeins. He tipped her head back. "Dare me."

Everything within her, all the pent-up desire, the love, the frustration, every stinging bit of it clamored for her to do as he challenged. To dare him, give in to the mad passion that threatened to consume her. But pride was an unrelenting beast, and so too was a wounded heart.

"I told you that I'll not share your bed, and I meant those words." She forced herself to say it, to remind them both. The old hurts ran too deep.

He released her, the motion jerky, abrupt. "Let down your goddamn walls, Helen. Or are you too afraid of what might happen if you do?"

Of course she was afraid. She was terrified of the way he made her feel, of how close he could bring her to unraveling. They stared at each other for a moment of charged silence. "You built these walls, not me," she said at last.

"Then I will dismantle them. One by one. However I must." He tipped up her chin, seeing far too much, it seemed, with that piercing gaze of his. "I'll do it, wife. Don't think I won't."

246

Levi sank his tired body into the deep, porcelain imperial bath he'd shipped from New York City for just this purpose. He had one identical to it in his Fifth Avenue home, in a bathroom that was easily three times the size of this one. He'd had the best company in the city design and plan his bathrooms, perfecting the layout, making the best use of the space. His Fifth Avenue home held a separate bath for his suites and another for his wife's suites, prepared at the time for Miss VanHorn's comfort. In Belgravia, he had made do with one bathroom shared between the master and mistress's suites, supposing that Miss VanHorn would never accompany him on London business trips.

But life had changed considerably since those plans, and now it wasn't Miss VanHorn he shared a bathroom with in Belgravia but Helen. His Helen, a woman who was equal parts angel and spitfire. The woman whose trust he'd spent the last fortnight attempting to regain.

He sighed and rested his head on the rim of the tub, closing his eyes. He had begun a slow and steady assault on her defenses. He'd been attentive and courteous. He joined her for every dinner. He stopped commenting upon her refusal to wear the gowns he'd given her. He sent a small army of staff to assist her at her House of Rest. He'd even decided to stay in England for a spell, to allow her to acclimate to the change ahead of her.

And she had remained impervious. Unmoving. When he tried to touch her, she withdrew. She was polite but cold. Present but not. Hang it, he was trapped in a prison of his own making, the woman he loved just a chamber away and yet, it seemed, somehow always out of reach.

The water of his bath was hot. A pleasant luxury, hot water, one he never did without these days. His bathroom in New York City was a true marvel. Plumbed pipes, a bidet, an imperial bath fashioned of porcelain and mahogany, a foot bath, water closet, and a wash stand with hand-painted Italian tiles and electric lights. But what the hell did he care? Once, these trappings, as Helen had called them, had made him feel as though he belonged to a world that had seemed so far out of reach in his youth. They'd made him feel important. They had even seemed, somehow, necessary.

Not any longer. He would settle for his warm bath, but all he truly wanted was his wife to look upon him as she once had. All he wanted was her kisses freely given, her hands on him of her own accord, her body beneath his because she couldn't bear to go another night without him.

That didn't seem likely. His wife was frosty as Wenham Lake ice. Perhaps the damage he'd done was irreversible. Perhaps she needed time. Either way, he'd reached a grim realization. He needed to give her a choice.

"Oh dear, I'm so sorry."

The dismayed voice had him opening his eyes and sitting up at attention, rivulets of warm water running down his back. Helen stood on the threshold in a dressing gown, her hair unbound, a wild net of curls tumbling around her shoulders. Her eyes went wide, her hand pressed to her heart. She took a step in retreat.

"I hadn't realized you were in here," she said. "That is, I thought you were asleep." Her hands went to the door, ready to snap it closed, sever the small link of intimacy between them before it could even begin.

"Wait," he called out softly. "Don't go, Helen."

She hesitated, her expression a mask of uncertainty. "I don't think—"

"Then don't," he interrupted quickly. "Don't think, sweetheart."

Helen didn't close the door on him and flee, but neither did she move. "You're at your bath. I don't wish to disturb you."

"Afraid to stay?" he asked, knowing it would nettle her.

And it did, if her reaction was any indication. Her chin went up, her eyes narrowing. The stubborn in her wouldn't allow her to walk away now. "I'm not afraid of you, if that is what you mean."

"Not me." He shook his head, allowing his gaze to drop to her lips, then the sweet swell of her breasts, the curve of her waist and hips. No nightdress or robe could sufficiently hide the beauty he knew lay beneath them, waiting for his hands and mouth. "You're afraid of yourself, of what you might do. What you might feel."

Pink tinged her cheeks. "I'll feel the same thing that I have felt ever since you reappeared in my life."

He hung his arms over the marble surround encompassing the tub and leaned back, affecting a relaxed air to goad her even more. Her eyes lowered to his bare chest, lingering. It would seem the lady wasn't as immune as she pretended. "And what is that, darling? Lust?"

Her gaze snapped back to his, her flush deepening. Damn, but she was lovely, his English rose. "Don't be absurd."

"Prove you don't want me." He raised a brow. "My back needs to be washed. How fortuitous that you've interrupted my bath."

"Ring for a servant," she said coolly.

"No, I don't think I will." He grinned at her.

Her lips compressed into a tight frown. "Then I suppose your back will not be washed this evening."

"I don't want a servant," he said lowly. "I want you."

She didn't mistake the wealth of meaning behind his words, and she wasn't unaffected. He knew her well enough to note the way she drew in a quick breath, the way her lips parted. "You cannot have me. I'm not yours to command."

"But you are my wife," he pointed out. And that had to mean something to her. How could it not? "It's never been my wish to command you, Helen. You have your own mind, and you always have. So either step over the threshold or run back to your chamber and hide."

That did it. She finally crossed the tiled floor to him, her eyes flashing as she took up his soap and a cloth. "I don't hide. If it suits your whims for me to scrub your back, then I will."

Keeping her gaze averted carefully away, she dunked the soap into the tub, wetting it before scrubbing the cloth over its surface with more force than necessary. He bent forward at the waist to allow her better access, holding his tongue as she ran the cloth lightly over his skin. She moved with haste, three quick swipes, and then dropped the cloth into the water.

"There you are," she announced, her voice tight.

Did she think she could escape that easily? That he would allow her to flee now that he finally had her where he wanted her? He caught her around the waist when she would have left again and hauled her toward him, settling her bottom on the marble slab.

"Why are you so eager to run, Helen?" He nuzzled through the fragrant locks of her hair, putting his mouth close to her ear. "Don't you trust yourself?"

"Unhand me, you brute!" She twisted, attempting to break free of his hold. "You're making my dressing gown all wet."

He ignored her, giving in to temptation and kissing the shell of her ear. "I'd be happy to remove it for you and hang it somewhere to dry."

"Levi." Her hands clamped on his forearm, trying to tug free, and the touch of her bare skin on his sent a bolt of unadulterated lust straight through him. "This is most indecent of you."

"I'm an indecent kind of man, it seems, because I'm not about to let you slip back into the night so swiftly." He kissed her creamy throat, licked her skin. "Why don't you stay for a bit? This tub is large enough for two."

She swallowed, another small sign of her inner struggle, and he felt the slight movement against his lips. "Perhaps you should invite someone else into the tub, then. Someone who wishes to be there. A maid, maybe? An opera singer or an actress? There must be plenty of women who would eagerly join you."

So she thought to use his own ploys against him, trying to goad him into releasing her. Her breasts were full and heavy against his arm, larger than he remembered. No, that he would not do. He had her precisely where he wanted her, and he meant to take his good, sweet time.

He raked his thumb over her left nipple, enjoying her swift intake of breath. "I've never taken to maids or opera singers or actresses." He kissed her neck again, scored the sensitive flesh lightly with his teeth. "Oddly enough, there's only one woman I'd want in this tub with me, and she happens to be in my arms right now. Isn't that luck?"

"Lucky for you that I was too foolish to realize I shouldn't cross the threshold with you in here," she said tartly. "Luckier still that I was foolish enough to think I could ever trust you."

There it was again, her sword raised between them. But he grew tired of doing battle with her. "You can trust me. I wronged you, and for that I'm deeply sorry." Another kiss, another lick, a nibble. She didn't move away and he couldn't seem to stop. "Let me in, sweetheart. Let me show you."

She angled her body toward him just a bit, and rested her head back against his shoulder. "Your water will soon cool and you'll grow weary of holding me hostage." Her words were prim and unruffled.

Her skin was hot, her body responsive, belying her façade. He relaxed his hold on her waist, kissed her ear, tugged the soft lobe with his teeth. "Go if you want. Go now, Helen. I won't stop you."

Helen went still. He watched her profile, holding his breath, awaiting her decision. Her nose was perfect and dainty, her lips full and lush. Her cheekbones high and regal. Even from the side, her beauty was undeniable. With her hair a moist tangle about her face, she looked wild and wanton. A pagan goddess come to earth to taunt him, make him love her, make him want her, and forever keep him beyond reach.

Abruptly, she turned toward him, threw her arms around his neck, and pressed her mouth to his. He hauled her against his chest, not giving a damn that half her wrapper and nightdress sank into the water, instantly sodden. He kissed her back, showing her with his lips and tongue how much he worshiped her, how much he wanted her. How much he loved her. She tasted of tea and herself and every dark fantasy he'd entertained for the last year, alone in his bed with little hope of ever having her in his arms again.

Impossible, was all he could think. Impossible that her mouth moved against his, her tongue sweeping the seam of his lips, that a deep, throaty purr came from within her as if to say she craved more. Even more impossible that she sidled farther into the tub until nearly her entire body was submerged, her gowns plastering to his chest like a second skin as displaced water splashed aver the rim and marble surround and onto the floor. She clutched at him, her fingers in his hair, kissing him with a ferocity that mirrored what he felt inside. It had been too long, far too long, and her kiss was like the sweetest homecoming.

When their mouths broke apart, they were both short of breath. He tipped his forehead to hers, staring into her eyes. "Helen, sweetheart."

Something bubbled forth from her kiss-swollen lips then, something equally impossible. Laughter. She was laughing. Laughing with the abandon of a lunatic, her shoulders shuddering, her breath catching. "I think I've gone mad."

He kissed her again. Hang it all, he loved this woman. He cupped her jaw. "You're not mad, my love."

"I must be mad, for there's no other explanation for this." She glanced down at the water. Her dressing gown floated around her. Her nipples were plainly visible now, pointed and hard through the twin layers of wet fabric.

"You're not mad," he said again. "I warned you I would dismantle your walls. And I will continue, Helen. I will not stop. Brick by brick. Stone by stone."

252

"My walls were built for good reason," she reminded him, not quite yet ready to surrender. No, she wouldn't make it easy on him. But she never had.

He wouldn't want her to. He didn't want to convince Helen to forgive him. He wanted her to convince herself, to make the decision on her own. He wanted her to realize that he was a husband worthy of her. That he would go to the ends of the earth to make her happy and proud, to show her how much he loved her.

"I'll take them down," he said again. "Be warned that I'm laying siege."

"Then do your worst," she challenged him.

He grinned. "To the contrary, darling. I'll do my very best."

He kissed her again, his hand tangling in the damp knot of her hair. He wanted the cumbersome layers of her wet garments gone. He wanted her, naked and slick, beautiful and his. In his bed. Beneath him. Atop him. However she desired, whatever she desired. As desperately as he longed for her, as much time that had passed since the last time they'd made love, this night was about Helen.

He dragged his mouth back down her throat, palmed one of her heavy breasts. She moaned. His thigh dipped between her legs, and then his fingers found her there too, seeking, thwarted by the barrier of wet fabric. She arched into him, her body responding as sweetly as ever. She hadn't forgotten after all.

"Levi," she whispered. "I don't want to feel this way. It isn't fair."

"It would be far simpler, would it not, if you felt nothing for me and if I felt nothing for you?" he asked, stroking her beneath the cooling water. She arched against him, seeking, wanting, the same as he. "Life isn't simple, nor fair. If it were, we'd never experience joy or love or desire or anything worth a damn. We'd be bovine and complacent, too stupid to realize what we were missing."

She kissed his jaw. "You aren't wearing a stitch beneath

this bath water."

The breath hissed from his lungs when her fingers found his cock and stroked. "No."

Helen nipped at his lips. "I don't want to be bovine and complacent."

"You never could be," he assured her, pleasure robbing him of further words as she tightened her grip.

"May we raise a white flag of truce for now?" She kissed him, slow and lingering.

"Hell yes." His answer was instant. "Come to my bed tonight, Helen. You're my wife, and it's been far too long."

Her gaze was unreadable, but her answer was all he needed to hear. "Yes."

Levi helped her from the tub with great care, as if she were fashioned of thinnest porcelain rather than flesh and bone. She stood dripping on the exquisite painted tiles, her dressing gown and nightdress plastered to her. Something had happened and she couldn't say with precision what it was, but when he'd given her the choice of leaving or remaining, she hadn't been able to go. It was as if some missing key had been fitted into a lock inside her. The door opened, and forward she went. Straight into his arms and straight into his tub.

He climbed from the tub with a leonine grace she couldn't help but admire, his muscles and strength on display. He didn't even bother to dry himself or hide his body from her. His dark hair was wet. Water kissed his broad shoulders, ran down his honed chest, over his flat abdomen and lower still. Her gaze dipped there. He was ready, thick and hard. Desire simmered through her. She was ready too. There remained much to be settled between them, if indeed it ever could, but tonight she reveled in remembering what it had been like to be his. To make him hers. Tonight they were husband and wife, their pains and enmity laid aside.

Her fingers flew to the cord holding her dressing gown in place, untying the knot. The drenched garment hit the floor with a vigorous splat. He stood before her, working the line of buttons on her night dress, peeling it away, kissing every swath of skin he exposed along the way. His mouth was everywhere, his hands stroking, soothing, peeling the cold wet fabric from her skin and setting her aflame instead. Kisses all over her body. Her neck, the curve of her breast, collarbone, inner elbow, fingertips, and then to the place where her skin had stretched to miraculous size while she'd been pregnant with Theo.

He tugged her nightdress over her hips and stopped there, where she would never quite be the same. But she loved those marks, the little reminders of the blessing of her son, the miracles of life and love. He kissed her there, his hand passing over her in a tender caress.

"I told you I've changed," she said softly, unashamed.

"You're more beautiful." He kissed her again. "More beautiful than I deserve."

The nightdress joined her dressing gown on the floor. Chill air struck her, giving her gooseflesh. Or perhaps it was what he was doing to her that gave her the gooseflesh. "Are you cold, darling?" Another kiss. His hands branded the curve of her hips, his head dipping to the center of her. Down her thighs he trailed his touch, stopping at her knees, urging her legs apart. And then his tongue was upon her, licking her, flicking over her. She forgot to be cold.

"No," was all she could say, for she didn't want him to stop.

She reached for his shoulders, his skin smooth and supple over sculpted muscle. Yes, dear heavens, this was what she wanted. What she needed, this exquisite abandon, sweet and delicious pleasure. An elixir to her tattered soul. Her mind struggled to process thoughts. Nothing made sense. Everything made sense. His tongue sank inside her, then played over the most tender part of her.

He gripped her hips, licking, angling her, knowing what she liked, how to please her. He worshiped her as if she were precious to him. She didn't want to notice, didn't want to think it, but a sliver of awareness splintered the pleasure overtaking her. And then, his tongue again.

It took her fast and swift, her body shaking, crumpling. She sagged into him, nearly toppling over as the intensity of her climax slammed into her. Levi hadn't released his hold. He stayed where he was, absorbing every last ripple, drinking her in. She wanted to be precious to him. God, how she wanted to be precious to him.

Levi kissed his way back up her body until he stood and took her into his arms. He didn't speak and neither did she as he carried her from the bath chamber and into his own suite. Across the rich carpet he went, leaving a trail of wet footprints in his wake, all the way to his bed.

He laid her on her back and then joined her. His fingers threaded through her hair, weighing the long locks. "I'll never grow tired of admiring you with your hair unbound," he said solemnly, his gaze pinned to hers. "Not for as long as I live."

She raked her touch over his prickly jaw. "I've missed you, Levi." She didn't know where the admission had come from, but it was too late to take it back.

He kissed her, and it was a crushing, possessive kiss. Her mouth moved against his, opening for his tongue. *More.* His fingers slid between her thighs. She jerked into him, clutching at his back, pulling him closer to her. She couldn't seem to get him close enough. *More.* Her hands found his hips. He rolled atop her. She guided him. *Yes.*

Levi thrust inside her. They moved as one, bodies wet and heated, their skin slick. She pressed against him, urging him deeper. *Yes, more.* And then, surrender, as sudden as it was delicious. He rocked into her, spending himself. She came undone with almost violent splendor.

He broke their kiss and eased from her body, pressing his mouth to her brow before he rolled onto his back. Helen stared at the gilt ceiling as the world returned to her. The electric lights burned brightly around them as it wasn't yet time for his dynamo to go down for the night. She wished for darkness, a way to cloak her emotions, if not her body.

But there was only light. And there was Helen, and there was Levi, side by side. Their bodies still touched from shoulder to hip. He was her husband, and there was no shame in what they'd done, but she hadn't intended for them to ever share a bed again. She thought of Theo, sleeping soundly in her chamber, and the tingling in her breasts that told her he would soon wake.

"I must return to my chamber," she said into the silence. "Theo will need me soon."

He caught her hand and raised it to his lips, forcing her to meet his gaze when she would've retreated like a coward, refusing to look at him for fear of what she might see. "You can't undo this, Helen."

No, she could not. "The white flag was only temporary." She reminded him as much as herself.

"No indeed, Mrs. Storm." He tugged her to him for a lingering kiss that had her melting into him in spite of her determination to remain unmoved. "Tonight was your Appomattox Court House. This war between us is done."

She rose from the bed. "We shall see about that, Mr. Storm." Head held high, she retreated from his chamber, cold and nude, all too aware that he watched every step she took.

Chapter Sixteen

HE THOUGHT SHE WAS READY TO SURRENDER. But lovemaking was not a panacea. Helen took breakfast in her chamber the next morning with Theo, determined to avoid Levi and give herself some time and space to think. Her heart was hopelessly confused, her mind in even more desperate straits. She'd spilled her tea, dropped her fork, upended a chair, and forgotten to fasten Theo's nappy properly after changing him. With stains marring her dress from the tea, the leaking nappy, and the fork, she'd had to call her lady's maid back and dress all over again. On a whim, she'd chosen one of the gowns Levi had bought for her.

It was fashioned of vibrant Ottoman silk, its kilted skirts pinned with small bows and a bouffant at the back, and she had to admit that it fit her surprisingly well. The fabric was fine, and she hadn't worn a dress so dear since nearly the last time she'd seen him. Wearing it felt rather odd, yet also somehow right.

Oh, perhaps choosing the gown had not been a whim after all, she thought now as she hastened down the hall to his workshop. Perhaps it had been her heart telling her head what it ought to have realized by now. She would never stop loving him. Going to his bed may have been unwise, but it had proved to her in ways that nothing else could that the passion burning between them remained, as hot and consuming as any flame. She could not continue to ignore it.

Didn't, in fact, wish to.

Where did that leave her? She didn't know, but she stopped before the closed door separating her from him and knocked twice just the same. He hadn't sought her out that morning as she'd thought he might. Initially, she'd been relieved. But as time had stretched, her mind wandering, her emotions spinning into painful knots, she'd decided she would wait no longer.

No answer. She knocked again. Only quiet from within. Perhaps he had gone to his office for the day. Somehow, she'd thought he might remain after all they'd shared. Disappointment wafted over her. Unless he was inside the chamber after all and merely too caught up in his task to hear her?

Helen turned the knob before thinking better of invading his domain. The door swung open, and she tentatively poked her head inside. The curtains had been tied back, allowing a generous, cheerful sunshine to pour forth and spill over the room's intriguing contents. There was no sight of her husband, but she stepped inside anyway, leaving the door ajar.

This chamber, his private domain, was where she'd gotten her best glimpse of him. It was where he'd dropped his guard, allowing her to see inside his mind, where the walls she'd carefully built had begun their initial crumble. After last night, they lay in rubble at her feet. She paced the length of the spacious workshop, careful not to touch anything, her eyes drifting over dissected machines, parts and pieces, metal and wood, wires and tools, sheets of handwritten notes. His scrawl was tidy but bold, much like him. Slowly, she made her way through the room until she reached his desk. Unlike the scattered pieces of machines littering nearly every other available table, his desk was a meticulous presentation of order. And it was then that she accidentally caught sight of the journals he kept there in tidy stacks. *The Telegraphic Journal & Electrical Review, Engineering, The Electrical World.*

Nothing overly surprising about his reading material, she thought with a smile that faded when she noticed the corner of a newspaper jutting out from beneath the stack, the only source of disorder on an otherwise spartanly kept surface. It bore her name. Knowing a bit of guilt for prying in his personal effects but too curious to allow it to stop her, she slid the paper out of its hiding place.

It was one of her articles. Passages had been underlined as though he'd given her words a great deal of thought. As though her words had interested him. Meant something to him. The paper bore the signs of having been re-read, its creases well worn. In fact, it looked quite as if it had traveled with him for some time. The date on the paper confirmed her suspicion. Why, it was nearly six months old.

That meant...dear heavens, it meant he had been reading her articles in New York City, before he'd ever known about Theo. He had brought her article with him to London. But why?

And why did the discovery make her heart give a great pang inside her chest? A pang of, what was it? Surprise? Longing? Hope? Perhaps all of those emotions simultaneously, tumbling over each other, each clamoring to be felt the most. Oh, but she dared not hope. Dared not long. Hoping and longing were dangerous pursuits indeed when it came to Levi Storm.

The workshop door slid softly over the thick carpet, and she spun, heart in her throat, to find him standing at the threshold. He wore his work clothes, a simple dark suit and white shirt, black waistcoat beneath devoid of ornamentation. No hat, his rich mahogany hair on full display. His whiskers had not been trimmed this morning, and the effect was quite maddening. He looked splendid, rugged, and handsome all at once.

"Mrs. Storm," he said formally, surprise coloring his voice. "While I'm gratified to see you're no longer disguising yourself as a washer woman, I do have one question. Would you care to explain what you're doing riffling through my desk?"

Her cheeks went hot with embarrassment. Oh dear. Perhaps she had been trespassing where she had no right. "I was not riffling," she rebutted, however.

He directed a pointed look at the newspaper in her hands. "One might argue that the evidence of your guilt is in your hands."

Yes, there was that. She placed the newspaper back on his desk but her gaze remained fastened on him. "Will you bring the law upon me? Have me hauled off for my crimes?"

"I can think of better punishments." His lips quirked into a smoldering smile, dimples appearing the better to taunt her.

Her heart thumped. "Indeed? What punishment is that, Mr. Storm?"

He closed the door at his back and stalked toward her with slow purpose. "It depends, Mrs. Storm, upon the nature of the crime. Tell me, what were you reading just now?"

He already knew, of course he did. But he wanted to hear her say it.

"One of my articles." A warm sensation stole over her again, and this time embarrassment was most definitely not its source.

"Ah." He stopped just short of her, saying nothing more.

"Did you read all of them?" she had to ask. Very much depended upon his answer, it seemed.

"You refused to publish your articles with the *Beacon* even though I wrote you to say that I hoped you would not abandon your cause for loathing of me. So I discovered the paper you'd chosen instead."

He spoke as if it were of no greater import than buttoning his waistcoat. But Helen's heart, so conflicted earlier, felt now as if it would burst. "Why?"

His smile turned self-deprecating. "You have a sharp mind, Helen, and the world could use more of your forward thinking."

"Thank you, but you didn't answer my question." She knew that he too could be liberal in his ideas, but he was not the sort of man to carry reform journals about with him. The engineering and electrical journals she could well understand. The reform journal? Not really. And she needed to know why he'd read her articles, carried them with him. Her heart needed to know why.

His smile dissipated, his jaw tightening. "What do you want me to say? That it was because I wanted to hear your voice, and I could not? Because I longed for you so badly this last year that I was willing to settle for typeset words? Or should I say that I missed your mind, your thoughts, and reading your articles was the closest I could get?"

She pressed her hand to her heart as if the action would stay its frantic beats. She wanted nothing more than to throw herself into his arms. "I would want you to say all that if it were true."

"Of course it's true, hang it." His voice was as dark as his expression. He stepped forward before she could, hands clamping on her waist and dragging her into his chest. "Of course it's all true, you stubborn, maddening woman. I wanted nothing more than to come back to you, but I was too proud to beg. Too stupid, maybe, to beg."

"I wouldn't have wanted you to beg." She locked her arms around his neck, leaning into him for the first time since his return without thinking that she ought not, that she should keep her distance. He was so beautiful, so masculine and brash. She was fiercely glad in that moment that she had chosen to invade his territory and riffle through his desk, as he had mockingly phrased it.

"What would you have wanted then?" He pinned her with his gaze, searching, seeking. "Tell me, Helen, and I'll give it to you. You have the world at your fingertips if you but ask."

"I would have wanted to know how you felt," she confessed softly, feeling unaccountably shy. They had shared the magic of each other's bodies and yet somehow this seemed the most intimate act between them of all. "And I want to know how you feel, now."

He cupped her face as if she were beloved. "How can you not see, Helen? I loved you then. I didn't understand it for what it was, not well enough to treat you as you deserved, and for that I will have eternal regret. I've discovered that I know a great deal about business. I know how electricity works, how to harness it and make rooms and train stations light up. I know how to improve upon virtually any machine or invention there is. But I don't know a goddamn thing about love other than that it can eat a man alive from the inside out. This isn't the pretty speech you ought to get, and Lord knows you could've found a hundred men more worthy to be your husband than I, but all I know is that I loved you then, Helen, and I love you now."

He loved her.

She stared at him, words failing her. The stern businessman who had once locked her out of his office, who had looked down his nose at her articles without reading them, who had been aloof and cold, perfect and unflappable, who had raged through her life like his surname, that same man loved her. Impossible. This was the man who cared only about his business, about furthering his own goals.

Or was he?

The man before her now, the man who held her as delicately as if she were their baby son, who had carried her article around with him for six months, who had kissed every part of her body and who had transformed everything she'd thought she'd known about herself…this man loved her.

And she loved him. She loved him enough to move beyond their past wounding of each other. Love was stronger than pain, she realized then, and forgiveness was the greatest healer of all.

"Levi." Her fingers sank into his hair. "Tell me again."

"I love you, Mrs. Helen Storm." His mouth came down on hers, swift and hungry. "I love you, hang it."

His last declaration was so utterly Levi that she couldn't help but smile and kiss him once more. His tongue dipped inside to tease hers. All the pent-up emotion of the last year without him crashed over her and her hands fisted in his hair. She never wanted to let him go. She never would. Not ever.

He broke the kiss. "I wish to God I'd never hurt you, Helen. I hope that, in time, you may learn to trust me. That you may even enjoy my company outside the bedchamber. I'm willing to wait, my love. I'll wait for however long it takes." He kissed her again. "I need to go back to New York City soon. The lawsuit I told you about will be tried in court, and I need to be present for the case. My life's work depends on winning it. But I don't want to rush you. If you and Theo are more comfortable here, this is where you will remain. You will have all my funds at your disposal, to dispense with as you like, and this house is yours to run as you see fit."

The thought of seeing his New York, surely a city as bold and as untamed as he, both daunted and thrilled her. But see it she would, for she wasn't about to let him go anywhere without her.

"No," she said. "We will go where you go. Theo and I are your family. If you're in New York City, then we will be."

"You needn't feel obligated—"

She pressed a finger to his lips, stopping his words. "Hush. I want to be where you are. We've spent too much time apart, and I don't want to lose another minute. I love you, Levi."

He stilled, dragging her back to arm's length so he could look at her. "What did you say?"

"I said that I love you." She was smiling and crying happy tears all at once, but ever since she'd had Theo, her emotions had been rather uncontrollable. "I love you, you maddening man. I love that you know how machines work when they look like worthless lumps of wood and metal to me, how you've fashioned yourself into the man you are today by nothing but your own hard work and persistence. I love the father you are to Theo. I loved you then, and I love you now. I was too proud to accept that you'd made a mistake, and I pushed you away, and that will be *my* everlasting regret."

He crushed her to him and kissed her. "No regrets between us. Not from this point forward."

"None," she agreed, and kissed him again.

Levi was precisely where he wanted to be, in his bed, his naked wife pressed to him. Her breasts were against his chest, his hip thrown over hers as if to hold her to him forever. They'd made love twice. Once, with fierce abandon and then with tender slowness, a sense of wonderment. Damn it all, he'd thought he'd been fortunate to have her as his wife. But nothing compared to her love.

She loved him. Electricity was no enigma to him. There was nothing he could not comprehend, given time and patience. How he had earned this woman's heart, though, would ever be a mystery. He buried his face in Helen's gleaming tresses and inhaled. Bergamot and rose. His favorite scent.

"Levi." She caressed his chest, watching her fingers work their path of fire across his skin. "There's something that's been troubling me. Your mother died when you were so young. How did you manage? A little boy, all alone?"

He tensed. This hadn't been a topic he'd expected her to broach, not after they were spent with passion. His fingers sifted idly through her hair. "I managed." His ma had been ill for days and she'd told him what to expect. She'd given him into the care of a fellow prostitute, who'd neither the money nor the disposition to take care of an unruly, motherless lad.

"Won't you tell me?" She touched his jaw, stroked him. "Or is it too painful to speak of?"

"Yes," he said, and it was his answer to both of her questions. He pulled her even closer as though he could absorb her love, wear it like a shield. "She left me in a woman's charge, another whore. She was not kind or patient, this woman, and she didn't want another mouth to feed. I found out she wanted to sell me to a man who liked to misuse children, and I ran away. For some time, I lived as a thief. When the war began, I enlisted with false papers because I was too young. I'd always been tall, and the war machine needed able-bodies. I was that, and no one asked questions."

"My God, you went off to war as a boy?" Her exquisite face was stricken. For all that she was a reformer, a woman who didn't shy from the ugliness of life, she was still the sheltered daughter of an earl.

But he loved the goodness in her, that it had not been ruined. "I survived, sweetheart." He cupped her cheek, lowered his mouth to her already kiss-swollen lips for a moment. "While I was a soldier, I learned to read and write exceptionally well from some of my comrades, and when the war ended, I was a changed man. I've never broken the law since except for our wedding day, but that I will not regret. I'd do anything to protect you and Theo."

She pressed her forehead to his. "As I'd do anything to protect you. You will never be alone again in this world, Levi. Not as long as I've breath in my body."

Her fervent words warmed him as nothing else could. Dredging up the specters of his past never failed to shake him, but she was real and sweet and soft in his arms. "I'll hold you to that, my love. Don't think I won't."

"Thank you for telling me."

He kissed her again because he couldn't not, especially not when she was looking at him as if he were an angel come down to walk among men. But he was no angel, and he had sinned too many times to count. "Thank you for loving me," he said when at last the kiss had ended. "I don't deserve it."

"Yes," she said with just as much vehemence, "you do."

Levi thought then of the day they'd first met, when she had invaded his office, golden and beautiful and every inch a lady. And he'd been a boor, tossing her over his shoulder, carting her to the door. He'd wanted her even then, with a need that had only grown over time rather than lessening. It was like a river, cutting deeper into the earth with each passing year.

He was about to kiss her again when he remembered something else about the day she'd stormed his offices, wielding her article and her reticule like weapons. Gently, he disentangled himself from her, flipping back the bedclothes and rising to his feet.

"What in heaven's name are you doing?" she demanded, sitting up and clutching the coverlet to her chest for modesty's sake. Her hair was an untamed curtain about her shoulders, and he couldn't wait to bury his face and his hands in it once more.

But there was something he needed to do first.

"I have something that belongs to you," he said cryptically, and strode across the chamber without a thought for his nudity. He threw open his wardrobe and reached inside, extracting his memento of their first day together. Levi carried it to her like an offering, the hat she'd left behind. His albatross, the bit of frippery he'd carried with him ever since. The only piece of her he'd had left.

"My hat," she exclaimed, reaching out to take it from him and turn it in her hands. "It's rather crumpled, I'm afraid. Did you find it beneath the wheel of a carriage?"

Levi laughed, easing his hip back onto the bed alongside her. "It has traveled a great deal since you saw it last, from London to Paris to New York City. And now back to London."

"You carried my hat with you?"

"Packed inside my trunk." He made the admission without a hint of embarrassment. Yes, she had wreaked so much havoc upon him that he had carried her hat across the globe. But now he had an infinitely better prize to treasure. The woman herself.

She smiled, love shining from her eyes, and opened her arms to him. "Come here, you vexing, wonderful man."

And he very willingly obliged.

Dear Reader,

Thank you for reading *Sweet Scandal!* I hope you enjoyed Helen and Levi's story as much as I loved writing it.

If you'd like to keep up to date with my latest releases, sign up for my email list at:

http://www.scarsco.com/contact_scarlett

As always, please consider leaving a review of *Sweet Scandal.* All reviews are greatly appreciated!

If you'd like a preview of Book Five in the Heart's Temptation series—featuring the infamous Earl of Ravenscroft and a lady who refuses to behave—do read on.

Until next time,

Scarlett

Restless Rake

Heart's Temptation Book Five

She wants her freedom…

Clara Whitney is desperate to leave London and return to her native Virginia. She'll do anything, even if it means striking a deal with the most notorious earl in England, to get what she wants. How could she anticipate just how much his melting kisses and knowing hands would tempt her?

He wants her…

The Earl of Ravenscroft is infamous for his prowess in the bedchamber and for earning his living by entertaining bored society widows and wives. When the innocent and lovely Miss Whitney seeks him out with the daring proposition of a marriage in name only in return for a generous share of her dowry, Julian accepts. After the vows, however, he isn't ready to part with his prickly Southern belle. At least not without taking her to bed.

A restless rake no more…

Julian knows the game of seduction all too well, but this time, the rules are different, and he just may lose the one thing he thought he no longer had to give. His heart.

Chapter One

London, 1884

HE WAS POCKETS TO LET AND HE WAS BLOODY well tired of whoring himself for the well-to-do ladies of the Marlborough House set. Drinking seemed an excellent course of action for the moment.

"Lord Ravenscroft, you've a visitor."

Julian finished pouring his brandy before flicking a glance to his grim-faced butler. Osgood's expression was one of distaste, as though a fly had flown into his mouth and his august bearing wouldn't allow him to spit it out. Osgood was a relic of the previous earl's days. A gargoyle made of stone, guarding against evil spirits and indiscreet late-night apparitions with unsavory intentions.

Oh, this wasn't the first time an unexpected visitor had made her way to Julian's front door. Nor, he suspected, would it be the last. It was a certainty that the visitor was female. They always were.

Osgood was far too loyal a retainer to make his thoughts about such callers known. He was a third generation butler who had served the Earls of Ravenscroft for the entirety of his life, and he was above reproach. But Julian could read him like a bad gambler.

No face for *vingt-et-un* on that one. Indeed, Julian thought as he sipped his brandy with great care, eying the old fellow, no face for much of anything save being a wilted stickler for propriety. Even if his employer was living on credit and bad debts, every sign indicating that he ought to flee the proverbial sinking ship like a rat.

But Osgood wasn't a rat. And Julian wasn't in the mood for visitors, especially not the unexpected variety.

He frowned at his butler. "I'm not at home. I believe I made that known."

The butler cleared his throat. His expression remained suitably dour and pinched. "Yes, my lord, of course. Forgive me, but the visitor in question refuses to leave. Would you care for me to have some footmen brought round, my lord, to extricate her?"

Some devil in Julian rather enjoyed watching Osgood squirm. After all, with ruin so certain a future, this may well prove his final opportunity to needle the man. Another sip of brandy. He enjoyed the burn down his throat, wished it was enough to numb him. It never was.

"Surely such persistence ought to be rewarded, Osgood?" His tone was carefully mild. "Do you not think so?"

Osgood remained immovable, however. "I do not presume to think, my lord."

"No?" Julian was feeling perverse tonight, dredged in the freeing wickedness of a man who was about to lose everything. "Terrible shame, that. Not to think. Or perhaps it's a lie, Osgood? Surely it cannot be said that a man does not think. You must have an opinion. Tell me, should I be at home to this creature who dares to call so late at night?"

His butler paled, clearly not relishing the untenable position of being forced to comment on his disreputable master's social niceties. "My lord, I'm certain I will be pleased to follow your instructions, whatever they may be."

Ah, perhaps it had been a whimsical notion on his part to believe he could wrangle a concession from the block of ice before him. "Bring her in, then, Osgood. The night grows late and I'm in need of diversion."

His butler's expression didn't alter, but Julian could sense the disapproval like a clap on his back. No matter. Disapproval had haunted him his entire life. He wore it like a mantle rather than a shroud. Osgood bowed and disappeared. Julian took another long sip of brandy and contemplated the visitor who wouldn't leave. He wondered, for a brief, fanciful moment if it was Lottie.

Not Lottie, his instincts told him, for Osgood would have recognized her. It hadn't been that long ago. What, a year? Not a great deal of time when one considered the span of a lifetime.

The door to his study opened. His butler did the pretty. A feminine figure entered, clad in a luxurious pelisse overtop a promenade gown that was, unless he missed his guess, a Worth. His visitor was petite but curved in all the right places. Her nipped waste was visible even beneath her layers of fabric, so too her generous bosom. An ostentatious hat adorned with a stuffed bird and veil hid the woman's identity from his view, but he scarcely cared. He'd find out who she was soon enough.

He stood. "Thank you, Osgood. That will be all." The door had only just snicked closed before he bowed to her. He wondered what lie beneath that veil. The little he could discern of her features seemed even, unremarkable. "Madam, if I may be so bold, please be seated and make the reason for your unexpected visit known."

Her steps were not those of a confident woman. Rather, they were mincing. Hesitant. As though she feared him. She stopped a notable length from his desk. "My lord, I'm here to make you an offer."

Her voice was soft and sweet, her enunciation rounded like pebbles worn smooth by a stream. There was beauty in that honeyed voice, and it rolled over his senses like a touch. Unless he missed his guess, she was an American. Perhaps one of the many heiresses who had exchanged her immense dowry for a title and now found herself ensnared by ennui. Or disillusioned, her girlish dreams of snagging a coronet and living a fairytale dashed by the reality of a balding duke with a paunch and a penchant for bedding servant girls.

Julian supposed he shouldn't be surprised. He frowned. "I fear I'm no longer interested in offers of any sort." He'd long ago grown tired of playing this role. Of whoring himself to wealthy widows for enough money to keep from utter penury. A man could only swallow his pride for so many years before it choked him.

She clasped her hands at her waist, the sole outward indication of apparent indecision. "Perhaps you would care to hear my offer before you so summarily dismiss it, my lord."

Bold of her. Now he could place her accent, the leisurely drawl. A Virginian, unless he missed his guess. Julian closed the distance between them, not stopping until her pelisse brushed his trousers. "I daresay it couldn't be an offer I haven't already heard before."

"You may be surprised." She held her ground, tipping up her chin.

Feisty as well as bold, he thought, studying her with new interest. The veil was an unwanted deterrent that kept him from seeing if her face matched the lilting beauty of her voice.

He stepped closer, her skirts crushing against him, and hooked an arm around her waist. She stiffened. "What is it, love? You want me to join you and your husband in bed? You want him to watch as I fuck you? No? Perhaps you want to feel pleasure for the first time. Is that it? You've settled for a title but he doesn't make you come."

Her quick intake of breath told him he'd shocked her. She sounded young. Perhaps she was a novice to this sort of game. He should be merciful and send her on her way, but his mood was dark. A man on the edge had little to lose, and he needed distraction badly. Here was a plaything, a well-dressed naïf who had landed in his study like a benediction.

He reached beneath her veil, cupped her cheek. The contact jolted him. Her skin was smooth and warm, soft. His thumb found her lower lip, lush and full, stroking. Her lips parted. He'd consumed too much brandy tonight, it was certain. Otherwise, why would he feel such heat, such unadulterated attraction for a faceless woman with a Virginia drawl and an atrocity of a hat?

She didn't say a word, just held very still, allowing his touch but not reacting. Her breath fanned over his skin, quick and shallow, the only sign she was affected. Was her lack of response borne of shock? He couldn't be sure.

"You've heard I'll do anything for a price, yes?" His thumb dipped ever so slightly inside her mouth. "That is why you're here, is it not?"

She swallowed, and he absorbed the ripple in his fingertips that rested lightly beneath her jaw. Then, her drawl, steady and calm, cut into the silence. "Do you think to frighten me into fleeing, my lord?"

The lady was even more audacious than he'd supposed. Fine. How far would she take their gamble before she broke? The hand that held her waist slid with unerring precision to the buttons lining the front of her gown. He could undo buttons faster than the most skilled lady's maid. With one hand, with his teeth, with a knife—whatever the moment and the woman required.

He watched his handiwork. Her pelisse hung open. Her bodice gaped. He could see the elegant embroidery of her corset cover, the white ribbon at the top of her chemise. Her breasts were full and high, straining against the constriction of her tight lacing. She still hadn't moved. "Are you not frightened yet, love?"

Perhaps he would consider her offer after all, if only for the night.

"Would it please you if I were?"

Her cool question stayed him in the act of removing the final button from its moorings. Damn it, what was he about, practically ravaging some poor sod's wife merely because she'd appeared in his study? And for what gain? To prove a point to himself? To the enigmatic lady whose face he'd yet to behold?

Part of him wanted her to run away into the night and take with her all reminders of the man he'd become. Shouldn't she be terrified of him, of what he could do to her? Or was she not as innocent as she seemed? Did a depraved heart beat beneath her ivory breast? He had to know. "Does fear excite you?"

"No, and neither does your posturing."

He could so easily make a lie of her words. Julian knew when a woman was attracted to him, and this one was no different than a hundred others before her. She wanted him. He trailed his hand down her throat, feeling tension in the corded muscles. Tenderly, he caressed her as if she were already his lover. Some part of him understood that she would be, that this pull between them was inevitable. If not tonight, another.

The time for playing games was at an end. "What is your offer then, love? The night grows late and I'm tired of entertaining my whims."

Her hands remained clasped at her waist, just below the last button he'd yet to undo. The knuckles rose in stark relief from her fine-boned fingers, belying the ease with which she spoke. "I thought you were no longer interested in offers."

She possessed a considerable amount of mettle. He smiled, for he was thoroughly enjoying himself now, in a way he had not done in quite some time. "Can a man not change his mind?"

"Of course. Man is rarely constant, I've discovered."

There was a reproach in her words, though whether it was aimed at him or another, he couldn't be certain. "Your offer, madam. What is it?"

"My offer is simple." She unclasped her hands and reached up to remove the hideous hat and veil.

Good God, the face didn't match the voice at all.

No indeed, it surpassed the mellifluous lure by leaps and bounds. She was beautiful, more exquisite than any goddess he'd ever seen splashed across a canvas. Her golden hair was plaited into basket weaves. Her eyes were wide, blue, unblinking. Her mouth full and lush, her cheeks pink, her cheekbones high. She was the most gorgeous creature he'd ever seen. Who was she, and how had he never set eyes upon her before? For he couldn't have ever crossed her path. He would have remembered a splendor so rare.

"Marry me," she said.

Author's Note

The 1880s was a fascinating decade filled with great sociological and technological change that heralded the arrival of the modern era. In researching this book, I found real-life inspiration in Josephine Butler, W.T. Stead, Thomas Edison, George Westinghouse, and Nikola Tesla, among others, all of whom changed the course of history forever with their fierce devotion to upending the status quo.

Helen and Gussie's reform work is based loosely on Josephine Butler, who dedicated her life to championing the rights of women—particularly disenfranchised women trapped in lives of prostitution. It was Josephine Butler who helped form the Ladies' National Association for the Repeal of the Contagious Diseases Acts in 1869 to fight legislation that enabled forced state inspections of suspected prostitutes and their subsequent detention in lock hospitals. To Josephine and her fellow reformers—notably Florence Nightingale among them—the Contagious Diseases Acts were an egregious violation of civil rights, and the fight to repeal the CD Acts spanned from 1869 until their suspension in 1883 and final, full repeal in 1886.

Wherever possible, I've remained true to historical integrity in an effort to preserve the authenticity of electricity's progress in the 1880s. Thomas Edison began the Edison Electric Light Company in 1878 and within a few years, had successfully installed his low voltage direct current (DC) generators—known then as dynamos—in New York and abroad. Edison's DC stations, however, were limited in the sense that the power they generated could only be transmitted within a small radius geographically.

Enter George Westinghouse, an indisputable genius

who had already transformed railway travel by inventing air brakes. In 1885, he learned of a secondary generator—the term then for what we now refer to as a transformer—developed and exhibited by Lucien Gaulard and John Gibbs. Westinghouse, unlike many of his contemporaries who viewed alternating current (AC) as far too dangerous, realized the potential for AC systems to transmit electrical power over a great distance using a transformer to safely step down the voltage for end use. He secured American patent rights for the Gaulard-Gibbs secondary generator and developed it into the modern-day transformer.

The rest, as they say, is history.

About the Author

Award-winning author Scarlett Scott writes contemporary and historical romance with heat, heart, and happily ever afters. Since publishing her first book in 2010, she has become a wife, mother to adorable identical twins and one TV-loving dog, and a killer karaoke singer. Well, maybe not the last part, but that's what she'd like to think.

A self-professed literary junkie and nerd, she loves reading anything but especially romance novels, poetry, and Middle English verse. When she's not reading, writing, wrangling toddlers, or camping, you can catch up with her on her website www.scarsco.com. Hearing from readers never fails to make her day.

Scarlett's complete book list and information about upcoming releases can be found on her website, www.scarsco.com.

Follow Scarlett on social media:

www.instagram.com/scarlettscottauthor/
www.twitter.com/scarscoromance
www.pinterest.com/scarlettscott
www.facebook.com/AuthorScarlettScott

Other Books by Scarlett Scott

HISTORICAL ROMANCE

Heart's Temptation

A Mad Passion (Book One)
Rebel Love (Book Two)
Reckless Need (Book Three)
Sweet Scandal (Book Four)
Restless Rake (Book Five, Coming Soon)

Wicked Husbands

Her Errant Earl (Book One)
Her Lovestruck Lord (Book Two)
Her Reformed Rake (Book Three, Coming Soon)

CONTEMPORARY ROMANCE

Love's Second Chance

Reprieve (Book One)
Perfect Persuasion (Book Two)
Win My Love (Book Three)

Coastal Heat

Loved Up (Book One)

Made in the USA
Middletown, DE
26 December 2023